I0588771

William Gilpin

The Lives of John Wicliff and of the Most Eminent of His Disciples

Lord Cobham, John Huss, Jerome of Prague, and Zisca

William Gilpin

The Lives of John Wicliff and of the Most Eminent of His Disciples
Lord Cobham, John Huss, Jerome of Prague, and Zisca

ISBN/EAN: 9783337383916

Printed in Europe, USA, Canada, Australia, Japan

Cover: Foto ©Raphael Reischuk / pixelio.de

More available books at **www.hansebooks.com**

THE
LIVES

OF

JOHN WICLIFF;

AND OF THE MOST EMINENT OF HIS
DISCIPLES;

LORD COBHAM,

JOHN HUSS,

JEROME of PRAGUE,

AND

ZISCA.

After the way, which they call Herefy, fo worfhip *we* the God of *our* Fathers.

ACTS, 24. 14.

By WILLIAM GILPIN, M.A.

LONDON:

Printed for J. ROBSON, Bookfeller to Her Royal Highnefs the Princefs Dowager of Wales, in *New-Bond-Street*.

M.DCC.LXV.

T O

The Right Reverend

T H O M A S,

Lord Bishop of BRISTOL.

My Lord,

I HAVE taken the liberty to present the following work to your Lordship; the fruit of the little leisure of many years. It may put in a distant claim to your protection, as a kind of appendix to some of your Lordship's valuable *Dissertations on the Prophecies*. The *man of sin* was never more apparent than at the time, when these Reformers lived; who began to strip him of his disguises; and gave the first, and fairest illustration of that prophecy, which your Lordship has so ably explained.

a 2

In

In whatever light this work may be confidered by the public, your Lordſhip, with
your uſual candour, will accept it as an
acknowledgment of the reſpect, with
which

  I am,

   My Lord,

    Your Lordſhip's

     Obliged, and moſt obedient,

     Humble ſervant,

    WILLIAM GILPIN.

Cheam, Feb. 20, 1765.

Houſe of SUPERSTITION.

A VISION.

By *Thomas Denton*, M. A. Rector of *Aſhted*,
in *SURREY*.

I.

WHEN Sleep's all ſoothing hand with fetters ſoft
    Ties down each ſenſe and lulls to balmy reſt;
    The internal pow'r, creative fancy, oft
    Broods o'er her treaſures in the formful breaſt.
Thus when no longer daily cares engage,
  The buſy mind purſues the darling theme;
Hence Angels whiſper'd to the ſlumb'ring ſage,
  And gods of old inſpir'd the heroe's dream;
Hence as I ſlept, theſe images aroſe
To fancy's eye, and join'd this fairy ſcene compoſe.

II.

As, when fair morning dries her dewy tears,
  The mountain lifts o'er miſts its lofty head;
Thus new to ſight a Gothic dome appears,
  With the grey ruſt of rolling years o'erſpread.
On ſolid baſe of ever-during ſtone,
  Which erſt was laid by workmanſhip divine,

a 3

Diſtorted

Diſtorted fancy's way-ward freaks are ſhewn,
    To hide with airs grotefque the grand defign :
With fragil ftraw and reeds the front is lin'd :
Vain prop of tott'ring age, the fport of every wind.

III.

In flocks unnumbered, like a pitchy cloud,
    Birds of ill omen round the fabric fly,
Here build their nefts, and nurfe their callow brood,
    And fcare the timorous foul with boading cry.
Here SUPERSTITION holds her dreary reign,
    And her lip-labour'd Orifons ſhe plies
In Tongue unknown, when morn bedews the plain,
    Or evening ſkirts with gold the weftern ſkies ;
To the dumb ſtock ſhe bends, or fculptur'd wall,
And many a crofs ſhe makes, and many a bead lets fall.

IV.

Near to the dome a magic pair refide
    Prompt to deceive, and practic'd to confound ;
Here hood-winkt *Ignorance* is feen to bide
    Stretching in darkfome cave along the ground ;
No object dawns upon his ftupid eyes,
    Nor voice articulate arrefts his ears,
Save when beneath the moon pale fpectres rife,
    And haunt his foul with vifionary fears ;
Or when hoarfe winds incavern'd murmur round,
And babbling echo wakes, and iterates the found.

V.

Where boughs entwining form an artful ſhade,
    And in faint glimmerings juft admit the light,
There *Errour* fits in borrow'd white array'd,
    And in Truth's form deceives the tranfient fight.

Her

Her beaming luftre when fair Truth imparts,
  A thoufand glories wait her opening day;
Thus *Errour* fain would cheat with mimic arts
  Th' unpractic'd mind, and pours a fpurious ray;
She cleaves with magic wand the liquid fkies,
Bids airy forms appear, and fcenes fantaftic rife.

VI.

A porter deaf, decrepid, old and blind
  Sits at the gate, and lifts a liberal bowl
With wine of wondrous power to lull the mind,
  And check each vig'rous effort of the foul:
Whoe'er unwares fhall ply his thirfty lip,
  And drink in gulps the lufcious liquor down,
Shall haplefs from the cup delufion fip,
  And Objects fee in features not their own;
Each way-worn traveller that hither came,
He lav'd with copious draughts, and *Prejudice* his name.

VII.

Within a various race are feen to wonne,
  Props of her age, and pillars of her ftate,
Which erft were nurtur'd by the * wither'd crone,
  And born to *Tyranny*, her griefly mate:
The firft appear'd in pomp of purple pride,
  With triple crown erect, and throned high;
Two golden keys hang dangling by his fide
  To lock or ope the portals of the fky;
Crouching and proftrate there (ah fight unmeet!)
The crowned head would bow, and lick his dufty feet.

VIII.

With bended arm he on a book reclin'd
  Faft lock'd with iron clafps from vulgar eyes;

a 4

Heav'n's

* Superftition.

Heav'n's gracious gift to light the wand'ring mind,
   To lift fall'n man, and guide him to the fkies!
A man no more, a GOD he would be thought,
   And 'mazed mortals blindly muft obey:
With fleight of hand he lying wonders wrought,
   And near him loathfom heaps of reliques lay:
Strange legends would he read, and figments dire
Of Limbus' prifon'd fhades, and purgatory fire.

IX.

There meagre *Penance* fat, in fackcloth clad,
   And to his breaft clofe hugg'd the viper, fin;
Yet oft with brandifh'd whip would gaul, as mad,
   With voluntary ftripes his fhrivel'd fkin.
Counting large heaps of o'er abounding good
   Of Saints that dy'd within the church's pale,
With gentler afpect there *Indulgence* ftood,
   And to the needy culprit would retail;
There too, ftrange merchandize! he pardons fold,
And treafons would abfolve, and murders purge with gold.

X.

With fhaven crown in a fequefter'd cell,
   In dortour fad a lazy lubbard lay;
No work had he, fave fome few beads to tell,
   And indolently fnore the hours away.
No patriot voice awakes his languid eye;
   No calls of honour raife his drowfy head:
Impure he deems chafte Hymen's holy tie;
   To all life's elegant endearments dead:
No focial hopes hath he, no focial fears,
But fpends in lethargy devout the ling'ring years.

XI.

Gnafhing his teeth in mood of furious ire
   Fierce *Perfecution* fits, and with ftrong breath

Wakes

Wakes into living flame huge heaps of fire,
   And feafts on murders, maffacres and death.
Near him is plac'd *Procruftes'* iron bed
   To ftretch or mangle to a certain fize;
To fee the victims pangs each heart muft bleed,
   To hear their doleful fhrieks and piercing cries;
Yet he beholds them with unmoiftned eye,
Their writhing pains his fport, their moans his melody.

XII.

A gradual light diffufing o'er the gloom,
   And flow approaching with majeftic pace,
A lovely maid appears in beauty's bloom,
   With native charms and unaffected grace:
Her hand a clear reflecting mirrour fhows,
   In which all objects their true features wear,
And on her cheek a blufh indignant glows
   To fee the horrid forc'ries practis'd there;
She fnatch'd the volume from the tyrant's rage
Unlock'd it's iron clafps, and ope'd the heavenly page.

XIII.

Marching in goodly row, with fteady feet,
   Some reverend worthies followed in her train,
With love of truth whofe kindred bofoms beat,
   To free the fettered mind from error's chain.
Wicliff the firft appeared, and led the croud,
   And in his hand a lighted torch he bore,
To drive the gloom of fuperftition's cloud
   And all corruption's mazes to explore.
Next noble *Cobham,* on whofe honoured brow
The martyr's crown is placed, wreath'd with the laurel bough.

XIV.

Hufs mild and firm next dares the tyrant's fires;
   And fweet-tongu'd *Jerome,* fkilful to perfuade;

And

And *Zifca*, whom fair liberty infpires,
    Blind chieftain ! waves around his burnifh'd blade.
Uuwearied paftor, with unbating zeal,
    Next † *Gilpin* comes, on fhepherd's ftaff reclin'd;
He of his much-loved flock each want can feel,
    And feeds the hungry mouth, and famifh'd mind :
Worfter's good ‡ prelate laft, with artlefs fmile,
Surveys each magic fraud, and eyes the flaming pile.

XV.

" My name is TRUTH, and you, each holy feer,
  " Who thus my fteps with ardent gaze purfue,
" Unveil, fhe faid, the facred myfteries here,
  " Give the celeftial boon to public view.
" Tho' blatant *Obloquy* with leprous jaws
  " Shall blot your fame, and blaft the generous deed,
" Yet in revolving years your liberal caufe
  " Shall meet in glory's court its ample meed,
" Your names, illuftrious in the faithful page,
" With each hiftoric grace fhall fhine thro' ev'ry age.

XVI.

" What tho' the tyrant's fierce relentlefs Pow'r
  " Exerts in torment all its horrid fkill;
" Tho' premature you meet the fatal hour
  " Scorching in flames, or writhing on the wheel;
" Yet when the † dragon in the deep Abyfs
  " Shall lye, faft bound in adamantine chain,
" Ye with the lamb fhall rife to ceafelefs blifs,
  " Firft-fruits of death, and partners of his reign;
" Then fhall the great fabbatic reft repay
" The noble ftrife fuftained, the fufferings of a day."

---

† BERNARD GILPIN.   ‡ Bp. LATIMER.
† See Revel. Chap. 20. and the learned and ingenious
Bifhop of BRISTOL's Comment upon it, in the the 3d Vol.
of his Differtation on the Prophecies.

[11]

✵✵✵✵✵✵✵✵✵✵✵✵✵✵✵✵✵✵

CONTENTS

Of the Life of

WICLIFF.

anſwers

CONTENTS

CONTENTS

Of the Life of

Lord *COBHAM*.

OF his firſt oppoſition to the church of Rome, 102—he gives offence to the clergy, 104—his oppoſition to the court, 105—ſent with an army into France, 110—the clergy intrigue againſt him, 112—the king reaſons with him on matters of religion, 115—cited before the primate, 116—implores the king's protection, 117—brought to a trial, 119—his confeſſion, 120—brought to a ſecond trial, 123—eſcapes out of the tower, 135—maligned as the author of an inſurrection, 137—cleared of that charge, 139—he is ſeized in Wales, 147—and put to death, 148.

CONTENTS

Of the Life of

HUSS.

CONTENTS

THE

LIFE

OF

JOHN WICLIFF.

ABOUT the thirteenth and fourteenth centuries the ufurpations of the church of Rome had arifen to their greateft height. That amazing fyftem of fpiritual tyranny had drawn within its influence, in a manner, the whole government of England. The haughty legate, ftriding over law, made even the minifters of juftice tremble at his tribunal: parliaments were over-awed; and fovereigns obliged to temporize: while the lawlefs ecclefiaftic, intrenched behind the authority of councils and decrees, fet at naught the civil power; and opened an afylum to any, the moft profligate, difturbers of fociety.

A   In

In the mean time the taxes gathered, under various pretences, by the agents of the conclave, exceeded, by above two thirds, the produce of the royal treafury: and when men confidered how one claim after another had arifen, and from flender pretences had taken the forms of legal eftablifhments, they could not but be alarmed at an evil teeming with fuch ruin; and faw delufion even through the gloom of ignorance. The people, in fpite of fuperftition, cried out againft fuch fcandalous exactions; and the legiflature began to think ferioufly of checking thefe enormities by refolute laws.

The rapacity of the court of Rome firft fet the fufpicions of men afloat. The votaries of the church bore with temper to fee the extenfion of its power; and its advocates had always to obtrude upon the people the divine fanctions of its dominion; and could on that topic defcant plaufibly enough. But when this holy church, the facred object of veneration, became immerfed in temporal things; when it plainly appeared to be fully inftructed in all the arts of grafping and fquandering, which were found among mere human beings, its mercenary

views

views were evident; and serious men were led to question opinions, which came accompanied by such unwarrantable practice.

The first person of any eminence, who espoused the cause of religious liberty, was John Wicliff. This reformer was born about the year 1324, in the reign of Edward II. Of his extraction we have no certain account. His parents designing him for the church, sent him to Queen's-college in Oxford, then just founded by Robert Eaglesfield, confessor to queen Philippa. But not meeting with the advantages for study in that new-established house, which he expected, he removed to Merton-college; which was then esteemed one of the most learned societies in Europe.

Here he applied with such industry, that he is said to have gotten by heart the most abstruse parts of the works of Aristotle. The logic of that acute philosopher seems chiefly to have engaged his attention; in which he was so conversant, that he became a most subtile disputant, and reigned in the schools without a rival.

Thus prepared, he began next with divinity. The divinity of those times corres-

ponded

ponded with the logic. What was fartlieſt from reaſon, appeared moſt like truth: at leaſt moſt worth a ſcholar's purſuit. In that age flouriſhed thoſe eminent doctors, who mutually complimenting each other with ſounding titles, the profound, the angelic, and the ſeraphic, drew upon themſelves the reverence of their own times, and the contempt of all poſterity. Wicliff's attention was a while engaged in this faſhionable ſtudy; in which he became ſo thorough a proficient, that he was maſter of all the niceties of that ſtrange jargon, which is commonly called ſchool-divinity.

His good ſenſe, however, ſeems to have freed him early from the ſhackles of authority and faſhion. He ſaw the unprofitableneſs of ſuch ſtudies; and having been miſled, rather than bewildered, he diſengaged himſelf from them without much difficulty.

From this time he ſeems to have chalked out for himſelf a ſimpler path. He took the naked text of ſcripture into his hands, and became his own annotator. The writings of the ſchoolmen, he ſoon found, were calculated only to make ſectaries; the bible alone to make a rational chriſtian. Hence
he

he attained that noble freedom of thought, which was afterwards fo confpicuous in all his writings; and among his contemporaries was rewarded, after the fafhion of the times, with the title of the evangelic doctor.

To thefe ftudies he added that of the civil and canon law; and is faid alfo to have been well verfed in the municipal laws of his country.

In the mean time his reputation increafed with his knowledge: and he was refpected not only as an able fcholar, but efteemed as a ferious and pious man; a fincere en-quirer after truth; and a fteady maintainer of it when difcovered.

The firft thing, which drew upon him the public eye, was his defence of the uni-verfity againft the begging friars. The affair was this.

Thefe religious, from the time of their firft fettlement in Oxford, which was in the year 1230, had been very troublefome neighbours to the univerfity. They fet up a different intereft, aimed at a diftinct jurif-diction, fomented feuds between the fcholars and their fuperiors, and in many other ref-pects became fuch offenfive inmates, that

A 3

the

the univerfity was obliged to curb their li-
centioufnefs by fevere ftatutes. This infolent behaviour on one fide, and the oppofition it met with on the other, laid the foundation of an endlefs quarrel. The friars
appealed to the pope; the fcholars to the
civil power: and fometimes one party, and
fometimes the other prevailed. Thus the
caufe became general; and an oppofition to
the friars was looked upon as the teft of a
young fellows affection to the univerfity.

It happened, while things were in this
fituation, that the friars had gotten among
them a notion, of which they were exceedingly fond; that Chrift was a common beg-
gar; that his difciples were beggars alfo;
and that begging, by their example, was
of gofpel-inftitution. This notion they propagated with great zeal from all the pulpits,
both in Oxford, and the neighbourhood, to
which they had accefs.

Wicliff, who had long held thefe religious in great contempt, on account of the
lazinefs of their lives, thought he had now
found a fair occafion to expofe them. He
drew up therefore, and prefently publifhed,
a treatife *Againft able beggary*; in which he

firft

firſt ſhewed the difference between the poverty of Chriſt and that of the friars, and the obligations which all chriſtians lay under to labour in ſome way for the good of ſociety. He then laſhed the friars with great acrimony, proving them to be an infamous and uſeleſs ſet of men, wallowing in luxury; and ſo far from being objects of charity, that they were a reproach not only to religion, but even to human ſociety. This piece was calculated for the many, on whom it made a great impreſſion. At the ſame time it increaſed his reputation with the learned; all men of ſenſe and freedom admiring the work, and applauding the ſpirit of the author.

From this time the univerſity began to conſider him as one of her firſt champions; and in conſequence of the reputation he had gained, he was ſoon afterwards promoted to the maſterſhip of Baliol-college.

About this time, archbiſhop Iſlip, founded Canterbury-hall in Oxford, where he eſtabliſhed a warden, and eleven ſcholars. The warden's name was Wodehall; who with three of his ſcholars were monks; the reſt were ſecular. The prudent archbiſhop, un-

A 4

willing

ing to irritate either side, chose in this way to divide his favours. Wodehall, though brought from a diftant monaftery, rufhed immediately into the quarrel, which he found fubfifting at Oxford; and having vexed the unhappy feculars incorporated with him, by every method in his power, he became next a public difturber; and made it his particular employment to raife and foment animofities in colleges, and difputes in the convocation. The archbifhop, hearing of his behaviour, and finding the report well-grounded, apologized to the univerfity for placing among them fo troublefome a man; and immediately ejected both him, and the three regulars, his affociates. The primate's next care was to appoint a proper fucceffor: and in this view he applied to Wicliff, whom he was greatly defirous of placing at the head of his new foundation. Wicliff, whether through an inclination to cultivate the archbifhop's acquaintance, or to put in order a new-eftablifhed houfe, accepted the propofal, and was immediately chofen warden of Canterbury-hall.

But

But his new dignity foon involved him in difficulties. He was fcarce eftablifhed in it, when the archbifhop died, and was fucceeded by Simon Langham, bifhop of Ely. This prelate had fpent his life in a cloyfter, having been firft a monk, and afterwards an abbot. The ejected regulars failed not to take advantage of fo favourable an opportunity; and made inftant application to the new archbifhop; expecting every thing from a man whom they imagined fo well inclined to their order. Their expectations were juftly founded. Langham efpoufed their caufe with great readinefs; ejected Wicliff, and the regulars his companions; and fequeftered their revenues.

So flagrant a piece of injuftice, raifed a general out-cry. " If the very act of a " founder might be thus fet afide by a pri- " vate perfon, how precarious was college- " preferment!" In fhort, Wicliff was advifed by his friends to appeal to the pope; who durft not, they told him, countenance fo injurious a proceeding. Urban forefeeing fome difficulty in the affair, prudently ftepped behind the curtain, and commiffioned a cardinal to examine it. The archbifhop being

ing cited put in his plea; and each fide accufed and anfwered by turns, protracting the bufinefs into great length.

While this matter was in agitation, an affair happened, which brought it to a fpeedy conclufion. Edward the III. who was now king of England, had for fome time withdrawn the tribute, which his pre-deceffors, from the time of king John, had paid to the pope. The pope menaced in his ufual language: but he had a prince to deal with of too high a fpirit to be fo intimi-dated. Edward called a parliament, laid the affair before them, and defired their advice. The parliament without much de-bating refolved, that king John had done an illegal thing, and had given up the rights of the nation: at the fame time they advifed the king by no means to fubmit to the pope; and promifed to affift him to the utmoft of their power, if the affair fhould bring on confequences.

While the parliament was thus calling in queftion the pope's authority, the clergy, efpecially the regulars, fhewed their zeal by fpeaking and writing in his defence. His undoubted right to his revenue was their

fubject;

ſubject; which they proved by a variety of arguments, drawn from the divinity, and adapted to the genius of thoſe times.

Among others who liſted themſelves in this cauſe, a monk, of more learning, and of a more liberal turn of thought than common, publiſhed a treatiſe, written in a very ſpirited and plauſible manner. His arguments met with many advocates, and helped to keep the minds of the people in ſuſpence. Wicliff, whoſe indignation was raiſed at ſeeing ſo bad a cauſe ſo well defended, undertook to oppoſe the monk, and did it in ſo maſterly a way, that he was no longer conſidered as unanſwerable.

Soon after this book was publiſhed, the ſuit at Rome was determined againſt him: and when men ſaw an effect correſponding ſo exactly with a probable cauſe, they could not avoid aſſigning that probable cauſe, as a real one. In a word, nobody doubted but his oppoſition to the pope, at ſo critical a time, was the true cauſe of his being nonſuited at Rome.

Notwithſtanding his diſappointment, Wicliff ſtill continued at Oxford; where his friends, about this time, procured him a benefice.

benefice. Soon after, the divinity profeſſor's chair falling vacant, he took a doctor's degree, and was elected into it, the univerſity paying him this compliment, not only as the reward of his merit, but as a compenſation for his loſs.

Dr. Wicliff had now attained the ſummit of his hopes. His ſtation afforded him that opportunity, which he wanted, of throwing ſome new lights, as he imagined, upon religious ſubjects. A long courſe of reaſoning had now fully convinced him, that the Romiſh religion was a ſyſtem of errors. The ſcandalous lives of the monaſtic clergy firſt led him into this train of thinking; and an inquiry into antiquity had confirmed him in it. But it was a bold undertaking to encounter errors of ſo long a ſtanding; errors, which had taken ſo deep a root, and had ſpread themſelves ſo wide. The undertaking at leaſt required the greateſt caution. He reſolved therefore at firſt to go on with the popular argument, which he had begun, and continue his attack upon the monaſtic clergy.

It was a circumſtance in his favour, that the begging friars were at this time in the
higheſt

higheft difcredit at Oxford. The occafional oppofition he had already given them, had by no means hurt his reputation; and as he really thought the monaftic clergy, the principal inftruments of the prevailing corruption, he was fully determined not to fpare them. In his public lectures therefore he reprefented them as a fet of men, who profeffed indeed to live under the rule of holy faints, but had now fo far degenerated from their firft inftitution, that they were become a fcandal to their founders. Men might well cry out, he faid, againft the decay of religion; but he could fhew them from whence this decay proceeded. While the preachers of religion never inculcated religious duties, but entertained the people with idle ftories, and lying miracles; while they never inforced the neceffity of a good life, but taught their hearers to put their truft in a bit of fealed parchment, and the prayers of hypocrites, it was impoffible, he faid, but religion muft decay. Such treacherous friends did more hurt than open enemies.—— But a regard for religion, he added, was not to be expected from them: they had nothing in view but the advancement of

their

their order. In every age they had made it their practice to invent, and multiply such new opinions and doctrines as suited their avaritious views: nay they had, in a manner, set aside christianity, by binding men with their traditions in preference to the rule of Christ, who, it might well be supposed, left nothing useful out of his scheme.

In such language did Dr. Wicliff inveigh against the monastic clergy; and opened the eyes of men to a variety of abuses, which were before hidden in the darkness of superstition.

He had not, however, yet avowedly questioned any doctrine of the church. All he had hitherto attempted was to loosen the prejudices of the vulgar. His success in this warranted a further progress; and he began next to think of attacking some of the fundamentals of popery.

In this design he still proceeded with his usual caution. At first, he thought it sufficient to lead his adversaries into logical and metaphysical disputations; accustoming them to hear novelties, and to bear contradiction. Nothing passed in the schools but learned arguments on the form of things, on the

increase

increafe of time, on fpace, fubftance, and identity. In thefe difputations he artfully intermixed, and pufhed as far as he durft, new opinions in divinity; founding, as it were, the minds of his hearers. At length, finding he had a great party in the fchools, and that he was liftened to with attention, he ventured to be more explicit, and by degrees opened himfelf at large.

He began by invalidating all the writings of the fathers after the tenth century. At that time, he faid, an age of darknefs and error commenced; and the honeft enquirer after truth could never fatisfy himfelf among the opinions and doctrines, which then took their birth.

The fpeculative corruptions, which had crept into religion were the firft fubject of his enquiry. Many of thefe he traced out, from their earlieft origin; and with egrat accuracy and acutenefs fhewed the progrefs they had made, as they defcended through the ages of fuperftition. He proceeded next to the ufurpations of the court of Rome. On this fubject he was very copious: it was his favourite topic; and feldom failed, however coolly he might begin, to give him

warmth

warmth and spirit as he proceeded. On these, and many other subjects of the same kind, he insisted with great freedom, and a strength of reasoning far superior to the learning of those times.

This spirited attack upon the church of Rome hath been attributed by his enemies to motives of resentment. His deprivation, it is said, was the unlucky cause of all this heat and bitterness. And indeed his conduct, in this instance, hath unquestionably the appearance of being influenced by his passions. But the candid of all parties will be very cautions in assigning motives; and the friends of Wicliff may with truth remonstrate, that he began his attack upon the church of Rome, before he had been injured by the pope. They may add too, that he never before had so proper an occasion to question publickly the erroneous tenets of religion.

From whatever motives however, this spirited attack proceeded, we are not surprised to find a violent clamour raised against him by the romish clergy. The archbishop of Canterbury, taking the lead, resolved to prosecute him with the utmost vigour. But

herefy

herefy was a new crime: the church had
flept in its errors through fo many ages, that
it was unprepared for an attack. Records
however were fearched, and precedents examined; till, with fome difficulty, at length
Dr. Wicliff was deprived and filenced.

Edward III. after a glorious, and active
reign, was, at this time, too much impaired
both in body and mind, to bear the fatigues
of government. The whole adminiftration
of affairs was in the hands of his fon the
duke of Lancafter, commonly known by
the name of John of Ghent.

This prince had a fpirit anfwerable to his
birth, and preferved the forms of royalty
as much as any monarch of his time. He
had violent paffions, of which his enemies
and friends were equally fenfible. In religion he had free notions; and whether his
creed gave offence to the popifh clergy; or
whether he had made fome efforts to curb
the exorbitance of their power, it is certain
they were vehemently incenfed againft him;
and fome of * the leading churchmen, it

B

is

* This is particularly charged upon William of Wickham,
Bifhop of Winchefter; but a late very accurate and ingenious writer hath fufficiently exculpated him on this head.

is faid, had ufed very bafe arts to blacken his character.   With equal fire the duke retorted their ill-treatment; and having long defpifed them, and being now fo exceedingly provoked, he conceived a fettled prejudice againft the whole order; and endeavoured by all the means in his power to bring them into the fame contempt with others, in which he held them himfelf.

This quarrel between the duke of Lancafter and the clergy, was the occafion of introducing Dr. Wicliff into public life; and this introduction afforded him afterwards an opportunity of fignalizing himfelf ftill more in the great caufe of religious liberty.   The duke, it feems, had heard with pleafure, of the attack he had made upon the church of Rome; and had waited the confequences of it with great attention: and when he now found, that Dr. Wicliff was likely to be the fufferer, he interpofed, refcued him out of the hands of his enemies, who were perfuing their advantage, and brought him to court; where, through a paffionate vibration of temper, from one extreme to another, he took him into his confidence, and treated

him

him with a kindnefs proportioned to the enmity which he bore the clergy.

The oppreffions of the court of Rome were,
at this time, feverely felt in England. Many
things were complained of; but nothing
more than the ftate of church-preferments;
almoft all of which, and even rectories, and
vicarages of any value, in whomfoever originally vefted, were now, through one fiction
or another, claimed by the pope. With
thefe he penfioned his friends and favourites;
moft of whom, being foreigners, refided a-
broad; and left their benefices in the hands
of ill-paid, and negligent curates. By thefe
means religion decayed; the country was
drained of money; and what was looked
upon as moft vexatious, a body of infolent
tythe-gatherers were fet over the people,
who had their own fortunes to make out of
the furplus of their exactions.

Thefe hardfhips, notwithftanding the blind
obedience paid at that time to the fee of
Rome, created great unquietnefs. The nation faw itfelf wronged; and parliamentary
petitions, in very warm language, were preferred to the conclave: but to little purpofe;
the pope lending a very negligent ear to any

motion

motion which fo nearly affected his revenue.

The duke of Lancafter, however, at this time, though the nation had now complained in vain during more than 30 years, was determined, if poffible, to obtain redrefs. And, in the firft place, to open the eyes of the people in the moft effectual manner, he obliged all bifhops to fend in lifts of the number and value of fuch preferments and benefices in each of their dioceffes, as were in the hands of foreigners. From thefe lifts it appeared what immenfe fums, in that one way, were conveyed every year out of the kingdom.

The next ftep taken was to fend an embaffy to the pope to treat of the liberties of the church of England; at the head of which embaffy were the bifhop of Bangor, and Dr. Wicliff. They were met at Bruges, on the part of Rome, by the bifhops of Pampelone and Semigaglia, and the provoft of Valenza. Thefe agents, practifed in the policy of their court, fpun out the negotiation with great dexterity; fome hiftorians mention the continuance of it during the fpace of two years. The romifh ambaffadors however, finding them-

themselves hard pressed by their antagonists; and prudently considering, that it would be easier to evade a treaty when made, than in the present circumstances not to make one, determined at last to bring matters to a conclusion. Accordingly it was agreed, that the pope should no longer dispose of any benefices belonging to the church of England. No mention was made of bishopricks: this was thought a voluntary omission in the bishop of Bangor; and men the rather believed so, when they saw him twice afterwards translated by the pope's authority.

But though Dr. Wicliff failed in his endeavours to serve his country by this treaty, (for indeed it was never observed) he made his journey however of some service to himself. It was his great care to use the opportunity it afforded him of sifting out the real designs of the court of Rome, not only in this affair, but in all its other negotiations: he inquired into the ends it had in view, and the means it employed: and by frequent conversations with the ambassadors upon these subjects, he penetrated so far into the constitution and policy of that corrupt court, that he began to think of it in a much harsher

B 4   manner

manner than he had ever yet done, and to be more convinced of its avarice and ambition. Prejudiced as he had long been againſt its doctrines and miniſtry, he had never yet thought ſo ill of its deſigns.

Thus influenced, when he came home, we find him inveighing in his lectures againſt the church of Rome, in warmer language than he had hitherto uſed. The exemption of the clergy from the juriſdiction of the civil power was one of his topics of invective: the uſe of ſanctuaries was another: indulgences a third: in ſhort there has ſcarce been a corrupt principle or practice in the Roman church, detected by later ages, which his penetration had not at that early day diſcovered; and though his reaſonings want much of that acuteneſs and ſtrength, with which the beſt writers of theſe times have diſcuſſed thoſe ſubjects; yet when we conſider the uninlightened age in which he lived, we rather ſtand aſtoniſhed at that force of genius, which carried him ſo far, than in any degree wonder at his not going farther.

The pope himſelf was often the ſubject of his invective: his infallibility, his uſurpations, his pride, his avarice, and his tyranny,

were

were his frequent theme; and indeed his language was never warmer than when on thefe topics. The celebrated epithet of *antichrift*, which in after ages, was fo liberally beftowed upon the pope, feems to have been firft given him by this reformer.

The pomp and luxury of bifhops he would frequently lafh; and would afk the people, when they faw their prelates riding abroad accompanied with fourfcore horfemen in filver trappings, whether they perceived any refemblance between fuch fplendor, and the fimplicity of primitive bifhops?

Where thefe lectures were read, does not certainly appear. It is moft probable however, that they were read in Oxford; where Dr. Wicliff feems by this time to have recovered his former ftation, and where he had ftill a confiderable party in his favour.

In the mean time he was frequently at court, where he continued in great credit with the duke of Lancafter. Many indeed expected, fome high preferment in the church was intended for him; but we meet with no account of his having had the offer of any fuch, whether he himfelf declined it, or the duke thought an eminent ftation in the

church

church would only the more expofe him to the malice of his enemies. The duke however took care to make him independent by conferring a good benefice upon him, the rectory of Lutterworth in Leicefterfhire; whither he immediately repaired, and fet himfelf faithfully to difcharge the duties of it. We hear nothing more of his other benefice, fo that it is probable he gave it up when he accepted Lutterworth.

Dr. Wicliff was fcarce fettled in his parifh, when his enemies, taking the advantage of his retirement, began to perfecute him again with frefh vigour. At the head of this perfecution were Sudbury, archbifhop of Canterbury, and Courtney, bifhop of London. The former was a man of uncommon moderation for the times in which he lived; the latter was an inflamed bigot. The archbifhop indeed feems to have been preffed into this fervice; to which he afforded only the countenance of his name. Courtney, took upon himfelf the management of it; and having procured proper letters from Rome, Dr. Wicliff was cited to appear before him on a day fixed, at St. Paul's in London.

This

This was an unexpected summons to Dr. Wicliff; who imagined probably that the obscurity of his retreat would have screened him from his enemies. He repaired however, immediately to the duke of Lancaster, to consult with him on a business of such importance. The duke did what he could to avert the prosecution; but finding himself unable to oppose a force composed of little less than the whole ecclesiastical order, he thought it more probable that he should be able to protect his friend from the future consequences of the clergy's malice, than to screen him from the present effects of it. Determined however, to give him what countenance he could, he attended him in person to his trial; and engaged also the lord Piercy, earl-marshal of England, to accompany them.

When they came to St. Paul's, they found the court sitting, and a very great croud assembled, through which the earl-marshal made use of his authority to gain an entrance.

The arrival of such personages, with their attendants, occasioned no little disturbance in the church; and the bishop of London piqued to see Dr. Wicliff so attended, told the

the earl with a peevifh air, that if he had known before what difturbance he would have made, he fhould have been ftopped at the door. He was greatly offended alfo at the duke for infifting that Dr. Wicliff fhould fit during his trial; and let fall fome expreffions, which that haughty prince was ill able to bear. He immediately fired; and reproached the bifhop with great bitternefs. Warm language enfued. The prelate however, had the advantage; of which the duke feeming confcious, from railing began to threaten; and looking difdainfully at the bifhop, told him, that he would bring down the pride, not only of him, but of all the prelacy of England: and turning to a perfon near him, he faid in a half whifper, that rather than take fuch ufage from the bifhop, he would pull him by the hair of his head out of the church. Thefe words being caught up by fome, who ftood near, were fpread among the croud, and in an inftant threw the whole affembly into a ferment; voices from every part being heard, united in one general cry, that their bifhop fhould not be fo ufed, and that they would ftand by him to their laft breath. In fhort, the confufion

arofe

arofe to fuch an height, that all bufinefs was at an end, the whole was diforder, and the court broke up without having taken any ftep of confequence in the affair.

The tumult however did not fo end. The duke, agitated by his paffions, went directly to the houfe of peers; where inveighing againft the riotous difpofition of the Londoners, he preferred a bill, that very day, to deprive the city of London of its privileges, and to alter the jurifdiction of it.

The city of London was never more moved than on this occafion. The heads of it met in confultation; while the populace affembled in a riot, and affaulted the houfes of the duke, and the earl marfhal, who both left the city with precipitation.

Thefe tumults, which continued fome time, put a ftop to all proceedings againft Wicliff; nor indeed do we find him in any farther trouble, during the remainder of king Edward's reign.

In the year 1377 that prince died, and was fucceeded by his grandfon Richard II. Richard being only eleven years of age, the firft bufinefs of the parliament was to fettle a regency. The duke of Lancafter afpired to

be

be fole regent ; but the parliament thought otherwife : much was apprehended from the violence of his temper; and more from his unpopular maxims of government. The regency therefore was put into commiffion, and he had only one voice in the management of affairs.

The duke of Lancafter's fall from his former height of power was a fignal to the bifhops to begin anew their perfecution againft Wicliff. Articles of accufation were immediately drawn up, and difpatched to Rome. How very heartily the pope engaged in this bufinefs may be imagined, from his fending upon this occafion not fewer than five bulls into England : of thefe, three were directed to the archbifhop of Canterbury and the bifhop of London; a fourth to the univerfity of Oxford ; and a fifth to the king.

Together with his bulls to the bifhops, he fent a copy of the heretical articles ; requiring thofe prelates to inform themfelves, whether Wicliff really held the doctrines therein contained ; and, if he did, forthwith to imprifon him ; or if they failed in that, to cite him to make his perfonal appearance at Rome within three months.

In his bull to the chancellor, and other heads of the univerſiy, he expoſtulates with ſome warmth upon their ſuffering tares to ſpring up with the wheat, and even to grow ripe without rooting them out. It gives him great uneaſineſs, he ſays, that this evil was publicly ſpoken of at Rome, before any remedy had been applied in England. He bids them conſider the conſequences of Wicliff's doctrines; that they tended to nothing leſs than the ſubverſion both of church and ſtate: and injoins them laſtly, to forbid the preaching of ſuch tenets for the future within their diſtricts; and to aſſiſt the biſhops in bringing Wicliff to condign puniſhment.

To the king he addreſſed himſelf in very obliging language; and exhorted him to ſhew his zeal for the faith, and the holy ſee, by giving his countenance to the proſecution commencing againſt Wicliff.

Of the ſucceſs of theſe bulls the pope had little doubt. The court of Rome had never been accuſtomed to contradiction. Deſpotic in all its commands, it had only to dictate, and the proudeſt monarch was ready to obey. But a new ſcene of things was now opening; and a more liberal ſpirit taking poſſeſ-

ſion

fion of the minds of men. It muſt have been a ſenſible mortification to the haughty pontiff, to ſee the neglect with which he was treated on this occaſion. Oppoſition to his exactions he had ſometimes found before; but this was the firſt occaſion, on which he had ever been treated with contempt. The univerſity deliberated, whether it ſhould even receive his bull; and by what appears it did not. And the regency were ſo little diſpoſed to ſhew him any reverence, that they joined with the parliament at this very time, in giving a ſignal inſtance of their confidence in Dr. Wicliff, as if on purpoſe to make their contempt as notorious as poſſible. The inſtance was this.

· A truce with France at this juncture expiring, that nation took the advantage of a minority, and was making mighty preparations to invade England. As the country was far from being in a poſture of defence, all the money that could be raiſed was wanted. The parliament deliberating about the means, it was debated in the houſe, whether, upon an emergency, the money collected in England for the uſe of the pope, might not be applyed to the ſervice of the nation.

nation. The expediency of the meafure was acknowledged by all, but the legality of it was doubted. At laft it was agreed both by the regency and the parliament, to put the queftion to Dr. Wicliff. It appears as if they only wanted the authority of an able cafuift to give a fanction to a refolution already made; a fanction very eafily obtained from the cafuift they confulted.

But whatever difrefpect was paid to the pope's bulls by the king and the univerfity of Oxford, the zeal of the bifhops made ample amends. The bifhop of London efpecially complyed not only with the letter, but entered into the fpirit of the pontiff's mandate.

He had taken however only the firft ftep in this bufinefs, when he received a peremptory order from the duke of Lancafter, not to proceed to imprifonment. To imprifon a man for holding an opinion, the duke told him, could not be juftified by the laws of England: he took the liberty therefore to inform him, that if he proceeded to any fuch extremity, he muft abide the confequences.

This menace alarmed the bifhop: he dropt the defign of an imprifonment; and contented himfelf with citing Wicliff to make

his

his appearance, on fuch a day, before a provincial fynod in the chapel at Lambeth;
fending him at the fame time a copy of the
articles, which had been objected to, and de-
firing his explanation of them.

On the day appointed Dr. Wicliff appeared; and being queftioned about the articles,
he delivered in a paper, which explained the
fenfe, in which he held them.

It would be tedious to tranfcribe this collection of antiquated opinions; many of
which, at this day, would feem of very little importance.   The curious reader may fee
them at large in the firft volume of Fox's acts
and monuments. We cannot however avoid
obferving, that Dr. Wicliff by no means appears in the moft favourable light on this occafion *.   He explains many of the articles

in

---

* The ingenious Mr. Hume, alluding to this paffage of
his life, tells us, that " Wicliff, notwithftanding his enthu-
" fiafm, feems not to have been actuated by the fpirit of
" martyrdom; and in all fubfequent trials before the pre-
" lates, he fo explained away his doctrine by tortured mean-
" ings, as to render it quite innocent and inoffenfive."
Mr. Hume's cenfure, without queftion, hath fome foundation in hiftory; which affords in this inftance a very good
handle to any one, who is glad of an opportunity of tra-
ducing the memory of the reformer.

in a forced, unnatural manner, with much art, and in a very unmanly ftrain of compliment. On the other hand, it muft not be concealed, that his advocates call in queftion the authenticity of this explanation ; and have at leaft to fay for themfelves, that it is folely conveyed down through the channel of popifh writers.

While the bifhops were deliberating upon Wicliff's confeffion, which (however cautioufly worded) was far, it feems, from being fatisfactory, (an argument, by the way, againft the authenticity of that confeffion, which is handed down to us) the people both within doors, and without, grew very tumultuous, crying aloud, that they would fuffer no violence to be done to Wicliff.

At this juncture Sir Lewis Clifford, a gentleman about the court, entered the chapel, and in an authoritative manner forbidding the bifhops to proceed to any definitive fentence, retired. Sir Lewis was very well known to many there prefent; and the bifhops taking it for granted, that he came properly authorized, (which yet does not appear) were in fome confufion at the meffage. The tumult at the door, in the mean time increafing,

 and

and adding to their perplexity, at length they diffolved the affembly; having forbidden Dr. Wicliff to preach any more thofe doctrines which had been objected to him. To this prohibition, it feems, he paid little refpect; going about barefooted, as we are informed, in a long frieze-gown, preaching every where occafionally to the people, and without any referve in his own parifh. His zeal, it is probable, might now break out with the greater warmth, as he might tax his late behaviour, if the account we have is genuine, with the want of proper freedom.

In the year 1378, pope Gregory the XIth died, and was fucceeded by the archbifhop of Barri, a Neapolitan, who took upon him the name of Urban VI. This pontiff, a man of an haughty temper, began his reign in fo arbitrary a manner, that he alienated from him the affections of his fubjects. The cardinals in particular fo highly refented his behaviour, that a majority of them refolved to run any lengths rather than bear it longer. They found therefore, or pretended to find, fome flaw in his election; and affembling at Avignon, where the popes had often refided, they declared the election of Urban void, and

chofe

chose Clement VII. This was a paffionate meafure; and produced, as paffionate meafures generally do, deftructive confequences. The two popes, laying an equal claim to St. Peter's chair, began to ftrengthen their refpective parties; their quarrel immediately became the caufe of God, found adherents in all parts of Europe, occafioned deluges of blood, and gave a more fatal blow to popery than any thing had yet done.

Dr. Wicliff, it may eafily be fuppofed, was among thofe, who took moft offence at this unchriftian fchifm. He confidered it as a new argument againft popery; and as fuch he failed not to ufe it. A tract foon appeared in his name againft the fchifm of the Roman pontiffs, in which he fhewed what little credit was due to either of the contending parties. This tract was eagerly read by all forts of people, and tended not a little to open the eyes of the vulgar.

About the end of the year, Dr. Wicliff was feized with a violent diftemper, which, it was feared, might have proved fatal. Upon this occafion, we are told, he was waited upon by a very extraordinary deputation. The begging friars, it feems, whom he

had

had heretofore so severely treated, sent four of their order, accompanied with four of the most eminent citizens of Oxford, to attend him; who having gained admittance to his bed-chamber, acquainted him, that hearing he lay at the point of death, they were come in the name of their order, to put him in mind of the many injuries he had done them; and hoped for his soul's sake, that he would do them all the justice now in his power, by retracting, in the presence of those respectable persons, the many severe and unjust things he had said of them. Wicliff surprised at this solemn message, raised himself in his bed; and we are informed, with a stern countenance cried out, " I shall not " die, but live to declare the evil deeds of " the friars." The unexpected force of his expression, together with the sternness of his manner, the story adds, drove away the friars in confusion.

Soon after his recovery, Dr. Wicliff set about a great work, which he had often intended, the translation of the scriptures into English. It had long given him great offence, and indeed he always considered it as one of the capital errors of popery, that the

bible

bible fhould be locked up from the people. He refolved therefore to free it from
this bondage. But before his great work appeared, he publifhed a tract, in which, with
great ftrength of argument, he fhewed the
neceffity of engaging in it. The bible, he
affirmed, contained the whole of God's will.
Chrift's law, he faid, was fufficient to guide
his church; and every chriftian might there
gather knowledge enough to make him acceptable to God: and as to comments, he
faid, a good life was the beft guide to the
knowledge of fcripture; or, in his own language: " He that keepeth righteoufnefs hath
" the true underftanding of holy writ."

When he thought thefe arguments were
fufficiently digefted, his great work came a-
broad, much to the fatisfaction of all fober men.

Some have contended, that Dr. Wicliff
was not the firft tranflator of the bible
into Englifh. The truth feems to be, that
he was the firft, who tranflated the whole
together; of which, it is probable, others
might have given detached parts. It does
not however appear, that Dr. Wicliff underftood the Hebrew language. His method
was, to collect what Latin bibles he could find:

from

from thefe he made one correct copy; and from this tranflated. He afterwards examined the beft commentators then extant, particularly Nicolas Lyra; and from them inferted in his margin thofe paffages, in which the Latin differed from the Hebrew.

In his tranflation of the bible, he feems to have been literally exact. In his other works, his language was wonderfully elegant for the times in which he lived: but here he was ftudious only of the plain fenfe; which led him often, through the confufion of idioms, within the limits of nonfenfe. *Quid nobis & tibi, Jefu fili dei,* we find tranflated thus, *What to us, and to thee, Jefus the Son of God.*

This work, it may eafily be imagined, had no tendency to reinftate him in the good opinion of the clergy. An univerfal clamour was immediately raifed. Knighton, a canon of Leicefter, and a contemporary with Wicliff, hath left us, upon record, the language of the times. "Chrift intrufted his gofpel," fays that ecclefiaftic, "to the clergy, and doctors of the "church, to minifter it to the laity, and "weaker fort, according to their exigences, "and feveral occafions. But this mafter "John Wicliff, by tranflating it, has made

it

" it vulgar; and has laid it more open to the
" laity, and even to women, who can read,
" than it ufed to be to the moft learned of
" the clergy, and thofe of the beft under-
" ftanding: and thus the gofpel jewel, the
" evangelical pearl, is thrown about, and
" trodden under foot of fwine." Such language was looked upon as good reafoning
by the clergy of that day, who faw not with
what fatyr it was edged againft themfelves.

The bifhops, in the mean time, and mi-
tred abbots, not content with railing, took
more effectual pains to ftop this growing
evil. After much confultation, they brought
a bill into parliament to fupprefs Wicliff's
bible. The advocates for it, fet forth in their
ufual manner, the alarming profpect of herefy, which this verfion of the fcriptures opened; and the ruin of all religion, which muft
inevitably enfue.

Thefe zealots, were anfwered by the principal reformers, who judicioufly encountered
them with their own weapons. It appears,
faid the Wiclivites, from the decretals, that
more than fixty different fpecies of herefy
fprang up in the church, after the tranflation
of the bible into Latin. But the utility of that
tranflation

tranflation, notwithftanding its bad confequences, all parties acknowledge. With
what face therefore, they afked, could the
bifhops pretend to difcountenance an Englifh tranflation, when they could not produce
one argument againft it, which did not equally
conclude againft the Latin one? This reafoning filenced all oppofition; and the bill
was thrown out by a great majority.

The zeal of the bifhops to fupprefs Wicliff's
bible only made it, as is generally the cafe, the
more fought after. They who were able,
among the reformers, purchafed copies; and
they who were not able, procured at leaft
tranfcripts of particular gofpels, or epiftles, as
their inclinations led. In after times, when lollardy increafed, and the flames were kindled,
it was a common practice, to faften about
the neck of the condemned heretic, fuch of
thefe fcraps of fcripture as were found in his
poffeffion, which generally fhared his fate.

Before the clamour, which was raifed a-
gainft Dr. Wicliff, on the account of his bible, was in any degree filenced, he ventured
a ftep farther; and attacked that favourite
doctrine of the Roman church, the doctrine
of tranfubftantiation.

About

About the year 820 this ftrange opinion was firft heard of. It owed its birth to Paf-chafe Radbert, a wild enthufiaft, who pub-lifhed it, not as falfhood generally gains ground, by little and little; but at once glaring in its full abfurdity. He informed the world, in plain language, that in the facrament of the Lord's fupper, the elements after confecration, are entirely changed into the body and blood of Chrift; that very body, which was born of Mary, fuffered upon the crofs, and rofe from the dead. It is amazing, that an opinion fo big with abfurdity, and yet unaided by prejudice, could faften upon the minds of men, however rude of fcience. Yet the improbable tale, we find, went down, as if the greater the improbability, the more venerable the myftery. It was found a doctrine well adapted to imprefs the people with that awful and fuperftitious horror, which is the neceffary foundation of falfe religion : as fuch therefore the church of Rome with great zeal upheld it; and if any were ftaggered by the appearance of an impoffibility, they were prefently told, that, " The acci-
" dents, or forms of bread and wine, it was
" true, ftill remained after confecration; but
" by

" by the omnipotence of God they remain-
" ed without a fubject." This was the argument of the clergy; and it was thought con-
clufive, for who could doubt the omnipotence of God?

Dr. Wicliff, after a thorough examination
of this doctrine, was entirely fatisfied, that
it had no fcriptural foundation. In his lectures therefore before the univerfity of Oxford, in the year 1381, which he feems ftill
to have continued every fummer, as profeffor of divinity, he took upon him to con-
fute this error; and to explain the real defign
of the Lord's fupper. He principally endeavoured to eftablifh, that the fubftance of
the bread and wine in the Lord's fupper remained the fame after confecration; and that
the body and blood of Chrift were not fub-
ftantially in them, but only figuratively.
Thefe conclufions he offered to defend publicly in the fchools. But the religious, who
were now, it feems, getting ground in the
univerfity, would not fuffer any queftion of
this kind to be moved: upon which Dr.
Wicliff, without further ceremony, publifhed a treatife upon that fubject; in which he
went great lengths, and attacked the doctrine

of

of tranfubftantiation with all the freedom of a man, not hefitating, but fully convinced of the truth of what he maintained.

Dr. Barton was, at that time, vice-chancellor of Oxford. He was a perfon of great zeal againft innovations in religion; which he confidered as the fymptoms of its ruin; and had always ufed a bitternefs of expreffion in fpeaking of Dr. Wicliff; which eafily fhewed with how much pleafure he would take hold of any fair occafion againft him. An occafion now offered. He called together therefore the heads of the univerfity; and, finding he could influence a majority, obtained a decree, by which Wicliff's doctrine was condemned as heretical, and himfelf and his hearers threatened, if they perfifted in their errors, with imprifonment, and excommunication.

Dr. Wicliff, we are told, was greatly mortified on finding himfelf thus treated at Oxford, which had till now been his fanctuary. He had one refource however ftill left, his generous patron the duke of Lancafter; to whom he refolved to fly for protection, and through the hopes of whofe intereft he appealed

pealed to the king from the vice-chancellor's sentence.

While Dr. Wicliff and his followers, who were now very numerous, were thus censured at Oxford, a calumny was raised against them, which might have proved of more dangerous consequence. It took its rise from an insurrection, which at this time alarmed the whole kingdom.

Vexed by the severe exaction of a severe impost, the counties of Kent and Sussex took arms. Their body increased as it moved; and under the conduct of one Tiler, approached London with a force greatly superior to any tumultuary troops that could be brought against it. Here the rebels, having done infinite mischief, and brought even the government to a treaty, were dispersed by the mere address and resolution of the young king. The behaviour of Richard, on this occasion, ought never to be omitted even in a flight account of these things, as it is the only part of his behaviour, through his whole life, that deserves recording.

When all danger was over, and the thoughts of the ministry were now turned

upon

upon punishing the guilty, great pains were taken by the enemies of Wicliff, to fix the odium of this insurrection upon him; but with very little effect: for after the strictest scrutiny, nothing was produced to prove their accusation, but that one Ball, a priest, was seized among the rebels, whom the archbishop of Canterbury had formerly thrown into prison for preaching Wicliff's doctrines. But it appeared, that Ball was a conceited, empty fellow, who through motives of vanity was ready to adopt any singularity. And indeed the whole tenor of history has exculpated Wicliff, and his disciples on this head, by assigning other and more probable causes of this rebellion.

We left Dr. Wicliff, in the midst of his distresses, carrying up an appeal from the university to the king. But his appeal, it seems, met with no countenance. The duke of Lancaster finding his credit declining, supposed probably that the protection he afforded Wicliff might be the principal cause of its decline; perhaps too he might think this bold reformer, by attacking transubstantiation, had gone greater lengths than could well be warranted; it is certain however,

that

that he now for the firſt time deſerted him; and when Dr. Wicliff preſſed his highneſs in the affair, and urged him with religious motives, he was anſwered coolly, that of theſe things the church was the moſt proper judge, and that the beſt advice he could give him was to quit theſe novelties, and ſubmit quietly to his ordinary. Wicliff finding himſelf thus expoſed, had only to wrap himſelf in his own integrity, and puſh through the ſtorm as he was able.

It was a circumſtance greatly againſt him, that William Courtney was at this time promoted to the ſee of Canterbury; Simon of Sudbury, his predeceſſor, having been murdered by the rebels in the late inſurrection. Courtney, when biſhop of London, had been Wicliff's moſt active adverſary; and was now glad to find his hands ſtrengthened by the addition of ſo much power, were it only for the ability it gave him to cruſh the Wiclivites. He highly approved therefore of what the vice-chancellor of Oxford had done, and reſolved to go vigorouſly on with the proſecution.

His piety however allowed Wicliff ſome reſpite. So ſcrupulous was the primate, even

in

in matters of form, that he forbore any public exercife of his office, till he fhould receive
the confecrated pall from Rome; which did
not arrive till the May of the next year,
1382.

Being thus duly invefted, Dr. Wicliff was
cited to appear before him in the monaftery
of the grey friers, on the 17th day of the
fame month: fo eager was the archbifhop to
enter upon this bufinefs!

But before we proceed in the relation, it
may not be improper to inform the reader,
that we find great obfcurity in the accounts
of this part of Wicliff's life, many of thefe
accounts differing from each other; and
many being plainly contradictory. All therefore, which in fuch a cafe can be done, is to
felect, from a variety of circumftances, fuch
as feem moft probable, and beft founded.

Dr. Wicliff being thus cited before the
archbifhop, refufed to appear; alledging that
as he was a member of the univerfity, and
held an office in it, he was exempt from
epifcopal jurifdiction. The univerfity was
now, it feems, under different influence;
the vice-chancellor was changed; and the
determination of the majority was to fupport
their

their member. With this plea therefore the archbifhop remained fatisfied.

But though he could not proceed againft the perfon of Wicliff, he refolved however to proceed againft his opinions. When the court therefore met on the appointed day, a large collection of articles, extracted from his books and fermons, was produced.

In the inftant, as the bifhops and divines, of which this court confifted, were about to enter upon bufinefs, a violent earthquake fhook the monaftery. The affrighted bifhops threw down their papers; cryed out, the bufinefs was difpleafing to God; and came to a hafty refolution to proceed no farther.

The archbifhop alone remained unmoved. With equal fpirit and addrefs he chid their fuperftitious fears; and told them, that if the earthquake portended any thing, it portended the downfall of herefy; that as noxious vapours are lodged in the bowels of the earth, and are expelled by thefe violent concuffions, fo by their ftrenuous endeavours, the kingdom fhould be purified from the peftilential taint of herefy, which had infected it in every part.

This

This speech, together with the news, that the earthquake had been general through the city, as it was afterwards indeed found to have been through the iſland, diſpelled their fears. Dr. Wicliff would often merrily ſpeak of this accident; and would call this aſſembly, the council of the herydene; herydene being the old Engliſh word for earthquake.

The court, again compoſed, entred warmly into the buſineſs; and went through the examination of all the articles. In fine, they came to a determination, that ſome of them were erroneous; and ſome plainly heretical.

This determination was publiſhed, and afterwards anſwered by Dr. Wicliff, who ſhewed how much his enemies had miſrepreſented him in ſeveral points; and defended his opinions with a ſpirit of truth and freedom, which brought over many to his party.

The primate took new offence at this audacity, as he called it, of Wicliff; and being determined at all events to cruſh him, preferred a bill in parliament to enable ſheriffs (upon proper information from biſhops) to proceed as far as impriſonment againſt the preachers of hereſy. This bill paſſed the lords, but was rejected by the commons; who, being already jealous of the power of the clergy, were in no degree inclined to make any addition to it.

The archbishop, notwithstanding this check, applied to the king for his licence, which he imagined would be full as effectual, though not so plausible, as an act of parliament. The king, immersed in pleasures, thought only of tenths and subsidies, and could refuse nothing to the clergy, who were so ready on all occasions to comply with him. Letters patent therefore were immediately made out, granting the full powers, which the archbishop required.

The practice heretofore had been, in cases of this kind, for the king to grant special licences on particular occasions. This unlimited power therefore, before unheard of, was very disagreeable to the whole nation. Accordingly, when the parliament met, which it did soon after, heavy complaints came from every county to their representatives, setting forth, how much the people thought themselves aggrieved.

The alarm spread through the house, where the affair was taken up with a becoming
ing

ing zeal. " Thefe new powers, it was faid,
" were dangerous encroachments.—If the
" liberties of the people were thus put into
" the hands of the clergy, the nation be-
" came fubject to a new kind of defpotifm.
" —Herefy was an unlimited word, and
" might bear as wide a conftruction as a
" bifhop might chufe to give it : nor could
" it be doubted, but it would often be made
" to fignify whatever the pride, or avarice of
" the clergy might think expedient."

This language was carried in a petition
from the commons to the king. The king,
as was ufual, being in want of money, and
afraid at this time of difobliging the commons, revoked the licence through the hope
of a fubfidy from the laity, which he had
juft before granted through the hope of an
aid from the clergy.—Such were the weak
politics of Richard; and thus was the archbifhop's zeal baffled a fecond time.

In one point however the primate fucceeded better. He obtained letters from the king,
directed to the vice-chancellor and proctors
of the univerfity of Oxford, by which they
were required to make diligent fearch in their
colleges and halls for all who maintained he-

D 2

retical

retical opinions; particularly thofe condemned by the arch-bifhop of Canterbury; and for all, who had in their poffeffion the books of John Wicliff. Such delinquents were ordered to be expelled the univerfity; and the fheriff and mayor of Oxford were commanded to affift the academical magiftrates in the execution of this order. The arch-bifhop also, himfelf wrote to the vice-chancellor, injoining him to publifh in St. Mary's church the king's letter, and also thofe articles of Wicliff's doctrine, which had been condemned. The vice-chancellor modeftly anfwered, that party at this time ran fo high in Oxford, where the feculars, who generally favoured Dr. Wicliff, bore a principal fway, that fuch a publication would not only be very dangerous to himfelf, but would greatly endanger also the peace of the univerfity.

In anfwer to this, the violent primate called him before the council, where he was vexed and queftioned with all the inhumanity of infolent authority. This brought him to a compliance; and every thing was publifhed, and in what manner, the arch-bifhop required.

The

The vice-chancellor's fears however, were well grounded. The fecular clergy were fo exceedingly incenfed againft the religious, that the univerfity became a fcene of the utmoft tumult: all ftudy was at an end: and to fuch an height were the animofities of the two parties carried, that they diftinguifhed themfelves by badges, and were fcarce controuled from breaking out into the moft violent effects of rage.

Whether Dr. Wicliff was ever brought to any public queftion in confequence of thefe proceedings, we meet with no account. It is moft probable he was advifed by his friends to retire from the ftorm. It is certain however, that at this time he quitted the profeffor's chair, and took his final leave of the univerfity of Oxford; which till now he feems to have vifited generally once every year. —Thus the unwearied perfecution of the archbifhop prevailed; and that prelate had the fatisfaction of feeing the man whom he hated, and whom, for fo many years he had in vain purfued, retreating at length before his power into an obfcure part of the kingdom.—The feeds however were fcattered, though the root was drawn. Wicliff's opi-

nions

nions began now to be propagated so universally over the nation, that as a writer of those times tells us, if you met two persons upon the road, you might be sure that one of them was a lollard.

While these things were doing in England, the dissention between the two popes continued. Thus far they had fought with spiritual weapons only, bulls, anathemas, and excommunications; and thus far their contention had excited only contempt. But Urban perceiving how little the thunders of the church availed, had recourse to more substantial arms. With this view he published a bull, in which he called upon all, who had any regard for religion, to exert themselves at this time in its cause; and take up arms against Clement, and his adherents, in defence of the holy see. The times, he said, required violent measures; and for the encouragement of the faithful he promised the same pardons and indulgences, which had been always granted to those, who lost their lives in the holy wars. This bull met with great encouragement in England, especially as the pope chose an ecclesiastic of that nation for his general, Henry Spencer, bishop of Norwich;

wich; " a young and ftout prelate, fays Fox,
" fitter for the camping cure, than for the peace-
" able church of Chrift." This officer having obtained a parliamentary affiftance, and
made his levies, fet out with great eagernefs
upon his expedition.

A war, in which the name of religion was
fo vilely proftituted, roufed Dr. Wicliff's
indignation, even in the decline of years.
He took up his pen once more, and wrote
againft it with great acrimony. He expoftu-
lates with the pope in a very free manner,
and afks him boldly, " How he durft
" make the token of Chrift on the crofs
" (which is a token of peace, mercy, and
" charity) a banner to lead on to flay chriftian
" men, for the love of two falfe priefts;
" and to opprefs chriftendom worfe than
" Chrift and his apoftles were oppreffed by
" the Jews. When, fays he, will the proud
" prieft of Rome grant indulgences to man-
" kind to live in peace and charity, as he now
" does to fight and flay one another ?"

This fevere piece drew upon him the refentment of Urban, and was likely to have
involved him in greater troubles than he had
yet experienced : but God himfelf delivered

his

his faithful fervant. He was ftruck with a palfy, foon after the publication of this treatife; and though he lived fome time, yet he lived in fuch a way, that his enemies confidered him as a perfon below their refentment. To the laft he attended divine worfhip; and received the fatal ftroke of his diforder in his church at Lutterworth, in the year 1384.

The papifts of thofe times gloried much in the circumftances of his death., " It was " reported, one of them tells us, that he had " prepared accufations, and blafphemies, " which he intended, on the day he was " taken ill, to have uttered in his pulpit, a- " gainft Thomas a Becket, the faint and " martyr of the day; but by the judgment of " God he was fuddenly ftruck, and the palfy " feized all his limbs; and that mouth which " was to have fpoken huge things againft " God, and his faints, and holy church was " miferably drawn afide, and afforded a " frightful fpectacle to the beholders: His " tongue was fpeechlefs, and his head fhook, " fhewing plainly that the curfe of God was " upon him."

Thus did his enemies, in the true fpirit of fuperftition, turn the moft common fymptoms of a common malady into divine judgments; and difcover, by calling in fuch feeble aids, how much in earneft their caufe wanted a fupport.

Such was the life of John Wicliff; whom we hefitate not to admire as one of the greateft ornaments of his country; and as one of thofe prodigies, whom providence raifes up, and directs as its inftruments to enlighten mankind. His amazing penetration; his rational manner of thinking; and the noble freedom of his fpirit, are equally the objects of our admiration. Wicliff was in religion, what Bacon was afterwards in fcience; the great detecter of thofe arts and gloffes, which the barbarifm of ages had drawn together to obfcure the mind of man.

To this intuitive genius Chriftendom was unqueftionably more obliged than to any name in the lift of reformers. He opened the gates of darknefs, and let in not a feeble and glimmering ray; but fuch an effulgence of light, as was never afterwards obfcured. He not only loofened prejudices; but advanced fuch clear inconteftible truths, as, having once obtained footing, ftill kept their ground, and even in an age of reformation

mation

mation wanted little amendment. How nearly his fentiments, almoft on every topic, agreed with thofe of the reformers of the fucceeding century, hath been made the fubject of fet enquiries, and will eafily appear from a general view of his opinions.

As the opinions of Wicliff make a very material part of his life, I have thought it proper to give a fuller account of them, in a feparate view, than could well be introduced in the body of the work. The following therefore, which are all either collected from his own words, or by a fair deduction from them, are the principal opinions which this reformer held.

With regard to the church, he was not fond of applying the words *church* and *church-men,* merely to the clergy, as thefe were often men of bad lives, he thought fuch application a vile proftitution of thofe facred names. Befides, it had bad influence, he thought, upon the laity; feeming to exclude them from the pale of Chrift's church, and to give them a difpenfation for licentious practice. If they were not of Chrift's church, they were not under Chrift's laws. He would never therefore have any idea fixed to the

word

word *church*, but that of the whole body of
Chriftians. In fome of his writings he makes
a diftinction between the true church of Chrift,
and the nominal. By the true church he
means fuch perfons only as God fhall pleafe
to fave. Chrift's nominal church he calls a
net, yet undrawn to land, full of every kind,
which muft afterwards be picked and fepa-
rated.

He was a warm affertor of the king's fupremacy; to prove which he reafoned thus.
Under the old law, we read that Solomon
depofed one high prieft, and ordained another, by his own proper authority, without
the concurrence of any ecclefiaftical fynod:
and in the new teftament, though we meet
with no exprefs command on the point of
the king's fupremacy; yet in general we are
told, that magiftrates are ordained of God
to punifh evil doers, and that without any
limitation. If then they are ordained to punifh evil doers, certainly they are, in the
higheft degree bound to punifh thofe, who
do the moft evil: and who will contend,
that the wicked prieft is not a worfe citizen,
than the wicked layman? Chrift, fays he, and
his apoftles were obedient to the temporal

powers

powers then exifting: and not to mention the many precepts of the gofpel writers on this fubject, which feem to be generally directed to all Chriftians; we fee in one place our Saviour himfelf paying tribute to the emperor; and in another, anfwering before Pilate without claiming any exemption.— Againft thofe who maintained the pope's fupremacy to be an article of faith he was very warm. The faving faith of a chriftian, fays he, confifts in believing, that Chrift was the Meffiah : but the Roman church has multiplied articles of faith without number. It is not enough now to believe in Chrift; we muft believe in the pope of Rome. The holy apoftles never afcribed to themfelves any fuch honour: how then can a finful wretch require it, who knows not whether he fhall be damned or faved ? If the pope, fays he, fhould happen to be a wicked man, we profefs it as an article of our belief, that a devil of hell is head of the church—that he is the moft holy father, infallible, and without fin, who poifons the principles of the church, and corrupts its practice, who contributes what he is able to banifh out of it faith,

.   meeknefs,

meeknefs, patience, charity, humility, and every other virtue of a chriftian.

The authority likewife claimed by the church Dr. Wicliff ftrenuofly oppofed. It was a fcandal, he would fay, to the chriftian church, that any of its members fhould fet up their own authority againft that of their Saviour. The great argument of that day (which was indeed a fubtle one) for the authority of the church, was this. Many perfons, befides Matthew, Mark, Luke, and John, wrote gofpels; but the church rejected them all, excepting thefe four: and this it did by its own proper authority. It might by the fame authority have rejected thofe four gofpels, and have received others. It follows therefore, that the authority of the church is above that of any gofpel.—To this Dr. Wicliff replied, that the evidence for the received gofpels was fo ftrong, and that for the rejected ones fo weak, that the church could not have done otherwife than it did, without doing violence to reafon. But the beft argument, he faid, if it were proper to avow it, for fupporting the authority of the church, was the neceffity of that doctrine to fupport the tyranny of the pope.

This

This was what made it worth defending at the expence of truth.——In another place, fpeaking on the fame fubject, he fays, that the pope would not fubmit his actions to the fame criterion, by which Chrift was contented to have his actions tried. If I do not, fays Chrift, the works of my father which is in heaven, believe me not. But the pope's authority, it feems, muft be acknowledged, though he manifeftly does the works of the devil. Thus, fays he, Chriftians are in greater thraldom than the Jews under the old law; and that liberty, by which Chrift hath made us free, is by the wickednefs of defigning men, changed into the moft abfolute fpiritual bondage. The days, fays he, I hope, will come, when men fhall be wife enough to fhake from their necks the dominion of thefe human ordinances; and difdain fubmiffion to any ecclefiaftical injunctions, but fuch as are plainly authorized by the word of God.

Having thus fhewn Dr. Wicliff's opinions about the church, I fhall now give the reader fome of his opinions upon church doctrines.

He acknowledged feven facraments; but is very inaccurate in his definition of a facra-

ment;

ment; which he calls, *A token that may be feen of a thing that may not be feen.* This inaccuracy however, is not peculiar to Wicliff. We meet with it univerfally amongft the old writers in divinity, both before and after his time; whofe idea of a facrament feems to have been extremely vague: from Wicliff's logical exactnefs we might have expected a more accurate definition.

But though he thus acknowledges feven facraments, he exprefly fays, he does not efteem them all neceffary to falvation; and inveighs warmly againft the many idle ceremonies ufed by the church of Rome in the adminiftration of them all; ceremonies, he fays, which have no ufe in themfelves, nor any foundation in fcripture. When ceremonies are few and expreffive, he thinks, they may be of ufe; and enumerates, among others, kneeling, and beating the breaft in prayer.

With regard to baptifm, he thought it neceffary to falvation. This he grounded on the expreffion, *Except a man be born of water and of the fpirit, he cannot enter into the kingdom of God;* which he underftood of material water. But he oppofed the fuper-

ftition

ftition of three immerfions. In cafe of neceffity, he thought, any one prefent might baptize. The prieft, he faid, in baptifm (as
indeed in all the other facraments) admi-
niftered only the token or fign; but God,
who is the prieft, and bifhop of our fouls,
adminifters the fpiritual grace. This gave
occafion to his enemies to reprefent him
(which they did with great falfhood) as
denying any ufe of material water. When
he fpeaks of water, fay they, he means only
figuratively the water, which flowed from
the fide of Chrift.—With regard to the
queftion, whether unbaptized infants could
be faved, he waves it, adding, that he thinks
it probable, Chrift may fpiritually baptize
fuch infants, and confequently fave them.
This opinion too might afford fome foundation to the flander above-mentioned; though
he guards againft it by faying, that we muft
not neglect baptifm by water, on a fuppofition, that we are baptized by the fpirit.

Of the facrament of the Lord's fupper,
we have * already feen his opinion. But
though it appears from the account given

of

* See page 42.

of his creed in this point, that he thought bread and wine only figns of Chrift's body; yet in other parts of his writings we find him fpeaking of them in a much higher ftrain. The truth feems to be, that he was late in fettling his notions of the Lord's fupper: whence it is, that in different parts of his writings he contradicts himfelf. This appears to be the foundation of Melancthon's complaint. " I have looked, fays he, into " Wicliff; and find him very confufed in " this controverfy of the Lord's fupper."

With regard to confirmation, he thought the oil, and the veil made ufe of by the bifhop, had no foundation in fcripture, and were better omitted; and that the other ceremonies, together with all the parade and pomp, which accompany this facrament were ftill worfe, tending only to fix the minds of the people upon trifles, and to imprefs on them a fuperftitious veneration for the clergy. He could fee no reafon, why the prieft might not confirm, as well as baptize; baptifm, he faid, muft be acknowledged to be the facrament of greater dignity, inafmuch as it is of more authentic gofpel-inftitution.

E

Speaking

Speaking of matrimony, he inveighs warmly againſt granting divorces on ſlight occaſions, as was cuſtomary in the church of Rome; and ſays, that a divorce can be juſtified on no cauſe, but that of adultery.

In extreme unction he ſees nothing un-ſcriptural: at leaſt I meet with nothing of objection to it, in any part of his writings which I have ſeen. Only indeed, he blames the exorbitant fees, which the avarice of the prieſts of thoſe times exacted for the performance of it.

Speaking likewiſe of orders, he inveighs againſt the ſame avarice; and jocularly ſays, a man might have a barber to attend him a whole year for what he pays to have his crown ſhaven once.

With regard to confeſſion, his opinion was, that if a man be really contrite, exter-nal confeſſion is by no means of abſolute neceſſity; yet as it may be a means to bring on repentance, he would not reject it, if a proper choice be made of a confeſſor. But as confeſſion was practiſed in the church of Rome, he thought it a vile and ſcandalous method of getting into the ſecrets of fami-

lies,

lies, and tended only to advance the power of the church.

Pennance, he says, hath no fort of merit in God's fight, unlefs followed by a reformed life.

Of abfolution, as practifed in the church of Rome, he was a warm oppofer. It was the height of blafphemy, he faid, to afcribe to man the power of God. *Who can forgive fins, but God alone?* Inftead of acting as God's minifters, the Romifh clergy, he faid, took upon them, in their own names, to forgive fins. Nay in the plenitude of their power they will do, fays he, what God himfelf (if there is truth in fcripture) would not do—pardon unrepented fin. Exprefs paffages of fcripture in favour of the contrite heart are nothing : God's abfolution is of no effect, unlefs confirmed by theirs. Pre-fumptuous guides, fays he, they ought to urge the neceffity of repentance, inftead of abfolution ; and preach a future ftate of re-wards and punifhments, the deformity of fin, and the mercy of God, inftead of de-ceiving mankind by their ridiculous im-poftures.

E 2

Againft

Againſt indulgences, he was very ſevere.
A mere trick, he called them, to rob men
of their money. The pope, ſays he, has
the ſurplus of the merits of pious ſaints to
diſpoſe of. A profitable doctrine this; but
where found? Certainly not in ſcripture.
For my own part, ſays he, I meet not, in
the whole new-teſtament with one ſaint who
had more merit than was neceſſary for his
own ſalvation. And if Chriſt, who taught
all that was needful and profitable, taught
not this doctrine, it may be fairly preſumed,
that this doctrine is neither needful nor profitable. All men, as far as the merits of
another can avail, are partakers of the merits
of Chriſt: and no man can expect more.
How abſurd then is it to ſee men ſquander
away their money upon indulgences, inſtead
of laying it out properly in charitable uſes:
as if it were a more acceptable ſervice to
God, to add ſuperfluous wealth to a monaſtery, than to diſtribute alms among ne-
ceſſitous chriſtians.—Beſides, in how un-
charitable a light doth the pope appear, if
there be one ſoul left in purgatory. A turn
of his pen would deliver the ſinner, and if
he deny that, it can only be thought avarice

rice, and want of a good heart.—If he have not power to deliver all men, he is a deceiver; for he declares, that he has such power. But his pardons, it seems, are only to be had for ready money, and granted too, not for the good of mankind, but to promote diffention and war. Were this boafted power of pardoning an heavenly gift, like God's other favours, it would certainly be difpenfed in an impartial manner. Wealth could not command it: and the pope, like the apoftles, would cry out, " Thy money " perifh with thee." Whether the pope's pardons be difpenfed in this impartial manner, let the papift fay. They will tell you perhaps, he adds, that the pardons themfelves are a free gift; but that the bull occafions the expence. Such prevarication puts one in mind of the hoft, who profeffed to treat his guefts with a goofe for nothing; but charged them without confcience for the fauce.—Thus by the vile trade of indulgences are men deceived. Any one, who can pay for a pardon, may laugh at fin. He has found an eafy way to heaven; much eafier than by contrition, repentance, and works of charity. May we not then, fays

E 3

he,

he, safely conclude, that indulgences were an invention of anti-christ to magnify the sacerdotal power; and to bring in wealth to the church, at the expence of religion, and the souls of men?

With regard to purgatory, he believed in such a state; and, as it appears from some parts of his works, was once of opinion that pious prayers might be serviceable to souls imprisoned there: but in his later writings, he wholly renounces this opinion, and calls it a pernicious error; especially to pray for one person more than another, which he looks upon as a most unchristian practice; though he still seems to think we may pray in general for all those, whom God in his mercy intends for happiness. In short, upon this subject he does not seem to have absolutely fixed his opinion. He saw something extremely plausible in the Romish doctrine of purgatory; he likewise saw the absurdity of supposing, that God intrusted any man with a power to release sinners from such a state; but whether the souls of the dead might be profited by the prayers of the living, he seems to have been in doubt.

He

He was a great enemy to the endowments of chauntry-priefts. They led the people, he thought, to put their truft in fuch endowments, rather than in a good life: whereas no prayers, even of the holieft faints, he thought, could benefit a bad man. *That man*, faith he excellently, *who liveth beft, prayeth beft*. A fimple pater-nofter from a religious plowman, is of more value in the fight of God, than a thoufand maffes from a wicked prelate.

He had a great diflike to chaunting in divine worfhip, which was then commonly ufed in cathedrals and religious houfes; and was known by the name of the new fong. This fort of worfhip, he fays, was originally introduced to impofe on the underftanding, by fubftituting found in the room of fenfe; and fo to be one mean of keeping the people in ignorance. He owns it is a merry way of ferving God; and therefore, he fuppofes, it meets with fo much encouragement. But he would have men be of St. Auftin's opinion, who fays, that as often as found drew his attention from fenfe, fo often he worfhipped God improperly. If, fays he, the temple-mufic of the old law be

E 4   alledged

alledged as a fufficient warrant for cathedral worfhip, it may eafily be anfwered,
that Chrift, who was the beft commentator
upon the old law, gives us no inftruction
on this head; but tells his difciples, that he
requires no recommendation of prayer, but
the devotion of the heart.   Others again
will perhaps fay, that the angels praife God,
in heaven: to which, it may as eafily be
anfwered, that we know nothing of heavenly mufick.   Only this we know, that
the angels are in a triumphant ftate, and we
in a militant one; in a ftate of trial and affliction, where mufick diverts us from better
things.   It is grievous, fays he, to fee what
fums of money are yearly expended upon
thefe finging priefts, and how little upon
the education of children.   Befides, he adds,
how abfurd is it to hear, in a large congre-
gation, only two or three chaunting a piece
of devotion, while all the reft, not only
cannot join with them; but even do not
underftand what they fay.

He often inveighs againft prayers to faints,
and the ufe of any mediator except Chrift.
He even goes fo far as to wifh that all feftivals in the church were abolifhed, except
                                        Chriftmas-

Chriftmas-day, and eafter.   For the devotion of the people, fays he, being undivided, would be more fervent upon thofe folemn days.   As to modern canonizations, he fays, they owe their birth to nothing but exceſſive bigotry on one fide, or exceſſive avarice on the other.

With regard to images, he thought, that if they were exact reprefentations of the truth, they might be very ferviceable to give the vulgar ftrong impreſſions of the poverty, and fufferings, of Chrift, his apoftles, and martyrs.   But this ufe, he fays, could not be expected from them in the Roman church. Thofe gay reprefentations, decked in coftly apparel, inftead of giving us the idea of fuffering faints, exhibit to us perfons of pomp and expence; and fhould be confidered as heretical books, full of falfe doctrines; and as fuch fhould be condemned to the fire.—— Befides, fays he, how fhocking is it to fee thofe dumb idols covered with gold and filver; while Chrift's poor members are ftarving in the ftreets.——But of all the bad effects which attend images, the worft, he fays, is their leading the people into idolatry.   If Hezechiah broke in pieces the brazen ferpent,

pent, which God commanded to be made, becaufe it attracted the veneration of the people; how much more ought a chriftian king to break in pieces thofe images, which God is fo far from having commanded to be made, that we have in fcripture the moft exprefs commands againft making them.

He greatly difliked the ceremonies of confecration fo frequent in the church of Rome. Thefe confecrations, fays he, and benedictions, in which the Roman church is fo profufe upon water, oil, falt, wax, veftments, walls, pilgrims-ftaves, and a variety of other things, have more the appearance of necromancy, than of true religion. They are abfurd, becaufe thefe things are juft the fame after confecration as before : and they are idolatrous, becaufe they tend to make people pay a divine honour to them.

No man could be more ftrenuous than Dr. Wicliff againft refting upon the externals of religion; or faid more to convince men of the folly of expecting, that building and ornamenting churches, frequenting public worfhip, or any outward expreffion of religion, would fatisfy God without the heart, or make any atonement for a bad life. Holy

water,

water, says he, and the blessing of a bishop are mere impositions, tending only to blind the people, and make them rest in those externals, rather than in God's mercy, and their own repentance.

He asserted the necessity of being assisted by divine grace. Without this, he saw not how a human being could make himself acceptable to God.

With regard to pilgrimages, he says, that although visiting the shrines of saints might be suffered with a view to impress us strongly with a sense of their virtues, yet pilgrimages, as commonly used, are of most pernicious consequence. If idol-worship be bad, pilgrimages are equally so, leading the people into idolatry, and a misapplication of their charity.

Against sanctuaries he is still warmer. That the grossest crimes should be sheltered, under the safeguard of religion, was, in his opinion, such a perversion of all the principles of reason and Christianity, as could not be sufficiently exclaimed against.

He was a great advocate for the marriage of the clergy, and thought the celibacy pre-
scribed

fcribed by the Roman church one of the principal caufes of its corruption.

He denied the power of excommunication to the church; and ftiles fuch ecclefiaftical cenfures, punifhments inflicted by anti-chrift's jurifdiction. No man, fays he, can be excommunicated, unlefs he firft excommunicate himfelf.

Peter-pence, he calls an iniquitous impofition, without any foundation in fcripture.

Thefe are his principal opinions, with regard to church doctrines. The following are his opinions on feveral mifcellaneous fubjects.

He was a great enemy to the fuperfluous wealth of the clergy. He allowed the labourer to live by his labour; but he afferted, that he had a right to his hire from nothing elfe. Tythes, he faid, were only a fort of alms, no where of gofpel inftitution, which the people might either give or withdraw, as they found their paftor deferved. This opinion drew upon him the refentment both of papifts and proteftants. Melancthon, in particular, is very warm with him on this head; fays, he raved, and declares him plainly mad. But it is no wonder, if Wic-

liff's

liff's diflike to the prevailing luxury of the clergy, which was then fo exorbitant, led him into an extreme. His conftant advice to his brethren was, to exact their tythes by the holinefs of their lives. If thou be a prieft, fays he, contend with others, not in pomp, but in piety. Ill befits it a man, who lives on the labours of the poor, to fquander away the dear-bought fruits of their induftry upon his own extravagancies.

Church-endowments, he thought, were the root of all the corruption among the clergy. He often lamented the luxury they occafioned; and ufed to wifh the church was again reduced to its primitive poverty, and innocence.

With ftill greater warmth he exprefled himfelf againft the fecular employments of the clergy. This he feemed to think an unpardonable defertion of their profeffion.

In fome parts of his writings, he appears to have held, that ftrange doctrine, *That dominion is founded on grace*. His argument, if I underftand it all, feems to be, that as all things belong to God, and as good men alone are the children of God, they are of courfe the only true inheritors.

But

But in other parts of his writings, it appears, as if he only fpoke figuratively on this fubject, and of ideal perfection. That he did not hold the doctrine in its literal fenfe, feems plain from many paffages of his works. In his Trialogue particularly, he fays, " Duplici titulo ftat hominem habere " temporalia, fcilicet titulo originalis jufti- " tiæ, & titulo mundanæ juftitiæ. Titulo " autem originalis juftitiæ habuit Chriftus " omnia bona mundi. Illo titulo, vel titulo " gratiæ, juftorum funt omnia : fed longe " ab illo titulo civilis poffeffio." Upon the whole, however, what he fays on this fubject may be called whimfical.

He held fafting to be enjoined only for the fake of virtuous habits; and calls it therefore highly pharifaical to place a greater value upon bodily abftinence from food, than fpiritual abftinence from fin.

It was a conjecture of his, that this world was created to fupply the lofs in heaven occafioned by the fallen angels; and that when that lofs fhould be fupplied, the end of things fhould fucceed.

Upon a text in the revelations he founded an opinion, that the devil was let loofe about

a thoufand

a thoufand years after Chrift; from which period he dates the rife of the principal corruptions of the church.

With regard to oaths, he confidered it as plain idolatry to fwear by any creature. In this fenfe he underftood the prohibition of our Saviour againft fwearing by heaven and earth. It is not found, faith he, in the old law, that God at any time granted his permiffion to fwear by any creature.

He feems to have thought it wrong, upon the principles of the gofpel, to take away the life of man upon any occafion. The whole trade of war he thought utterly unlawful: nor did he think the execution of a criminal a more allowed practice.

In fome parts of his writings he fpeaks fo ftrongly of fate, that he appears an abfolute predeftinarian. In other parts he expreffes himfelf in fo cautious a manner, that we are apt to think he had no fixed principles on this fubject.

All arts, which adminiftred to the luxuries of life, he thought were prohibited by the gofpel. The fcriptures, fays he, tell us, that having food and raiment, we fhould be therewith content.

Herefy,

Herefy, according to Wicliff, confifted in a bad life, as well as in falfe opinions. No good man, he thought, could be an heretic.

His opinion, on this laft point, agrees with that of a prelate of later times, who generally fpeaks the language of true Chriftian freedom and charity. I fhall quote fome paffages at large from this celebrated writer, not only as they tend to fhew the juftnefs of Wicliff's own manner of thinking; but as they may ferve as a conclufion to this review of his opinions, in being a proper anfwer to all his adverfaries.

" No herefies, (fays bifhop Taylor, in his
" liberty of prophefying) are noted in fcrip-
" ture; but fuch as are errors practical. In
" all the animadverfions againft errors in the
" new teftament, no pious perfon was con-
" demned. Something was amifs in genere
" morum. Herefy is not an error of the
" underftanding, but an error of the will.
" And indeed, if we remember that St. Paul
" reckons herefy among the works of the
" flefh, and ranks it with all manner of
" practical impieties, we fhall eafily perceive,
" that if a man mingles not a vice with his
" opinions, if he be innocent in his life,
                              " though

" though deceived in his doctrine, his error
" is his misery, not his crime: he may be an
" object of pity, but by no means a person
" configned to ruin.——There are as many
" innocent causes of error, as there are
" weaknesses, and unavoidable prejudices.——
" In questions practical, the doctrine itself,
" and the person too, may be reproved; but
" in other things, which end in notion,
" where neither the doctrine is malicious,
" nor the person apparently criminal, he is
" to be left to the judgment of God. Opi-
" nions and persons are to be judged like
" other things. It must be a crime, and it
" must be open, of which any cognizance
" can be taken.——Let me farther observe,
" that since there are such great differences
" of apprehension concerning the confe-
" quences of an action, no man is to be
" charged with the odious consequences of
" his opinion. Indeed his doctrine may be,
" but the man is not, if he understand not
" such things to be consequent to his doctrine.
" For if he did, and then avows them, they
" are his direct opinions; and he stands as
" chargeable with them, as with his first
" proposition.——No error then, nor its con-

            " fequent,

" fequent, is to be charged as criminal upon
" a pious perfon, fince no fimple error is fin,
" nor does condemn us before the throne of
" God." *

Of

* A very ingenious hiftorian, hath charged Wicliff with
enthufiafm. " He denyed the doctrine, (fays he,) of the
" real prefence --- the fupremacy of the church of Rome ---
" the merit of monaftic vows. --- He maintained; that the
" fcripture was the fole rule of faith; --- that the church
" was dependent on the ftate, --- and ought to be reformed
" by it; --- that the clergy ought to poffefs no eftates; ---
" that the begging fryars were a general nuifance, and
" ought not to be fupported; --- that the numerous ceremo-
" nies of the church were hurtful to true piety. --- He
" afferted, that oaths were unlawful, --- that dominion was
" founded in grace; --- that every thing was fubject to fate
" and deftiny; and that all men were predeftinated either
" to eternal falvation or reprobation."
Having given this abftract of his opinions, which is in
general very juft, the hiftorian informs us, that " From the
" whole of his doctrines, Wicliff appears to have been
" ftrongly tinctured with enthufiafm."
Mr. Hume has certainly expreffed himfelf here in a very
unguarded manner, unlefs he meant to brand under the
name of enthufiam, the whole fyftem of the reformation.
He has given us twelve of the opinions of Wicliff, of which
only the feventh, and two laft, feem to be carried farther,
than was done by the more fober part of the reformers of
the fixteenth century; and indeed, Mr. Hume has been
ingenuous enough to own, that, " The doctrines of Wicliff,
" being derived from his fearch into the fcriptures, and
" into ecclefiaftical antiquity, were nearly the fame with
" thofe propagated by the reformers in the fixteenth cen-
" tury;

Of the Writings of Dr. Wicliff.

Having thus taken a view of Dr. Wicliff's
opinions, let us confider him next as a writer.

                    His

" tury; fome of them only carried farther." And yet,
notwithftanding this, we are told, that, " Upon the *whole*,
" they were *ftrongly* tinctured with enthufiafm."

This writer has been charged with refolving all revealed
religion into enthufiafm on one hand, or fuperftition on the
other. And indeed his treatment of Wicliff feems in fome
degree to juftify the charge: " He appears, (fays the hifto-
" rian,) to have been ftrongly tinctured with enthufiafm,
" and to have been thereby the better qualified to oppofe a
" church, whofe diftinguifhing character was fuperftition."
It was his enthufiafm, it feems, and not his rational arguments, (for our hiftorian appears to have thrown reafon out
of both fides of the queftion) that made him a formidable
adverfary to the church of Rome.

If Mr. Hume had not been under the influence of prejudice, it is impoffible but a perfon of his liberal caft of
mind, muft have admired the noble freedom, and rational
manner, with which this great reformer oppofed the flavifh
principles of his times. Had Wicliff lived in the days of
philofophy, this writer had been among his firft admirers;
but a religionift is a formal character; and what in a philofopher is a manly exercife of reafon, becomes in a modern
reformer, irrational zeal, and a ridiculous pretence to
infpiration.

If I have miftaken Mr. Hume's meaning, I heartily beg
his pardon. The reader, judging for himfelf, will lay no
farther ftrefs on what I have faid, than fair quotations will
authorize againft Mr. Hume; and fair reprefentations of
facts in favour of Dr. Wicliff.

His works are amazingly voluminous: yet he feems not to have engaged in any very large work: his pieces in general may properly be called tracts. Of thefe many were written in Latin, and many in Englifh: fome on fchool queftions; others on fubjects of more general knowledge; but the greateft part on divinity. It may be fome amufement to the reader to fee what fubjects he hath chofen. I fhall give a lift therefore of the more re-markable of them, from the various collections which have been made.

Trialagorum lib. 4.
De religione perfectorum.
De ecclefia & membris.
De diabolo & membris.
De Chrifto & Antichrifto.
De Antichrifto & membris.
Sermones in epiftolas.
De veritate fcripturæ.
De ftatu innocentiæ.
De dotatione ecclefiæ.
De ftipendiis miniftrorum.
De epifcoporum erroribus.
De curatorum erroribus.
De perfectione evangelicâ

De

De officio paftorali.
De fimonia facerdotum.
Super pænitentiis injungendis.
De feductione fimplicium.
Dæmonum aftus in fubvertenda religione.
De pontificum Romanorum fchifmate.
De ultima ætate ecclefiæ.
Of temptation.
The chartre of hevene.
Of ghoftly battel.
Of ghoftly and flefhly love.
The confeffion of St. Brandoun.
Active life, and contemplative life.
Virtuous patience.
Of pride.
Obfervationes piæ in X præcepta.
De impedimentis orationis.
De cardinalibus virtutibus.
De actubus animæ.
Expofitio orationis dominicæ.
De 7 facramentis.
De natura fidei.
De diverfis gradibus charitatis.
De defectione a Chrifto.
De veritate & mendacio.
De facerdotio Levitico.
De facerdotio Chrifti.

F 3

De

De dotatione Cæfareâ.

De verfutiis pfeudocleri.

De immortalitate animæ.

De paupertate Chrifti.

De phyfica naturali.

De effentia accidentium.

De neceffitate Inturorum.

De temporis quidditate.

De temporis ampliatione.

De operibus corporalibus.

De operibus fpiritualibus.

De fide & perñdia.

De fermone domini in monte.

Abftractiones logicales.

A fhort rule of life.

The great fentence of the curfe expounded.

Of good priefts,

De contrarietate duorum dominorum.

Wicliff's wicket.

De miniftrorum conjugio.

De religiofis privatis.

Conciones de morte.

De vita facerdotum.

De ablatis reftituendis.

De arte fophiftica.

De fonte errorum.

De incarnatione verbi.

Super

Super impofitis articulis.

De humanitate Chrifti.

Contra concilium terræ-motus.

De folutione Satanæ.

De fpiritu quolibet.

De Chriftianorum baptifmo.

De clavium poteftate.

De blafphemia.

De paupertate Chrifti.

De raritate & denfitate.

De materia & forma.

De anima.

Octo beatitudines.

De trinitate.

Commentarii in pfalterium.

De abominatione defolationis.

De civili dominio.

De ecclefiæ dominio.

De divino dominio.

De origine fectarum.

De perfidia fectarum.

Speculum de antichrifto.

De virtute orandi.

De remiffione fraterna.

De cenfuris ecclefiæ.

De charitate fraterna.

F 4

De

De purgatorio piorum.
De Pharifæo & Publicano.

I might have greatly enlarged this catalogue of the works of Wicliff, but the titles
I have inferted, will be fufficient to give the
reader an idea in general of the fubjects, on
which he wrote. To give him an idea of his
manner of writing, I have thought proper to
infert the following fhort treatife; in which
the reader will have a fpecimen of that
mafterly ftyle, that clearnefs, concifenefs, and
elegance, (confidering the times) with which
he treated every fubject. If the reader compare it with the original, he will find, that
a few fentences have been left out, but none
added.

Why many priefts have no benefices.
A treatife of John Wicliff.

Some caufes why poor priefts receive not
benefices. The firft for dread of Symony.
The fecond for dread of mifpending poor
mens goods. The third for dread of letting
of better occupation that is more light or
eafy, more certain and more profitable. ·

I. For

I. For firſt, if men ſhould come to benefices by gift of prelates, there is dread of
ſymony. For commonly they taken the firſt
fruits, or other penſions, or holden curates
in office in their courts or chapels, in offices
far fro prieſts life, taught, and enſampled of
Chriſt and his apoſtles. So that commonly
ſuch benefices comen not freely as Chriſt
commandeth, but rather for worldly winning, or flattering of mighty men, and not
for kunning of God's law, and true preaching of the goſpel, and enſample of holy life;
and therefore commonly theſe prelates, and
receivers ben fouled with ſymony, that is
curſed hereſie, as God's law and man's law
techen. And now whoever can run to Rome,
and bear gold out of the lond, and ſtrive,
and plead, and curſe for tithes, and other
temporal profits, that ben cleped with antichriſt's clerks rights of holy church, ſhall
have great benefices of cure of many thou-
ſand ſouls, tho he be unable, and of curſed
life, and wicked enſample of pride, of covetiſſe, glotony, leachery, and other great
ſins. But if there be any ſimple man, that
deſireth to live well, and teche truly God's
law, he ſhall ben holden an hypocrite, a new
teacher,

teacher, an heretick, and not fuffered to come to any benefice. But if in any little poor place he liven a poor life, he fhall be fo purfued, and flandered, that he fhall be put out by wiles, cantels, frauds, and world-ly violence, and imprifoned or brent. And if lords fhullen prefent clerks to benefices, they wolen have commonly gold in great quantity, and holden thefe curates in fome worldly office, and fuffren the wolves of hell to ftranglen mens fouls, fo that they have their office done for nought, and their chap-pels holden up for vain-glory or hypocrify; and yet they wolen not prefent a clerk able of God's law, and of good life, and holy enfample to the people; but a kitchen-clerk, or a penny-clerk, or one wife in building caftles, or other worldly doing; tho he kun not read his fauter, and knoweth not the commandments of God, ne facraments of holy church. And yet fome lords, to co-louren their fymony wole not take for them-felves, but kerchiefs for the lady, or a pal-fray, or a tun of wine. And when fome lords woulden prefent a good man, then fome ladies ben means to have a dancer pre-fented, or a tripper on tapits, or hunter, or

a hawker,

hawker, or a wild player of fummer gam-
)els. And thus it feemeth, that both pre-
ates, and lords commonly maken fome cured antichrift, or a quick fiend to be mafter
)f Chrift's people, for to leaden them to hell
o Sathanas their mafter; and fuffer not
Chrift's difciples to teche Chrift's gofpel to
iis children for to fave their fouls.

But in this prefenting of evil curates, and
iolding of curates in worldly office, letting
hem fro their ghoftly cure, ben three degrees of traitery agenft God and his people.
The firft is in prelates and lords, that thus
iolden curates in their worldly office; for
hey have their high ftates in the church,
ind lordfhips, for to purvey true curates to
he people, and to meyntene them in God's
aw, and punifh them, if they failen in their
ghoftly cure, and by this they holden their
ordfhips of God. Then if they maken evil
curates, and holden them in their worldly
office, and letten them to lead God's people
the rightful way to heaven, but helpen them,
ind conftreynen them to lead the people to
hell-ward, by withdrawing of God's word,
ind by evil enfample geving, they ben wei-
ward traytors to God and his people, and
vicars

vicars of Sathanas.——2. Yet more traitery is in falſe curates, that geven mede or hire to comen into ſuch worldly offices, and to get lordſhip and maintenance agenſt ordinances, and couchen in lord's courts for to get mo fatte benefices, and purpoſen not ſpedly to do their ghoſtly office. Woe is to the lords that been led with ſuch curſed heretics, an-tichriſts, traytors of God and his people; and traytors to lords themſelves; who ben ſo blinded, that they perceiven not that ſuch traitors, that openly ben falſe to God, wolen much more been falſe to them.—— 3. But the moſt traitery is in falſe confeſſors, that ſhulden by their office warn prelates, and lords of this great peril, and clerks alſo that they holden none ſuch curates in their worldly offices. For they don not this, leſt they leſen lordſhip, and friendſhip, and gifts, and welfare of their ſtinking belly; and ſo they fellen chriſten ſouls to Sathanas, and maken prelates and lords, and curates to live in ſin and traitery agenſt God and his people, and deceiven them in their ſouls health, and meyntenen them in curſed traitery of God and his people; and thus almoſt all the world goeth to hell for this curſed ſymony of falſe

confeſſors.

confeſſors. For commonly prelates, lords, and curates ben envenymed with this hereſy of ſymony, and never done very repentance, and ſatisfaction therefore. For when they have. a fat benefice geten by ſymony, they forſaken it not as they ben bounden by law, but wittingly uſen forth that ſymony, and liven in riot, covetiſſe, and pride, and don not their office neither in good enſample, ne in true teching. And thus antichriſt's clerks, enemies of Chriſt, and his people, by money, and flattering, and fleſhly love, gedring to them leading of the people, forbare true prieſts to teche God's law, and therefore the blind leadeth the blind, and both parts run-nen into ſin, and full many to hell: and it is huge wonder that God of his righteouſ-neſs deſtroyeth not the houſes of prelates, and lords, and curates, as Sodom and Go-mor for hereſie, extortions, and other cur-ſedneſſes. And for dread of this ſin, and many mo, ſome poor wretches receive no benefices in this world.

II. Yet tho poor prieſts mighten freely getten preſentation of lords to have bene-fices with cure of ſouls, they dreaden of miſpending poor mens goods. For prieſts

owen

owen to hold themfelves paide with food, and cloathing, as St. Paul techeth; and if they have more it is poor mens goods, as their own law, and God's law feyn, and they ben keepers thereof, and procurators of poor men. But for inftitution and induction he fhall give much of this good, that is poor men's, to bifhops officers, archdeacons, and officials, that ben too rich. And when bifhops and their officers comen, and feynen to vifit, tho they nourifhen men in open fin for annual rent, and don not their office, but fellen fouls to Sathanas for money, wretched curates ben neded to feaften them richly, and give procuracy and fynage, yea againft God's law, and man's, and reafon, and their own confcience, and yet they fhullen not be fuffered to teche truly God's law to their own fujects, and warn them of falfe prophets, who deceiven them both in belief and teching: for then they muften crie to the people the great fins of prelates; but they demen that fuch fad reproving of fin is envy, flandering of prelates, and deftroying of holy church. Alfo many times their patrons willen look to be feafted of fuch curates, elfe maken them

lefe

lefe that little thing, that they and poor men ſhullen live by. So that they ſhullen not ſpend their tithes and offerings after good conſcience, and God's laws, but waſte them on rich and idle men. Alſo eche good day commonly theſe ſmall curates ſhullen have letters fro their ordinaries to ſummon, and to curſe poor men for nought, but for covetiſſe of antichriſts clerks; and if they not ſumonen and curſen them, tho they know no cauſe why they ſhullen been hurted, and ſummoned fro day to day, fro far place to farther, or curſed, or leſe their benefits or profits. For elſe, as prelates feinen, they by their rebeldy ſhulden ſoon deſtroy prelates juriſdiction, power, and winning. Alſo, when poor prieſts, firſt holy of life, and devout in their prayers, ben beneficed, if they ben not buſy about the world to make great feaſts to rich perſons and vicars, and coſtly and gayly arrayed, by falſe doom of the world, they ſhullen be hated and hayned on as hounds, and ech man redy to peirc them in name, and worldly goods. So many curſed deceits hath antichriſt brought up by his worldly clerks to make curates to miſpende poor mens goods, and

not

not truly do their office; or elfe to forfaken
all, and let antichrift's clerks, as lords of
this world, rob the poor people by feyned
cenfures, and teche the fend's lore both by
open preching, and enfample of curfed life.
Alfo, if fuch curates ben ftirred to learn
God's law, and teche their parifhens the
gofpel, commonly they fhullen get no leave
of bifhops, but for gold; and when they
fhullen moft profit in their learning, then
fhullen they be clepid home at the prelate's
will.   And if they fhullen have any high
facraments, commonly they fhulle buy them
with poor mens goods; and fo there is full
great peril of evil fpending of thefe goods,
both upon prelates, rich men of the country, patrons, parfons, and their own kyn,
for fame of the world, and for fhame, and
evil deming of men.   And certes it is great
wonder that God fuffreth fo long this fin
unpunifhed, namely of prelates courts, that
ben dens of thieves, and larders of hell; and
fo of their officers, that ben fotil in malice
and covetiffe; and of lords, and mighty
men, that fhulden deftroy this wrong and
other, and meyntenen truth, and God's fer-
vants, and now meyntenen antichrift's falf-

nefs

nefs and his clerks, for part of the winning. But certes God fuffreth fuch hypocrites and tyrants to have name of prelates for great fins of the people, that eche part lead other to hell by blindnefs of the fend. And this is a thoufand time more vengeance, than if God fhud deftroy bodily both parts, and all their goods, and earth therewith, as he did by Sodom and Gomor. For the longer that they liven thus in fin, the greater pains fhullen they have in hell, unlefs they amenden them.——And this dread, and many mo, maken fome poor priefts to receiven none benefices.

III. But yet tho poor priefts mighten have freely prefentation of lords, and ben holpen by meyntening of kings, and help of good commons fro extortions of prelates, and other mifpending of thefe goods, that is full hard in this reigning of Antichrift's clerks, yet they dreden fore that by fingular cure ordained of finful men they fhulden be letted fro better occupation, and fro more profit of holy church. And this is the moft dread of all; for they have cure and charge at the full of God to help their brethren to heavenward, both by teching, praying, and exam-

G

ple-

ple-geving.   And it feemeth that they fhullen moft eafily fulfill this by general cure of
charity, as did Chrift and his apoftles.   And
by this they moft fikerly fave themfelves, and
help their brethren: and they ben free to flee
fro one city to another, when they ben purfued of antichrift's clerks, as biddeth Chrift
in the gofpel.   And they may beft without
challenging of men go and dwell among the
people where they fhullen moft profit, and
in covenable time come, and go after ftirring
of the holy ghoft, and not be bounden by
finful mens jurifdiction fro the better doing.
Alfo they purfuen Chrift and his apoftles
nearer, in taking alms wilfully of the people
that they techen, than in taking dymes and
offerings by cuftoms that finful men ordey-
nen, and ufen now in the time of grace.
Alfo this is more medeful on both fides as
they underftonden by Chrifts life, and his
apoftles: for thus the people giveth them
alms more wilfully and devoutly, and they
taken it more mekely, and ben more bufy
to lerne, kepe and teche God's law, and fo
it is the better for both fides.   Alfo by this
manner might and fhulde the people geve
freely their alms to true priefts that truly

kepen

kepen their order, and taughten the gospel; and withdrawen fro wicked priests, and not to be constreyned to pay their tithes, and offrings to open cursed men to meyntene them in their open cursedness. And thus shulde symony, covetisse, and idleness of worldly clerks be laid down; and holiness, and true teching, and knowing of God's law be brought in both in clerks and lewid men: also thus shulde striving, pleading, and cursing for dymes and offrings, and hate and discord among priests, and lewid men be ended; and unity, peace, and charity meyntened. Also these benefices, by this course, that men usen now, bring in worldliness, and needless business about worldly offices, that Christ and his apostles wolden never taken upon them, and yet they weren more mighty, more witty, and more brenning in charity to God, and to the people, both to live the best manner in themselves, and to teche other men. Also covetisse, and worldliness of the people shulden be done away; and Christs poverty, and his apostles, by ensample of poor life of clerks, and trust in God, and desiring of heavenly bliss, shulde regne in Christen people. Also then shulde priests study holy

 writt,

writt, and be devout in their prayers, and not be caried away with new offices, and mo facraments than Chrift ufed, and his apoftles, that taughten us all truth. Alfo mochil blafphemy of prelates, and other men of feyned obedience, and nedlefs fwearings made to worldly prelates fhulden then ceffen, and fovereyn obedience to God and his law, and efchewing of nedlefs othes fhulde regne among chriften men. Alfo then fhulde men efchew commonly all the perils faid before in the firft chapter, and fecond, and many thoufand mo, and live in clennefs, and fikernefs of confcience. Alfo then fhulde priefts be bufy to feke God's worfhip and faving of mens fouls, and not their own worldly glory and winning of worldly dritt. Alfo then fhulden priefts live like to angels, as they ben angels of office, whereas they liven now as fwine in flefhly lufts, and turnen agen to their former fins for abundance of worldly goods, and idlenefs in their ghoftly office, and overmuch bufinefs about this wretched life.

For thefe dreads and many thoufand mo, and for to be mo like to Chrift's life and his apoftles, and for to profit mo to their own

fouls

souls and other mens, some poor priests thinken with God to traveile about where they shulden most profiten, by evidence that God geveth them, while they have time, and little bodily strength and youth. Nethlefs they damnen not curates that don well their office, and dwellen where they shullen most profit, and techen truly and stably G d's law agenst false prophets, and cursed sends deceits.

Christ, for his endless mercy, help his priests and common people to beware of Antichrist's deceits, and go even the right way to heaven. Amen, Jesu, for thy endless charity.

The End.

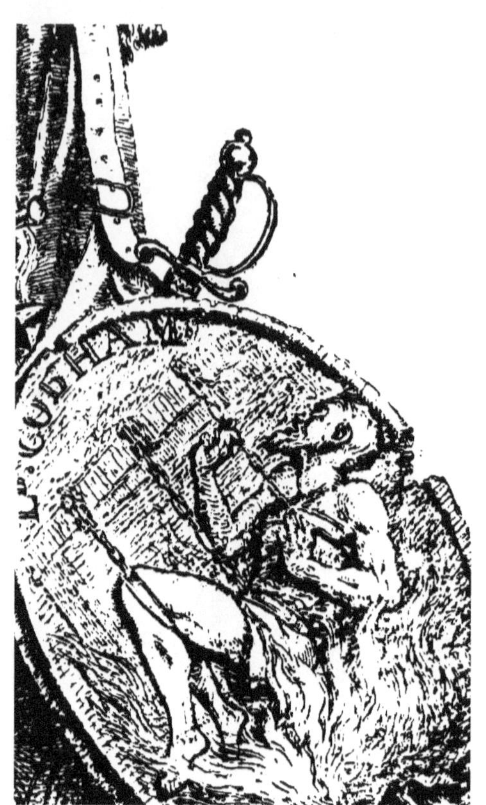

The Life of

Lord COBHAM.

WHEN we confider the circumftances of the times, in which Wicliff lived, the boundlefs ufurpations of the court of Rome, the additional power and glory of England, from its fuccefses againft the French; and the more liberal fpirit, which was daily getting ground in its national councils, we need not wonder, that a genius, like Wicliff, detecting errors, and holding up truths, of fuch infinite importance, fhould engage the attention of mankind. Though few had the courage or abilities to inveftigate thefe truths themfelves; yet many were ingenuous enough to clofe with them, when they were offered to their underftanding.

It is a common obfervation, that the vulgar are generally the moft open to conviction. The great are attached to eftablifhments, in which their interefts are concerned: the

learned

learned to fyftems, on which their time hath been fpent. We need not wonder therefore, if we find few of any confiderable eminence among the difciples of Wicliff.

Among his own countrymen, Sir John Oldcaftle, lord Cobham, is the moft remarkable. We meet indeed with greater names; as Joan dowager to the Black-prince, and Ann, queen to Richard II. But thefe, and fome others, were rather his favourers, than profeffed difciples.

Sir John Oldcaftle was born in the reign of Edward III. He obtained his peerage by marrying the heirefs of that lord Cobham, who with fo much virtue and patriotifm oppofed the tyranny of Richard II; with which nobleman he has been fometimes confounded.

With the eftate and title of his father in law, he feems alfo to have taken poffeffion of his virtue and independent fpirit. In the early part of his life we find him warmly diftinguifhing himfelf in the caufe of religious liberty. The famous ftatute againft provifors, which had been enacted in the late reign, was now become, during the languid government

ment of Richard, a mere dead letter. The lord Cobham with great spirit undertook the revival of it; and through his perfuafion it was confirmed by parliament, and guarded by feverer penalties.

The news of what the Englifh parliament was doing in this bufinefs gave a great alarm at Rome; and Boniface IX, who was then pope, difpatched a nuncio immediately to check their proceedings. This minifter at firft cajoled; and afterwards threatned; but the fpirit, which had been raifed in the parliament, fupported itfelf, againft both his artifices and his menaces.—This is the firft inftance we meet with of lord Cobham's avowed diflike to the church of Rome.

Four years after he made a farther effort. A rebellion having difcovered itfelf in Ireland, the king paffed over with an army. He had made one campaign, and was preparing to take the field early in the fpring of the year, 1395, when the arch-bifhop of Canterbury arriving at his camp, intreated his return into England, to put a ftop to the ruin of the church. By the ruin of the church the good primate meant the reformation of the clergy; which had been attempted, during the king's

abfence,

abfence, by the lord Cobham, Sir Richard Story, Sir Thomas Latimer, and others of the reforming party. Thefe leaders having collected their ftrength, had drawn up a number of articles againft the corruptions, which then prevailed among churchmen, and prefented them, in the form of a remonftrance, to the commons. As they had many friends in the houfe, and as their principal opponents were then abroad with the king, they thought it more than probable, that fomething might be done by the parliament, in confequence of their petition. But the zeal of the clergy prevailed; and the king, who came inftantly from Ireland, put an entire ftop to the affair.

The partiality, which the lord Cobham thus difcovered on all occafions for the reformers, eafily pointed him out to the clergy as the head of that party. Nor indeed did he make any fecret of his opinions. It was publickly known, that he had been at great expence in collecting and tranfcribing the works of Wicliff, which he difperfed among the common people without any referve. It was publickly known alfo, that he maintained a great number of the difciples of Wicliff, as itinerant preachers in many parts of the country, particularly in the diocesses of Canterbury, Rochester, London, and Hereford. These things drew upon him the resentment of the whole ecclesiastical order, and made him more obnoxious to that body of men, than any other person at that time in England.

Nine years had now elapsed, since Richard II. had taken the government into his own hands. This entire interval he had consumed in one steady incroachment (the only instance of steadiness he gave) upon the laws of his country. So many indeed, and so gross were his indiscretions, that it was commonly said by the people, their king was under some preternatural infatuation. But as old Speed very well remarks (a remark too which might equally have fallen, where that cautious writer in matters of kingship, would least have chosen it) " when princes are wilful and " slothful, and their favourites flatterers, there " needs no other enchantment to infatuate, " yea to ruinate the greatest monarchs." After repeated strokes upon the expiring liberties of the nation, a conclusive blow was struck. The whole legislative power was intrusted, trufted, by the act of a venal parliament, to the king, fix peers, and three commoners. An iron fceptre being thus forged, was immediately fhaken over the people. It were trifling to mention inftances of private oppreffion: towns and counties were feized at once. " For a while, (fays the judicious " Rapin, reafoning upon Richard's actions) " five or fix hundred perfons, who compofe " a parliament, and as many magiftrates of " towns and counties, may feem to an im- " prudent prince the body of a nation; but " a time will come, when every fingle per- " fon muft be taken into the account."

That time was now come. The nation exafperated beyond fufferance, caft their eyes upon the duke of Lancafter, who was now in exile. The archbifhop of Canterbury, who fhared the fame fate, undertook to inform him of the defigns of the malecontents in England. Henry, who had private, as well as public wrongs to revenge, put himfelf without delay at the head of the enterprize. His party foon became numerous, and was in general attended by the good wifhes of the nation.

Lord

Lord Cobham had always ſhewn himſelf equally a friend to the civil and religious liberties of his country. He had followed the ſteps of his father in law in oppoſing the tyrannical encroachments of Richard; whoſe reſentment he had felt oftner than once. Convinced therefore of the feeblenefs and wickedneſs of thoſe hands, by which the ſceptre was ſwayed, he was among the firſt who attached themſelves to the fortunes of Henry, and was received by that prince with thoſe marks of favour, which a perſon of his conſequence might naturally expect.

When Henry IV. came to the crown, it was imagined by all men, that in his heart he inclined to the opinions of the reformers. But Henry was a prudent prince; and maxims of policy were ever the rules of his conſcience. He found, upon examining the ſtate of parties in England, that the ecclefiaſtical intereſt was the moſt able to ſupport his pretenſions; and without farther heſitation attached himſelf to it. The clergy were high in their demands. Their friendſhip was not to be purchaſed but at the price of blood. Lollardy ſpread apace. The laws in being were unable to check its progreſs: and the

king

king was given to underftand, that his protection would fecure their loyalty. This language was intelligible enough; and it was
eafily interpreted, that by the protection of
the king, was meant a law to burn heretics.

The king difcovered no great reluctance;
but the commons, among whom many
thought favourably of Wicliff, were very
averfe from thefe fanguinary proceedings.
At length however an act paffed, impower-
ing the clergy to the extent of their defires :
yet it paffed not but with the utmoft ftretch
of the king's authority. By this act the civil
power was obliged to affift in the execution
of ecclefiaftical fentences. Mr. Fox indeed
tells us, that he cannot find, it ever did pafs
the commons; but fuppofes, that as parliamentary affairs were then managed with little regularity, it was huddled in among other
acts, and figned by the king without further
notice.

That wicked and ambitious men fhould
wade through blood to fupport either civil or
ecclefiaftical tyranny, is too common a fight
to be matter of furprize. But that any fet
of men fhould fo far pervert their notions of
right and wrong, as calmly to believe, that
a few

a few erroneous opinions could make a man in the higheſt degree criminal, however excellent his life might be, is a thing altogether amazing. And yet charity obligeth us to believe, that many of the popiſh perſecutors of thoſe times were thus perſuaded. "The "diſciples of Wicliff, (ſays Reinher, a popiſh "writer, are men of a ſerious, modeſt de- "portment, avoiding all oſtentation in dreſs, "mixing little with the buſy world, and com- "plaining of the debauchery of mankind. "They maintain themſelves wholly, (ſays "he,) by their own labour, and utterly "deſpiſe wealth: being fully content with "bare neceſſaries. They are chaſte, and "temperate; are never ſeen in taverns, or "amuſed by the trifling gaieties of life. "Yet you find them always employed, "either learning, or teaching. They are "conciſe, and devout in their prayers, "blaming an unanimated prolixity. They "never ſwear; ſpeak little; and in their "public preaching lay the chief ſtreſs on "charity." All theſe things this writer mentions, with great ſimplicity, not as the marks of a virtuous conduct, but as the ſigns of hereſy.——A ſtriking inſtance this,

among

among many others that might be produced from thofe times, of the little regard paid to morals, in comparifon of opinions and outward obfervances.

Notwithftanding Henry's determination, at any rate, to keep the clergy in good humour, he does not feem to have difcovered any change towards lord Cobham, who was indeed one of the principal ornaments of his court.

In the year 1407, the king had an opportunity of giving him a publick teftimony of his regard.

France was at this time a fcene of great diforder, through the competition of the Orlean and Burgundian factions. Henry remembring that the French had more than once infulted him, while he was in no condition to oppofe them, refolved, in the fpirit of retaliation, to avail himfelf of thefe troubles by affifting one of the contending parties. After balancing fome time, he thought it beft to join the duke of Burgundy. He raifed an army therefore with all fpeed, and giving the command of it to the earl of Arundel, and lord Cobham, tranfported it into France. Lord Cobham, it feems, was

not

not fo thorough a difciple of Wicliff, as to imbibe his opinions without referve. He had been bred to the profeffion of arms, and could not entirely reconcile himfelf to the peaceable tenets of his mafter. Perhaps, like many other cafuifts, he indulged a favourite point, and found arguments to make that indulgence lawful.

The Englifh army found the duke of Orleans befieging Paris, which was attached to the Burgundian intereft. The relief therefore of this city the Burgundian had greatly at heart. He communicated his views to the Englifh generals, who readily came into them. A bold pufh was accordingly made: the enemies lines were pierced; and the duke entered Paris at the head of his victorious army. This gallant action, in which the Englifh had a principal fhare, put an end to the conteft for this time. Orleans drew off his men; and waited for a more favourable opportunity of renewing the war.

Henry IV. died in the year 1413; in whom the clergy loft all their hopes. His fucceffor was a diffolute prince, carelefs even of appearances — without queftion therefore unconcerned about religion. Had heaven
granted

granted a few years more to his father's life, the church had been eftablifhed on a folid bafis. But now all was at an end.——Such were the fears and defponding murmurs of the clergy. But their hopes immediately revived. Henry V. was a perfon wholly different from the prince of Wales. He difmiffed the companions of his loofer hours; and with them his debauchery. No fentiments, but what were noble, great, and generous had any fway with him. And what was very remarkable, among his virtues, piety was confpicuous. This the clergy prefently obferved; and refolved to turn it to their own advantage.

Thomas Arundel was, at this time, archbifhop of Canterbury; and prefided over the church of England with as much zeal, and bigotry, as any of his predeceffors. By his councils the convocation, which affembled in the firft year of the new king, were directed. The growth of herefy was the fubject of their debate, and the deftruction of the lord Cobham the chief object which the archbifhop had in view. It was an undertaking however, which required caution. The lord Cobham was a perfon in favour

with

with the people; and, what was more, in favour with his prince. At prefent therefore the primate fatisfied himfelf with founding the king's fentiments, by requefting an order from his majefty to fend commiffioners to Oxford, to enquire into the growth of herefy. To this requeft the king made no objection.

Oxford was the feat of herefy. Here the memory of Wicliff was ftill gratefully preferved. His learning, his eloquence, his labours, and noble fortitude were yet the objects of admiration. His tenets had fpread widely among the junior ftudents, whofe ingenuity rendered them more open to conviction. Nor indeed was it an uncommon thing to hear his opinions publicly maintained even in the fchools. The governing part of the univerfity were however ftill firmly attached to the eftablifhed religion.

The commiffioners were refpectfully received; and having made their enquiry, returned with the particulars of it to the archbifhop, who laid them before the convocation. Long debates enfued—the refult was, that the increafe of herefy was particularly owing to the influence of the lord Cobham,

H

who

who not only avowedly held heretical opinions himſelf; but encouraged ſcholars from Oxford, and other places, by bountiful ſtipends, to propagate thoſe opinions in the country. In the end, it was determined, that without delay a proſecution ſhould be commenced againſt him.

Into this haſty meaſure the convocation had certainly run, had not a cool head among them ſuggeſted, that as the lord Cobham was not only a favourite, but even a domeſtic at court, it would be highly improper to proceed farther in this buſineſs, till application had been made to the king. This advice prevailed: the archbiſhop, at the head of a large proceſſion of dignified eccleſiaſtics, waited upon Henry; and with as much acrimony as decency would admit, laid before him the offence of his ſervant the lord Cobham, and begged his majeſty would ſuffer them, for Chriſt's ſake, to put him to death.

Some hiſtorians have charged this prince with cruelty. In this inſtance at leaſt he ſhewed lenity. He told the archbiſhop, he had ever been averſe from ſhedding blood in the cauſe of religion; ſuch violence he thought more deſtructive of truth than error.

He

He enjoined the convocation therefore, to
poſtpone the affair a few days; in which time
he would himſelf reaſon with the lord Cobham, whoſe behaviour he by no means approved; and if this were ineffectual, he
would then leave him to the cenſure of the
church.

With this anſwer the primate was ſatisfied;
and the king ſending for the lord Cobham,
endeavoured by all the arguments in his
power, to ſet before him the high offence
of ſeparating from the church; and pathetically exhorted him to retract his errors.
Lord Cobham's anſwer is upon record. " I
" ever was, (ſaid he,) a dutiful ſubject to
" your majeſty, and I hope ever will be.
" Next to God, I profeſs obedience to my
" king. But as for the ſpiritual dominion of
" the pope, I never could ſee on what foun-
" dation it is claimed, nor can I pay him any
" obedience. As ſure as God's word is true,
" to me it is fully evident, that he is the great
" antichriſt foretold in holy writ."

This anſwer of the lord Cobham ſo exceedingly ſhocked the king, that turning
away in viſible diſpleaſure, he withdrew from

that

that time, every mark of his favour from him.

The archbifhop, thus triumphant, immediately cited the lord Cobham to appear before him on a fixed day: but that high-fpirited nobleman, expreffing great contempt for the archbifhop's citation, would not even fuffer his fummoner (as he is called) to enter his gate. Upon this the archbifhop fixed the citation upon the doors of the cathedral of Rochefter, which was only three miles from Cowling-caftle, the lord Cobham's feat; but it was immediately torn away by unknown hands.

The day appointed for his appearance was the 11th of September, on which day the primate, and his affociates, fat in confiftory. The accufed party not appearing, the archbifhop pronounced him contumacious; and after receiving a very exaggerated charge againft him, which he did not examine, he excommunicated him without further ceremony. Having proceeded thus far, he armed himfelf with the terrors of the new law, and threatning direful anathemas, called in the civil power to affift him.

Now

Now firſt the lord Cobham thought himſelf in danger. He ſaw the ſtorm approaching in all its horrors; and in vain looked
round for ſhelter. Aided as the clergy were
by the civil power, he knew it would be
ſcarce poſſible to ward off the meditated
blow. Still however he had hope that the
king's favour was not wholly alienated from
him. At leaſt he thought it of importance
to make the trial. He put in writing therefore a confeſſion of his faith; and with this
in his hand, waited upon the king; begging
his majeſty to be the judge himſelf, whether
he had deſerved the rough treatment he had
found.

In this confeſſion he firſt recites the apoſtles
creed; then, by way of explanation, he profeſſes his belief in the trinity, and acknowledges Chriſt as the only head of the church,
which he divides into the bleſſed in heaven,
thoſe who are tormented in purgatory, (if,
ſays he, there is foundation in ſcripture for
any ſuch place) and the righteous on earth.
He then profeſſes to believe, that in the ſa-
crament of the Lord's ſupper are contained
Chriſt's body and blood under the ſimilitude
of bread and wine. " Finally, (ſays he,)
H 3

" my

" my faith is, that God will afk no more of
" a Chriftian in this life, than to obey the
" precepts of his bleffed law. If any pre-
" late of the church requireth more, or any
" other kind of obedience, he contemneth
" Chrift, exalteth himfelf above God, and
" becometh plainly antichrift."

This confeffion the lord Cobham offered
to the king in the manner as hath been mentioned. The king coldly ordered it to be
given to the archbifhop. Lord Cobham then
offered to bring an hundred knights, who
would bear teftimony to the innocence of
his life, and of his opinions. The king being filent, he affumed a higher ftrain, and
begged his majefty would permit him, as
was ufual in lefs matters, to vindicate his
innocence by the law of arms. The king
continued filent.

At this inftant a perfon entered the chamber, and in the king's prefence cited lord
Cobham to appear before the archbifhop.
It is probable this was a concerted bufinefs.
Startled at the fuddennefs of the thing, the
lord Cobham made his laft effort. " Since
" I can have, (faid he) no other juftice, I
" appeal to the pope at Rome." The king
firing

firing at this, cried out with vehemence, "Thou shalt never profecute thy appeal." and lord Cobham refufing to fubmit implicitly to the cenfure of the church, was immediately hurried to the tower by the king's exprefs order.

There is fomething uncommonly ftrange in the account here given us of lord Cobham's appeal to the pope, whofe fupremacy he had ever denyed. No confiftent reafon can be affigned for it. As to the fact however, we have only its improbability to alledge againft it.

On the 23d of September the primate, fitting in the chapter-houfe of Paul's, affifted by the bifhops of London and Winchefter, lord Cobham was brought before him by Sir Robert Morley, lieutenant of the tower.

The archbifhop firft broke filence. " Sir, " (faid he,) it was fufficiently proved in a late " feffion of convocation, that you held many " heretical opinions; upon which, agreeable " to our forms, you were cited to appear " before us; and refufing, you have been, " for contumacy, excommunicated. Had " you made proper fubmiffions, I was then " ready to have abfolved you, and am now."

Lord

Lord Cobham, taking no notice of the offer of abfolution, only faid in anfwer, that if his lordfhip would give him leave, he would juft read his opinion on thofe articles, about which he fuppofed he was called in queftion; that any farther examination on thofe points was needlefs, for he was entirely fixed, and fhould not be found to waver.

Leave being given, he read a paper, which contained his opinion on four points, the facrament of the Lord's fupper, penance, images, and pilgrimages.

With regard to the firft point, he held, as hath been already mentioned, that Chrift's body was really contained under the form of bread.— With regard to the fecond, he thought penance for fin, as a fign of contrition, was ufeful and proper.— With regard to images, he thought them only allowable to remind men of heavenly things; and that he who really paid divine worfhip to them, was an idolater.—With regard to the laft point, he faid that all men were pilgrims upon earth towards happinefs or mifery; but that as to pilgrimages undertaken to the

fhrines

fhrines of faints, they were frivolous, he thought, and ridiculous.

Having read this paper, he delivered it to the archbifhop; who having examined it, told him, that what it contained was in part truly orthodox; but that in other parts he was not fufficiently explicit. There were other points, the primate faid, on which it was expected he fhould give his opinion.

Lord Cobham refufed to make any other anfwer; telling the archbifhop, he was fixed in his opinions. " You fee me, (added he,) " in your hands; and may do with me what " you pleafe."

This refolution, which he perfifted in, difconcerted the bifhops. After a confultation among themfelves, the primate told him, that on all thefe points holy church had determined; by which determination all Chriftians ought to abide. He added, that for the prefent he would difmifs him, but fhould expect a more explicit anfwer on the monday following; and that in the mean time he would fend him, as a direction to his faith, the determination of the church upon thofe points, on which his opinion would be particularly required.

The

The next day he sent the following paper; which, as it will shew the grossness of some of the opinions of the church at that time, the reader shall have in its own language.

The determination of the archbishop, and the clergy.

" The faith and determination of the holy
" church touching the blissful sacrament
" of the altar, is this, that after the sacra-
" mental words be once spoken, the mate-
" rial bread, that was before bread, is turned
" into Christ's very body : and the material
" wine, that was before wine, is turned into
" Christ's very blood. And so there re-
" maineth, from thenceforth, no material
" bread, nor material wine, which were
" there before the sacramental words were
" spoken. — Holy church hath determined,
" that every Christian man ought to be
" shriven to a priest, ordained by the church,
" if he may come to him. — Christ ordain-
" ed St. Peter the apostle, to be his vicar here
" on earth, whose fee is the holy church of
" Rome; and he granted, that the same
" power, which he gave unto Peter, should
" succeed

" succeed to all Peter's successors, which we
" call now popes of Rome; by whose power
" he ordained, in particular churches arch-
" bishops, bishops, parsons, curates, and
" other degrees; whom Christian men ought
" to obey after the laws of the church of
" Rome.   This is the determination of holy
" church. — Holy church hath determined,
" that it is meritorious to a Christian man to
" go on a pilgrimage to holy places; and
" there to worship holy reliques, and images
" of saints, apostles, martyrs, and confessors,
" approved by the church of Rome."

On the day appointed the archbishop appeared in court, attended by three bishops, and four heads of religious houses. As if he had been apprehensive of popular tumult, he removed his judicial chair from the cathedral of Paul's, to a more private place in a dominican convent; and had the area crouded with a numerous throng of friars and monks, as well as seculars.

Amidst the contemptuous looks of these fiery zealots, lord Cobham, attended by the lieutenant of the tower, walked up undaunted to the place of hearing.

With

With an appearance of great mildnefs the archbifhop accofted him; and having curforily run over what had hitherto paffed in the procefs, told him, he expected, at their laft meeting, to have found him fuing for abfolution; but that the door of reconciliation was ftill open, if reflection had yet brought him to himfelf.

" I have trefpaffed againft you in nothing, " faid the high-fpirited nobleman: I have " no need of your abfolution."

Then kneeling down, and lifting up his hands to heaven, he broke out into this pathetic exclamation.

" I confefs myfelf here before thee, O " almighty God, to have been a grievous " finner. How often have ungoverned " paffions mifled my youth! How often " have I been drawn into fin by the tempta- " tions of the world.—Here abfolution is " wanted.—O my God, I humbly afk thy " mercy."

Then rifing up, with tears in his eyes, and ftrongly affected with what he had juft uttered, he turned to the affembly, and ftretching out his arm, cryed out with a

loud

loud voice; " Lo! thefe are your guides,
" good people. For the moft flagrant
" tranfgreffions of God's moral law was I
" never once called in queftion by them. I
" have expreffed fome diflike to their arbi-
" trary appointments and traditions, and I
" am treated with unparallel'd feverity.
" But let them remember the denunciations
" of Chrift againft the Pharifees; all fhall
" be fulfilled."

. The grandeur and dignity of his manner,
and the vehemence with which he fpoke,
threw the court into fome confufion. The
archbifhop however attempted an awkward
apology for his treatment of him : and then
turning fuddenly to him, afked, what he
thought of the paper, that had been fent
to him the day before? and particularly,
what he thought of the firft article, with
regard to the holy facrament ?

" With regard to the holy facrament,
" (anfwered lord Cobham,) my faith is, that
" Chrift fitting with his difciples, the night
" before he fuffered, took bread ; and blef-
" fing it, brake it, and gave it to them,
" faying, Take, eat, this is my body, which
" was given for you: do this in remem-
" brance

" brance of me. — This is my faith, fir,
" with regard to the holy facrament.   I am
" taught this faith by Matthew, Mark,
" Luke, and Paul."

The archbifhop then afked him, " Whether, after the words of confecration, he
believed there remained any *material* bread?"

The fcriptures, faid he, make no mention
of the word *material*.   I believe, as was expreffed in the paper I gave in, **that**, after
confecration, Chrift's body remains in the
form of bread.

Upon this a loud murmur arofe in the
affembly; and the words " Herefy, herefy,"
were heard from every part.   One of the
bifhops efpecially crying out with more than
ordinary vehemence, " That it was a foul
" herefy to call it bread;" lord Cobham,
who ftood near, interrupting him, faid,
" St. Paul, the apoftle, was as wife a man
" as you are, and perhaps as good a Chriftian;
" and yet he, after the words of confecra-
" tion, plainly calls it *bread*.   The *bread*,
" faith he, that we break, is it not the com-
" munion of the body of Chrift?   St. Paul,
" he was anfwered, muft be otherwife un-
" derftood; for it was furely herefy to fay
                                          " fo."

" fo." — Lord Cobham afked, " How that
" appeared ?"—" Why, faid the other, it is
" againſt the determination of holy church."
—" You know, ſir, interrupted the arch-
" biſhop, we ſent you the true faith on this
" point, clearly determined by the church,
" and holy doctors."—" I know none holier,
" replied lord Cobham, than Chriſt and his
" apoſtles ; and this determination is ſurely
" none of theirs. It is plainly againſt ſcrip-
" ture." — Do you not then believe in the
" determination of the church ? — " I do
" not. I believe the ſcriptures ; and all that
" is founded upon them : but in your idle
" determinations I have no belief. To be
" ſhort with you, I cannot conſider the
" church of Rome as any part of the
" Chriſtian church. Its endeavour is to
" oppoſe the purity of the goſpel, and to
" ſet up, in its room, I know not what ab-
" ſurd conſtitutions of its own."

This free declaration threw the whole
aſſembly into great diſorder. Every one
exclaimed againſt the audacious heretic.
Among others, the prior of the Carmelites,
lifting up his eyes to heaven, cried out,
" What

" What desperate wretches are these scholars
" of Wicliff?"

" Before God and man, (answered lord
" Cobham, with vehemence,) I here profess,
" that before I knew Wicliff, I never ab-
" stained from sin; but after I was acquainted
" with that virtuous man, I saw my errors,
" and I hope reformed them."

" It were an hard thing, replied the prior,
" if in an age so liberally supplied with pious
" and learned men, I should not be able to
" amend my life, till I heard the devil
" preach."

" Go on, go on, (answered lord Cobham
" with some warmth ;) follow the steps of
" your fathers, the old Pharisees. Ascribe,
" like them, every thing good to the devil,
" that opposes your own iniquities. Pro-
" nounce them heretics, who rebuke your
" crimes: and if you cannot prove them such
" by scripture, call in the fathers. — Am I
" too severe ?   Let your own actions speak.
" What warrant have you from scripture for
" this very act you are now about ? Where
" do you find it written in all God's law,
" that you may thus sit in judgment upon
                                " the

" the life of man ? — Hold — Annas and
" Caiphas may perhaps be quoted in your
" favour."

" Ay, (faid one of the doctors,) and Chrift
" too, for he judged Judas."

" I never heard that he did, (faid lord
" Cobham.)   He pronounced indeed a woe
" againft him, as he doth ftill againft you,
" who have followed Judas's fteps: for fince
" his venom hath been fhed in the church,
" you have vilely betrayed the caufe of real
" Chriftianity."
The archbifhop defired him to explain
what he meant by venom ?

" I mean by it, (faid lord Cobham,) the
" wealth of the church.   When the church
" was firft endowed, (as an author of your
" own pathetically expreffes it) an angel in
" the air, cryed out, woe, woe, woe: This
" day is venom fhed into the church of God.
" Since that time, inftead of laying down
" their lives for religion, as was common in
" the early ages, the bifhops of Rome have
" been engaged in a conftant fcene of per-
" fecution, or in curfing, murdering, poifon-
" ing, or fighting with each other. — Where
" is now the meeknefs of Chrift, his ten-

I

" dernefs,

" dernefs, and indulgent gentlenefs? not in
" Rome certainly."

Then raifing his voice, he cried out,
" Thus faith Chrift in his gofpel, woe unto
" you, fcribes, and pharifees, hypocrites,
" you fhut up the kingdom of heaven againft
" men: you neither enter in yourfelves,
" neither will you fuffer thofe to enter, who
" otherwife would.　You ftop the way by
" your traditions: you hinder God's true
" minifters from fetting the truth before the
" people.　But let the prieft be ever fo
" wicked, if he defend your tyranny, heis
" fuffered."

Then looking ftedfaftly upon the archbifhop, after a fhort paufe, he faid, " Both
" Daniel, and Chrift have prophefied, that
" troublefome times fhould come, fuch as
" had not been from the foundation of the
" world.—This prophefy feems in a great
" meafure fulfilled in the prefent ftate of the
" church.—You have greatly troubled the
" people of God: you have already dipped
" your hands in blood; and, if I forefee
" aright, will ftill farther embrue them. But
" there is a threat on record againft you:
" therefore look to it: your days fhall be
" fhortened,

" fhortened.——For the elects fake your days
" fhall be fhortened."

The very great fpirit, and refolution with which lord Cobham behaved on this occafion, together with the quicknefs and pertinence of his anfwers, Mr. Fox tells us, fo amazed his adverfaries, that they had nothing to reply. The archbifhop was filent. The whole court was at a ftand.

At laft one of the doctors, taking a copy of the paper which had been fent to the tower, and turning to lord Cobham, told him, That the defign of their prefent meeting was not to fpend the time in idle altercation; but to come to fome conclufion. "We " only, (faid he,) defire to know your opi-" nion upon the points contained in this " paper." He then defired a direct anfwer, whether, after the words of confecration, there remained any material bread. ?

" I have told you, (anfwered lord Cob-" ham,) my belief is, that Chrift's body is " contained under the *form* of bread."

He was again afked, whether he thought confeffion to a prieft of abfolute neceffity ?

He faid, he thought it might be in many cafes ufeful to afk the opinion of a prieft, if

he

he were a learned and pious man; but he thought it by no means neceffary to falvation.

He was then queftioned about the pope's right to St. Peter's chair.

"He that followeth Peter the nigheft in "good living, (he anfwered,) is next him "in fucceffion. You talk, faid he, of Peter; "but I fee none of you that followeth his "lowly manners; nor indeed the manners "of his fucceffors, till the time of Syl-"vefter."

"But what do you affirm of the pope?"

"That he and you together, (replied lord "Cobham,) make whole the great antichrift. "He is the head, you bifhops and priefts are "the body, and the begging friers are the "tail, that covers the filthinefs of you both "with lies and fophiftry."

He was laftly afked, what he thought of the worfhip of images and holy relicts?

"I pay them, (anfwered lord Cobham,) no "manner of regard.—Is it not, faid he, a "wonderful thing, that thefe faints, fo dif-"interefted upon earth, fhould after death "become fuddenly fo covetous?—It would "indeed

" indeed be wonderful, did not the pleasure-
" able lives of priests account for it."

Having thus answered the four articles, the archbishop told him, that, he found lenity was indulged to no purpose. " The day, " (says he) is wearing apace: we must come " to some conclusion. Take your choice of " this alternative; submit obediently to the " orders of the church, or endure the con- " sequence."

" My faith is fixed, (answered lord Cob- " ham aloud) do with me what you please."

The archbishop then standing up, and taking off his cap, pronounced aloud the censure of the church.

Lord Cobham, with great chearfulness, answered, " You may condemn my body: " my soul, I am well assured, you cannot " hurt."—Then turning to the people, and stretching out his hands, he cryed out with a loud voice, " Good Christian people, for " God's sake be well aware of these men; " they will otherwise beguile you, and lead " you to destruction." Having said this, he fell on his knees, and, raising his hands, and eyes, begged God to forgive his enemies.

He was then delivered to Sir Robert Morley, and sent back to the tower.

' These proceedings of the clergy were very unpopular. Few men were generally more esteemed than lord Cobham. His great virtues would have gained him respect, had his opinions been disreputable. But the tenets of Wicliff had, at this time, many advocates. The clergy therefore were in some degree perplexed. They saw the bad consequences of going farther, but saw worse consequences in receding. What seemed best, and was indeed most agreeable to the genius of popery, was, to endeavour to lessen his credit among the people. With this view many scandalous aspersions were spread abroad by their emissaries. Mr. Fox tells us, they scrupled not even to publish a recantation in his name; and gives us a copy of it. Lord Cobham, in his own defence, had the following paper posted up in some of the most public places in London.

" Forasmuch as sir John Oldcastle, lord
" Cobham, is untruly convicted, and im-
" prisoned, falsely reported of, and slandered
" among the common people by his adver-
" saries,

" faries, that he fhould otherwife fpeak of
" the facraments of the church, and efpe-
" cially of the bleffed facrament of the altar,
" than was written in the confeffion of his
" belief; known be it here to all the world,
" that he hath never fince varied in any point
" therefrom, but this is plainly his belief,
" that all the facraments of the church be
" profitable, and expedient alfo to all, taking
" them after the intent that Chrift and his
" true church hath ordained. Furthermore
" he believeth, that the bleffed facrament of
" the altar, is verily and truly Chrift's body
" in the form of bread."

Some months had now elapfed, fince lord
Cobham had been condemned : nor did the
primate and his clergy feem to have come to
any refolution. They thought it imprudent
yet to proceed to extremities.

Out of this perplexity, their prifoner himfelf extricated them. By unknown means
he efcaped out of the tower, and taking the
advantage of a dark night, evaded purfuit,
and arrived fafe in Wales; where, under the
protection of fome of the chiefs of the
country, he fecured himfelf againft the attempts of his enemies.

I 4

This,

This, it may easily be imagined, was a sensible mortification to the clergy; and great pains were taken to persuade the king to issue a proclamation against him. But the king, who probably thought, that enough had been done already, paid only little attention to what was urged; and shewed no inclination to afford his countenance in apprehending him.

This was still a greater mortification. They remembred the wicked attempts made against them by the commons in the last reign; and dreaded the revival of them. The least coolness in the king, they knew, would be a signal to their enemies: and it was the part of prudence, to spare no pains in alienating him from the Lollards.

Jealousy, the natural companion of usurped power, was the ruling foible of the house of Lancaster. This the clergy had observed; and thought they could not do better than to represent the Lollards as ill-inclined to the government. The king lent an ear to their whispers, and began to eye these unfortunate men with that caution, with which he guarded against his greatest enemies.

Among

Among other inftances of the zeal of the
lergy in propagating calumny, the follow-
ng ftory, attended by very extraordinary
ircumftances, is related.

The bifhops had lately obtained a procla-
nation, forbidding the Lollards to affemble
n companies; which they had commonly
lone for the fake of devotion. The pro-
lamation had in part only its effect: they
till continued to affemble; but in lefs companies, more privately; and often in the dead
of night. St. Giles's fields, then a thicket,
was a place of frequent refort on thefe occa-
ions. Here about an hundred of them had
met one evening, with an intention, as was
ufual, to continue their meeting to a very
ate hour. Emiffaries, mixing with them
under the difguife of friends, foon gave in-
elligence of their defign.

The king was then at Eltham, a few miles
from London. As he was fitting down to
upper, advice was brought him, that the
ord Cobham, at the head of 20,000 men,
had taken poft in St. Giles's fields, breath-
ng revenge, and threatening to murder the
king, the princes of the blood, and all the
lords,

lords, fpiritual, and temporal, who fhould oppofe him.

The king, not confidering how improbable it was, that fuch an army could have been gotten together without earlier notice; and having few about him to advife with, confulted only the gallantry of his own temper, and took a fudden refolution to arm what men he could readily mufter, and put himfelf at their head; hoping to furprize the rebels before they had concerted their fchemes. Soon after midnight he arrived upon the place, and fell with great fpirit upon what he fuppofed the advanced guard of the enemy. They were foon thrown into confufion, and yielded an eafy victory. About twenty were killed, and fixty taken; the chief leader of whom was one Beverly, a preacher. Flufhed with this fuccefs, the king marched on towards the main body. But no main body was found; and this formidable army was difperfed as eafily as it had been raifed.

This ftrange affair, we may imagine, is differently related by different party-writers. The popifh hiftorians talk of it, as of a real

confpiracy;

confpiracy; and exclaim loudly againft tenets, which could encourage fuch crimes. Among thefe the ingenious Mr. Hume has chofen to lift himfelf; and on no better authority than Walfingham, a mere bigot, hath without any hefitation charged lord Cobam with high-treafon.

On the other hand, the proteftant writers, in general, treat the whole as a fiction, and cenfure their adverfaries with great acrimony for fo malicious an afperfion.

The papifts, put to proof, alledge, that arms were found upon the field; and that many of the prifoners made open confeffion of the wickednefs of their intentions.

As to arms, reply the proteftants, it is a ftale trick to hide them on purpofe to ferve an occafion by finding them: and as to con-feffions, nothing is more common, than to extort them from innocent perfons. Befides, they might have been drawn from popifh emiffaries, mixing among the Wiclivites, with the very intention of being brought to confeffion. " In truth, (fays the judicious " Rapin, reafoning upon this fact) it is hardly " to be conceived, that a prince fo wife as " Henry, could fuffer himfelf to be impofed

" upon

" upon by fo grofs a fiction.   Had he found
" indeed, as he was made to believe, 20,000
" men in arms in St. Giles's field, it might
" have created fufpicion; but that fourfcore,
" or an hundred men, among whom there
" was not a fingle perfon of rank, fhould
" have formed fuch a project, is extremely
" improbable.   Befides, he himfelf knew
" fir John Oldcaftle to be a man of fenfe;
" and yet nothing could be more wild than
" the project fathered upon him; a project,
" which it was fuppofed he was to execute
" with a handful of men, and yet he him-
" felf abfent, and no leader in his room.
" Befides, notwithftanding the ftricteft fearch
" made through the kingdom, to difcover
" the accomplices of this pretended confpi-
" racy, not a fingle perfon could be found,
" befides thofe taken at St. Giles's.   Laftly,
" the principles of the Lollards were very
" far from allowing fuch barbarities.   It is
" therefore more than probable, that the
" accufation was forged to render the Lollards
" odious to the king, with a view to obtain
" his licence for their profecution."
It would be tedious to fay all that might
be faid in defence of Lord Cobham on this
occafion.

occasion. Mr. Fox, in the first volume of his acts and monuments, hath given us a very laboured, and satisfactory vindication of him. He examines first the statutes and authentic records, and afterwards the earliest historians, from all which he draws a very conclusive argument, that there was no conspiracy intended. The title of Mr Fox's tract is, *A defence of lord Cobham against Alanus Copus.*

As improbable however as this conspiracy was, it was, for a time at least, entirely credited by the king, and fully answered the designs of the clergy. It thoroughly incensed Henry against the Lollards; and gave a very severe check to the whole party. As for lord Cobham himself, the king was so persuaded of his guilt, that through his influence, a bill of attainder against him passed the commons, as appears from an old parliamentary record, preserved in the British Museum. And not satisfied with this, Henry set a price of a thousand marks upon his head; and promised a perpetual exemption from taxes to any town, that should secure him.——This affair happened in the year 1414.

In

In a few months after, a parliament was called at Leicefter. Hither the zeal of the clergy followed the king. In purfuance of their old fcheme of rendering the Lollards fufpected as enemies to the ftate, they had a bill brought in, by which herefy fhould incur the forfeitures of treafon. This bill likewife made thofe liable to the fame penalties, who had broken prifon, after having been convicted of herefy, unlefs they rendered themfelves again. This claufe was evidently aimed at the lord Cobham.

To this bill the clergy forefaw a furious oppofition from the Lollards, who bore no inconfiderable fway in the houfe. Great therefore was their furprize, when they found their bill paffed without any obftacle. Their pulpits rang with the praifes of the parliament; and they congratulated each other upon the glorious profpect of the church, when every branch of the legiflature united in their endeavours to extirpate herefy.—— But the clergy were much deceived in their opinion of the commons, who acted in this bufinefs with great addrefs.

It had long been the favourite fcheme of a majority in the houfe, to ftrip the clergy of

their

their poffeffions; and in this majority many were found, who were by no means inclined to the opinions of Wicliff. Thefe men were too much patriots to wifh their country en-flaved by an oppreffive hierarchy; and faw no way of efcaping fuch bondage, but by wringing from the church that wealth, which was the fource of its power. Friends to its fpiritual jurifdiction, they cavilled only at its temporal.

Full of thefe fentiments, the commons, though twice foiled in the late reign, were not difcouraged. Their difappointment put them only upon a change of meafures. The zeal which the reformers had fhewn in par-liament againft the unbounded wealth of re-ligious houfes, had heretofore furnifhed the clergy with a pretence for clamouring, " That all was virulence againft the church." To this clamour the late king paid great re-gard. The leading members therefore of this parliament refolved firft to exculpate themfelves of the charge of herefy; and having done this, they imagined they might with much greater facility, put their defigns in execution : and on this principle they gave way to the clergy in their late act.

Their

Their intention was not long a myſtery. In the midſt of the praiſes beſtowed upon them; while the clergy were every where extolling them as the wifeſt, and moſt reſpectable body of men that ever met together, how were they thunderſtruck, when they heard, that theſe wife and reſpectable men, had almoſt unanimouſly preſented a petition to the king to ſeize the revenues of the clergy? This was an unexpected blow. Something however was to be done, and that inſtantly. The king had difcovered no marks of difpleaſure at the petition; which was a dreadful omen.

It was matter of joy to all good catholics, that Henry Chicheley was now archbiſhop of Canterbury. This prelate had ſucceeded Arundel; and to the zeal of his predeceſſor, added a more artful addreſs in the management of affairs. Such addreſs was the principal thing, at that time, required in an archbiſhop of Canterbury.

Undaunted at the ſtorm, this able pilot ſtepped to the helm; and judging it advifeable to give up a part rather than hazard the whole, he went to the king; and with all humility hoped, " His majeſty did not mean

ſo

fo rafh a thing, as to put it out of the power
of his old friends to ferve him as they had
ever done: the clergy were his fure refuge
upon all occafions; and as a proof of their
zeal, they begged his majefty would accept
at their hands, a furrender of all the alien
priories; which being not fewer than an hundred and ten, would very confiderably augment his revenues." Henry paufed,——and
confidering the noble facrifice they had offered, and reflecting upon the old maxim of
prudence, that a fecurity, though of lefs value, is better than a contingence;——and
withal, dreading the confequences of irri-
tating fo powerful a body, he accepted their
offer; and the clergy had once more the
pleafure to fee their arts counterbalance the
defigns of their enemies.

The archbifhop, however, not yet fufficiently fecure, proceeded a ftep farther. He
obferved, from the times, a general inclination to a French war, and wanted thoroughly
to embark his fovereign in fuch an enterprize;
rightly judging, that fchemes abroad would
divert him from fchemes at home; and that
a war upon the continent would greatly in-

K   duce

duce him to leave all quiet in his own dominions.

Thus refolved, he took an early opportunity to addrefs the king in full parliament. In a ftudied harangue he proved the claim, which England had upon France, fince the time of Edward III. The neglect of that claim, he faid, fince that period, had by no means injured the right. He then launched out into a florid encomium upon the virtues of the king; and faid, the thunder of the Englifh nation, which had flept through two reigns, was referved folely for his arm; and God would profper the noble undertaking. He concluded with faying, that if his majefty fhould engage in this gallant enterprize, he would undertake, that the clergy fhould grant him a larger fubfidy than had been ever granted to an Englifh king; and he doubted not but the laity would follow their example.

Many hiftorians have attributed the conqueft of France to this fpeech. It is certain however, it greatly tended to reconcile the minds of men to this enterprize, and effectually put a ftop to the king's defigns

againft

againſt the church—Such were the vile politics of the clergy of thoſe times!

In the mean time lord Cobham, whoſe ſpirit in parliament had given birth to all this ferment, remained an exile in Wales, ſhifting frequently the ſcene of his retreat. In the ſimple manners of that mountainous country he found an aſylum, which he judged it imprudent to exchange for one, which might probably prove more hazardous beyond ſea.

But the zeal of his enemies was not eaſily baffled. After many fruitleſs attempts, they engaged the lord Powis in their intereſt, a very powerful perſon in thoſe parts; and in whoſe lands the lord Cobham was ſuppoſed to lie concealed.

This nobleman working upon his tenants by ſuch motives, as the great have ever in reſerve, had numbers ſoon upon the watch. This vigilance the lord Cobham could not eſcape. In the midſt of his fancied ſecurity, he was taken, carried to London in triumph, and put into the hands of the archbiſhop of Canterbury.

Lord Cobham had now been four years in Wales, but found his ſufferings had in no

degree

degree diminifhed the malice of his enemies. On the contrary, it fhewed itfelf in ftronger colours. Thofe reftraints, under which the clergy acted before, were now removed. The fuperiority which they had obtained, both in the parliament, and in the cabinet, laid every murmur afleep; and they would boaft, in the prophet's language, that not a dog durft move his tongue againft them.

Things being thus circumftanced, lord Cobham, without any divination, forefaw his fate. His fate indeed remained not long in fufpence. With every inftance of barbarous infult, which enraged fuperftition could invent, he was dragged to execution. St. Giles's fields was the place appointed; where both as a traitor, and a heretic, he was hung up in chains alive upon a gallows; and, fire being put under him, was burnt to death.

Such was the unworthy fate of this nobleman; who, though every way qualified to be the ornament of his country, fell a facrifice to unfeeling rage, and barbarous fuperftition.

Lord Cobham had been much converfant in the world; and had probably been engaged,

gaged, in the early part of his life, in the licence of it. His religion however put a thorough reſtraint upon a diſpoſition, natu- rally inclined to the allurements of pleaſure. He was a man of a very high ſpirit, and warm temper; neither of which his ſuffer- ings could ſubdue. With very little tempo- rizing he might have eſcaped the indignities he received from the clergy, who always conſidered him as an objeȼt beyond them: but the greatneſs of his ſoul could not brook conceſſion. In all his examinations, and through the whole of his behaviour, we ſee an authority and dignity in his manner, which ſpeak him the great man in all his afflictions.

He was a perſon of uncommon parts, and very extenſive talents; well qualified either for the cabinet or the field. In converſation he was remarkable for his ready and poignant wit.

His acquirements were equal to his parts. No ſpecies of learning, which was at that time in eſteem, had eſcaped his attention. It was his thirſt of knowledge indeed, which firſt brought him acquainted with the opini- ons of Wicliff. The novelty of them en-

gaged

gaged his curiofity. He examined them as a philofopher, and in the courfe of his examination became a Chriftian.

In a word, we cannot but confider lord Cobham as having had a principal hand in giving ftability to the opinions he embraced. He fhewed the world, that religion was not merely calculated for a cloifter, but might be introduced into fafhionable life; and that it was not below a gentleman to run the laft hazard in its defence.

The end.

VOLVIT·ANNIS·DEO·RESPONDEBIT·IS
V·ET·IV

HAVING given some account of the opinions of Wicliff in England; let us follow the course of them abroad. In Bohemia particularly, we shall find they obtained great credit; where they were propagated by John Huss, Jerome of Prague, and others of less note.

It must be confessed indeed, those Bohemian reformers made little change in the opinions they found prevailing in their own church. Every step they took was taken with extreme caution; and many of the Romish writers have been led from hence to question the propriety of ranking them in a catalogue of reformers. To rail at the popish clergy, we are told, hath ever been thought enough to give a man a place in this list. But this is making outcasts indeed of these celebrated enquirers after truth. The papists burnt their bodies, and damned their souls for being protestants, and would have

 protestants

proteftants damn their memory for being papifts.

Unconcerned at the reproach, the proteftants receive them with open arms, and confider them as thofe noble leaders, who made the firft inroads into the regions of darknefs; as thofe who held up lights, tho' only faint and glimmering, which encouraged others to purfue their paths.

If we confider fuch only as proteftant, whofe opinions were *thoroughly* reformed, it is hard to fay where the reformation began. Our Saviour confiders thofe as *for him, who were not againft him:* much more reafon have the proteftants to confider thefe Bohemians of their party, who, for the fake of opinions, which have been fince adopted by proteftants, fuffered the extremes of malice from papifts; and who maintained principles, which would have led them, if they had not been cut off by their enemies, to a full difcovery of that truth they aimed at.

John Hufs was born near Prague, in Bohemia, about the year 1376, at a village called Huffinez, upon the borders of the black foreft; from which village he had his name.

His

His father was a perfon in low circumftances; but took more care than is ufually
taken among fuch perfons, in the education
of his fon. He lived not however to fee the
fruit of his pains. After his death, his
widow purfued his intention; and found
means to fend her fon, though with difficulty enough even in the loweft ftation, to
the univerfity of Prague.

Here a very extraordinary piety began to
diftinguifh him. Among other inftances of
it, a ftory is recorded, the truth of which
is the rather to be fufpected, as we meet with
frequent relations of the fame kind in mar-
tyrologies. As he was reading the life of
St. Lawrence, we are told, he was fo ftrongly affected with the conftancy of that pious
man in the midft of his fufferings, that he
thruft his hand into the flame of a fire, by
which he fat, and held it there, till his fellow difciple, who was fitting by him, in great
terror interfered. " I had only, (faid Hufs,)
" an inclination to try, whether I had con-
" ftancy to bear an inconfiderable part of
" what this martyr underwent."

In the year 1396 he took the degree of
mafter of arts; and, foon after, that of
batchelor

batchelor of divinity. In 1400 his abilities and piety had so far recommended him, that he was chosen confessor to the queen : and eight years after he was elected rector of the university.

During the course of these honours, he obtained a benefice likewise. John Mulheym, a person of large fortune in Prague, built a chapel, which he called Bethelem; and having endowed it in a very ample manner, appointed Hus the minister of it.

Whatever religious scruples he might at this time have had, he had thus far kept them to himself. It is more than probable he had none of consequence. The superstitions of popery reigned still, in all tranquillity, in Bohemia; where the opinions of Wicliff, which had long been fermenting in England, were yet unknown.

In the year 1381, Richard II of England married Ann, sister of the king of Bohemia. This alliance opened a commerce between the two nations; and many persons, during an interval of several years, passed over from Bohemia into England, on the account either of expectances, curiosity, or business: some on the account of study. With a view of

this

this latter kind, a young Bohemian nobleman, who had finifhed his ftudies in the
univerfity of Prague, fpent fome time at
Oxford. Here he became acquainted with
the opinions of Wicliff, read his books, and
admired both him and them. At his return
to Prague he renewed an acquaintance, which
grew into an entire familiarity, with John
Hufs; and put into his hands the writings of
Wicliff, which he had brought over with
him. They confifted chiefly of thofe warm
pieces of that reformer, in which he inveighs
againft the corruptions of the clergy.

Thefe writings ftruck Hufs with the force
of revelation. He was a man of great fanctity
of manners himfelf, and had the higheft
notions of the paftoral care. With concern
he had long feen, or thought he faw, abufes
among the clergy of his time, which were
truly deplorable. But his diffidence kept
pace with his piety; and he could not perfuade himfelf to *caft the firft ftone*. He now
found that he had not been fingular. He
faw thefe abufes and corruptions dragged
into open light; and it even mortified him
to fee that freedom in another, which he had
been

been withheld, by a mere fcruple, from exerting himfelf.

As to the more alarming opinions of Wicliff, though it is probable Hufs became at this time acquainted with fome of them, yet it doth not *appear* they made any impreffion upon his mind; they were lefs obvious, and required more examination. From the language however, in which he always fpoke of this reformer, we cannot imagine he had taken offence at any thing he had heard of him. He would call him an angel fent from heaven to enlighten mankind. He would mention among his friends his meeting with the works of Wicliff, as the moft fortunate circumftance of his life; and would often fay, he wifhed for no better eternity, than to exift hereafter with that excellent man.

From this time, both in the fchools, and in the pulpit, as he had opportunity, he would inveigh, with great warmth, againft ecclefiaftical abufes. He would point out the bad adminiftration of the church, and the bad lives of the clergy; and would pathetically lament the miferable ftate of the people,

ple,

ple, who were under the government of the one, and the influence of the other.

Indeed the state of the Bohemian clergy, as all their historians testify, was at this time exceedingly corrupt. Religion was not only converted into a trade; but this trade was carried on with the utmost knavery, and rapacity. Avarice was their predominant vice. One of their bishops, we are told, was so sordidly addicted to it, that, being asked, What was the most disagreeable noise in nature? he answered, That of mouths feeding at his own table. Stories of this kind are unquestionably exaggerated by the zeal of protestant writers. We may venture however to make large deductions, and yet still leave a very sufficient charge against the morals of the Bohemian clergy.

It is no wonder therefore if Huss was heard with attention on such an argument. Indeed, all sober and ingenuous men began to think favourably of him; and to see the necessity of exposing the clergy, were it only to open the eyes of the people, and prevent their being seduced by vile examples.

There were, at this time, in Prague, among the followers of Huss, two ingeni-

ous

ous foreigners; who, being unacquainted with the language of the country, invented a method of expofing the pride of the Romifh clergy, which fully anfwered their end, and was well fuited to the fimplicity of the times. They hung up, in the public hall of the univerfity, two large pictures, in one of which were reprefented Chrift and his apoftles, in that humility, and modefty of attire, with which they appeared upon earth; in the other, the pope and his cardinals, in all that flow of garment, gold, and embroidery, in which their dignity fo much confifteth. Thefe pictures, it is probable, as pieces of art, were of no value; but the contraft they exhibited was fo exceedingly glaring, that among the common people they had more than the force of argument.

The fchifm between the two popes, which hath already been mentioned, ftill continued. This religious quarrel, having raged with fufficient animofity during the reigns of the two pontiffs, who gave it birth, was bequeathed to their fucceffors. It had now maintained itfelf above thirty years, and had

been

been the common firebrand of Europe, through that whole tract of time.

The cardinals had made many attempts to put an end to this confusion; but without effect: the ambition of the reigning prelates interfered. To strengthen their hands, the sacred college at length applyed to some of the leading princes of Europe. Henry IV. of England seems to have interested himself as much as any in this affair. He wrote with great spirit to Gregory the XIIth; told him, that, at a moderate computation, 230,000 men had lost their lives in this quarrel; expostulated with him for upholding it; and advised him to submit to the decision of the council, which was then assembling at Pisa.

The intention of the council, it seems, was to elect a new pope, and to make the two other popes give up their claims; which, at the time of their election, they had agreed in such circumstances to do. Accordingly, in the year 1410 the cardinals of each party met at Pisa, where a new election was made in favour of Alexander V. This pontiff, to shew his gratitude to his good friend the king of England, granted his subjects a full remission of all manner of sins, which was to

be

be difpenfed on three fet days, at St. Bartho-lomew's in Smithfield. This was not done entirely gratis; but the indulgent pope had made the expence fo very eafy, that, except indeed the moft indigent, all might enjoy the benefit of his abfolution.

At the time of this pope's election, Hufs, and his followers, began to make a noife in the world. They had now gotten fome of the works of Wicliff tranflated into the Sclavonian tongue; which were read with great attention in every part of Bohemia; and though it doth not appear, that any of the more offenfive doctrines of that reformer had even yet obtained footing there; yet it is certain the eftablifhed clergy had in a great meafure loft that reverence, which had been hitherto paid them.

To check the growth of herefy, was the firft work in which Alexander engaged. He was fcarce feated in his chair, when he thundered out a very fevere bull, directed to the archbifhop of Prague, and it is probable, directed by him likewife; in which he orders that prelate to make ftrict enquiry after the followers of Wicliff; to apprehend, and

imprifon

imprifon them; and, if neceffary, to call in the fecular arm.

Nor was private caufe of pique wanting to engage the clergy in the fevereft meafures. Befides the fpirited language, in which Hufs had always treated them, he had, on the following occafion, made himfelf particularly obnoxious to the whole order.

Learning having been for many years very little the tafte of the Bohemian gentry, the Germans, who in great numbers frequented the univerfity of Prague, and enjoyed, by the ftatutes of the founder, a fourth part of the authority in it, had, by degrees, gotten poffeffion of the whole. This, when letters began to revive under the influence of Hufs, became inconvenient. The Germans ftuck together; and a Bohemian, even in a uni- verfity of his own country, could meet with little encouragement in literary purfuits. Hufs faw with regret thefe difficulties; and endeavoured with all his attention to remove them. Having put himfelf at the head of a confiderable party, he made an application at court; and by his intereft there, which with the queen efpecially was very great, obtained a decifion, by which the authority

of

of thefe ftrangers was abridged, and the government of the univerfity thrown into its natural channel. The Germans, piqued at this, left Prague in a body, (hiftorians rate the numbers of thefe difcontented ftudents at 3000) and fettled themfelves in other houfes of learning.

This temporary evil opened the mouths of Hufs's enemies. The clergy in particular took the alarm; and immediately fhewed their difguft at feeing more weight thrown into a fcale, which they had ever been de-firous of rendering as light as poffible. It is worth remarking, that this is the * fecond inftance, in the courfe of a few pages, in which the herd of the Romifh clergy have confidered a feat of learning as an intereft oppofite to their own. Indeed in this cafe, they had more to fay. Hufs, who was now fole leader of the univerfity, had long fhewn himfelf their avowed opponent; and if fin-gle, he had given them fo much caufe of alarm, he became an object of double terror fupported by a multitude. They refolved therefore to make a handle of the affair of

the

* See the beginning of Wicliff's life.

the univerſity ; and though it was purely of
a literary nature, it was plauſibly converted
into a buſineſs of religion.

Among thoſe who took offence at theſe
proceedings, none took more than the archbiſhop of Prague. Having publiſhed the
bull he had received from Rome, he ſoon
after publiſhed a reſcript of his own; which
ordered all, who were poſſeſſed of any of
the works of Wicliff, to bring them to him.
Accordingly, many copies of different parts
of his writings, (we are told above 200)
were brought ; which the archbiſhop immediately condemned to the flames. In this
buſineſs, it was generally ſuppoſed, he acted
at the ſame time a diſingenuous, an illegal,
and an unjuſt part.   In the firſt place, thro'
the ambiguity of the reſcript, it was imagined, he meant only to examine the books;
to which the honeſt poſſeſſors of them had
no objection ; not doubting but ſuch an examination would redound to the honour of
their maſter : Huſs himſelf tells us, that he
ſent in his books merely on this ſuppoſition.——
Beſides, they thought the primate had no
authority for what he had done. They knew
he had none from the pope ; and if the

action

action was his own, they could not but
esteem it as a very illegal stretch of power.——
And if it was illegal, as it appeared to be,
they thought it farther a very considerable
injury. For in those days, before printing
was invented, books had their value: and
many of these likewise were ornamented
with silver in a very expensive manner. It
was an unlucky circumstance too, in prejudice to the archbishop, that he was a most
illiterate man : we are told he was so to such
a degree, that, by way of ridicule, he was
commonly called *alphabetarius*, or the A, B,
C doctor. As it was well known therefore
he could not read these books himself, and
as no examination of them had been heard
of, what he had done seemed rather an attack upon learning itself, than upon the
doctrines of Wicliff.

This action of the archbishop gave great
offence ; and Hufs remonstrated against it
with as much warmth, as the candour and
native modesty of his temper would admit.
But notwithstanding the propriety of his own
behaviour, it is allowed, his followers acted
with great indecency. Irritated by the lofs
of their books, they resolved to retaliate a

little

little of that spirit, in which the injury had been done. Having procured a copy therefore of the archbishop's rescript, they burnt it with great pomp and ceremony in the public street.

Kindled at this treatment, the archbishop's zeal flamed out in all its violence; and eager to do more than he had the power to do himself, he hurried to the king, and laid his complaints at the foot of the throne.

Winceslaus, king of Bohemia, whom we shall have frequent occasion to mention, was a prince, who looked for nothing in royalty, but the free indulgence of his passions. Matters of government were little his concern: and matters of religion still less. He had been educated in the best school for improvement, the school of affliction; yet he had profited little by the lessons he had there received. He had good natural parts, and great talents for business; but dissimulation was the only talent which he employed. *Temporibus insidiari* was his great maxim. If he had one fixed principle of government, it was never to encourage the zealots of any party. He cajoled the archbishop therefore with that art, which was natural to him;

and

and endeavouring to convince him of the
impropriety of his own interpofition, left him
to manage the fectaries, as he was able.

The archbifhop was thoroughly mortified
at the king's indifference for religion; and,
as he found no redrefs from him, he determined to try the force of his own authority.
After mature deliberation, he prohibited
Hufs, by an interdict, from preaching in his
chapel of Bethelem. Hufs, as a member of
the univerfity, which held immediately of
the Roman fee, appealed to the pope.

Alexander V. was now dead; poifoned, as
was commonly fuppofed, by an ambitious
cardinal, who found the means to fucceed
him. This was Balthafar Coffa, who afterwards affumed the name of John XXIII. a
man, whofe vicious life was probably the
only foundation of the fufpicion. In his
youth he had exercifed piracy: but finding
this profeffion dangerous, he retired to Bo-
lognia, where he applied himfelf to ftudy.
His abilities, for he was mafter of many ufeful talents, foon found a patron in Benedict
IX; under whom he was initiated into all
the myfteries of the conclave.

John

John was presently made acquainted with the situation of affairs in Bohemia. Hufs had preached a sermon at Prague, in which, it was thought, he had spoken lightly of oral tradition. This was immediately caught by the orthodox clergy; and carried, among other things, in the form of an accusation to Rome. The appeal therefore, and the accusation accompanied each other.

John seems to have had something else in his head at this time, besides religion. Without examining the affair himself, he left it to his delegate, the cardinal de Columna; who appointed Hufs a day for his appearance.

The report of this commission spread a general alarm through Bohemia; where the whole party trembled for their chief. A powerful intercession, headed by the queen herself, was made to the king, requesting his interposition in the affair. Winceslaus complied; and difpatched ambaffadors to the pope, who in very prefling terms requested his holinefs to difpenfe with Hufs's perfonal appearance; alledging his innocence, and the dangers he would run in paffing through Germany, where he had many enemies.

L 4

With

With thefe ambaſſadors, Huſs ſent his Proctors; who were treated with great ſeverity, and in the end impriſoned. This was enough to give him a warning of his fate. The irritated pope excommunicated him, as it ſeems, on the mere accuſation of his enemies.

This treatment had no tendency to leſſen the popularity of Huſs. His ſufferings indeed gave him only the greater influence. The people conſidered him as ſtanding ſingle in a common cauſe; as having paid their forfeiture as well as his own. Gratitude and compaſſion therefore were added to their eſteem; and he never was ſo much the idol of popular favour, as he was now. He had his adherents too among the higher ranks. The nobility were in general diſpoſed to ſerve him; and he wanted not friends even among the clergy.

As he was thus ſupported, we need not wonder that the diſgrace he ſuffered ſat light upon him. We find him indeed no longer in the character of a public preacher; and ſome authors write that he retired from Prague. It is certain however, that, except preaching, he continued ſtill to diſcharge

every

every branch of the paftoral care. One method he ufed was to give out queftions, which
he encouraged the people to difcufs in private, and to come to him with their difficulties. Many of thefe queftions had a tendency to invalidate the pope's authority.

Every day made it now plainer, that the
gofpellers, as the followers of Hufs were, at
this time, called, had fcarce received any
check. The primate was wretched to the
laft degree. The pope's authority had appeared to be of little weight; his own of lefs:
the king was wholly indifferent: the emperor alone remained, to whom application
could be made. To him therefore he refolved to apply; but upon his journey he fell
fick, and died; fretted, as was commonly
fuppofed, beyond fufferance, at the perplexity of the affair.——The archbifhop of Prague
was a well intentioned, weak man; under
the influence of violent paffions: a moft
unhappy compofition to be intrufted with
power.

The new archbifhop, notwithftanding his
predeceffor had failed in his defign of crufh-
ing this rifing herefy, had the courage to
make a farther attempt. He called a council

cil of doctors; by whom, after much debating, some articles against Huss, and his adherents were drawn up, and published in form. They were intended to lessen his credit with the people; but they produced only a spirited answer, in which Huss recapitulated what the late archbishop had done, and shewed that he had never been able to prove any heresy against him: he concluded with begging, that he might be suffered to meet, face to face, any one, who pretended to bring such a charge against him, and doubted not but he should be able to purge himself, to the satisfaction of the whole kingdom of Bohemia.

Soon afterwards Huss published another piece against the usurpations of the court of Rome. To this the archbishop and his council replied; but in a manner so futile, that they did more injury to their cause, (especially where prejudice ran high against them) than even their adversaries themselves had done. They applyed to the pope too for assistance; but the pope satisfied himself with exhorting the king to suppress the pestilent doctrines of Wicliff; and, if possible,

to

to curb the infolence of Hufs and his followers.

Indeed the pope had not leifure at this
time to attend to controverfy. His ambition
had incited him to quarrel with his neighbour
the king of Naples, into whofe dominions
he was meditating an irruption. But he fell
into his own fnare. He declared himfelf
before he was well prepared; and the wary
Neapolitan taking the advantage of his ignorance in matters of war, invaded the patrimony, and dividing his forces, fat down before feveral of the papal towns at once. In
this perplexity John had recourfe to the eftablifhed manner of levying troops. He difpatched legates into various parts of Chriftendom, who were largely commiffioned to grant
pardons and indulgencies to all, who would
inlift under his banners.

Among other places, one of thefe recruiting officers came to Prague. Winceflaus
had his reafons for favouring the pope; and
forefeeing that the legate would be oppofed
by Hufs and the gofpellers, forbad them by
proclamation to interfere.

But the zeal of thefe fectaries was of too
high a temper to bear controul. They
thought

thought their confciences concerned; and would have looked upon themfelves as guilty, had they ftood aloof, and feen the people deluded. They took every opportunity therefore of expofing the legate and his bufinefs; and of fhewing the folly of trufting to the pardon of a finful man. Hufs in particular exerted himfelf with great fpirit, and difperfed among his friends many little tracts, which affifted them with proper arguments. His activity put an entire ftop to the levy.

This behaviour was greatly refented by the king; and the magiftrates, who acted by his direction, ventured to feize three of the moft zealous. The perfon of Hufs was too facred to be touched.

The imprifonment of thefe men threw the whole city into an uproar. The more forward of the gofpellers took arms, and furrounded the town-hall, where the magiftrates were then fitting. With loud cries they demanded to have their companions fet at liberty. The magiftrates alarmed, came forward to the ftairs, foothed them with gentle language, and promifed that their companions fhould be immediately releafed. The people went quietly home; and the unfortunate

fortunate prifoners were inftantly put to death.

Hufs difcovered, on this occafion, a true Chriftian fpirit. The late riot had given him great concern; and he had now fo much weight with the people, as to reftrain them from attempting any farther violence; though fo notorious a breach of faith might almoft have juftified any meafures.

This moderation was conftrued by the oppofite party into fear. The clergy, and magiftrates, who acted in concert, well knew on which fide the balance of power lay: they knew that, even at the found of a bell, Hufs could have been furrounded by thoufands of zealots, who might have laugh-ed at the police of the city. When they faw them therefore, notwithftanding this force, act in fo tame a manner, they eafily concluded they were under the influence of fear; — that the death of their friends had ftruck a terror into them, — and that this was the time entirely to fubdue them.

Full of thefe miftaken notions, the arch-bifhop waited upon the king; affuring him, that if he chofe to crufh the gofpellers, and

give

give peace to his kingdom, this was the time.

Winceſlaus, whatever appearances he might think it prudent to aſſume, was in his heart no friend to the novelties of theſe reformers. He conſidered the goſpellers as a neſt of hornets, which he durſt not moleſt. While he ſeemed to favour, he deteſted them; and would have ventured a conſiderable ſtake to have freed his kingdom from what he eſteemed ſo great a nuiſance.

He heard the archbiſhop therefore with attention: He entered into his ſcheme, and in *his* ſpirit, but with ſomewhat more of temper. He knew the inveteracy of the diſeaſe would admit of palliatives only: violent medicines at leaſt he thought improper. He reſolved therefore to take ſome ſtep, though not ſo vigorous as that the clergy dictated. After much heſitation he at laſt baniſhed Huſs from Prague. The late tumults were his pretence. This was the firſt public inſtance he had given of his diſlike to the goſpellers.

Huſs immediately retired to his native place, where the principal perſon of the

country

country being his friend, he lived unmolefted; and was greatly reforted to by all
men of a ferious turn in thofe parts; which
contributed not a little to fpread his opinions,
and eftablifh his fect.

Some hiftorians give a different account of
his leaving Prague; and make it a voluntary
act. It is poffible there may be fome truth
in both thefe accounts. The king might
exprefs his pleafure, which Hufs might
willingly comply with.

During his retreat at Huffinez, he fpent
much of his time in writing. Here he
compofed his celebrated treatife, *Upon the
church*; out of which his adverfaries drew
moft of thofe objections, which were afterwards fo fatally brought againft him at
Conftance.

From this place likewife he dated a paper,
intitled, *The fix errors*; which he fixed on
the gate of the chapel of Bethelem. It was
levelled againft *indulgencies*;——againft the
abufe of *excommunication*;——againft *believing*
in the pope;——againft the unlimited *obedience*
required by the fee of Rome;——againft
fimony; with which he charged the whole
church;

church; and againſt *making* the body of Chriſt in the maſs.

This paper was greedily received in Bohemia; and increaſed that odium which had been raiſed againſt the clergy. Many anecdotes alſo againſt the dignified eccleſiaſtics had found their way among the people; by whom they were dreſſed out in the moſt unfavourable colours. So many open mouths, and ſuch an abundance of matter to fill them, rendered the clergy, in a ſhort time ſo infamous, that few of them durſt appear in public.

The politic king ſaw an advantage. Papiſt and goſpeller were alike to him: he had already made an engine of one party; and he now ſaw a favourable opportunity of working with the other. In ſhort, he thought he had the means before him of repleniſhing his coffers.

He told the clergy, " He was ſorry to
" hear ſuch complaints againſt them;—that
" he was determined to put a ſtop to theſe
" enormities;—that Bohemia would be the
" ſcandal of Chriſtendom;—that he had
" already done juſtice upon the ſectaries;—
" and

" and that an *eftablifhment* fhould be no fe-
" curity to *them*." His language was eafily
underftood; and large commutations were
offered, and accepted.

One thing is too remarkable to efcape notice. " That tythes were mere temporal
" endowments, and might be refumed by
" the temporal lord, when the prieft was
" undeferving," was that doctrine of Wicliff,
which gave moft offence in England; and,
as it feems, in Bohemia likewife. It was
confidered by the churchmen of both king-
doms as an herefy of the moft peftilent kind.
On this occafion however, the king infifting
upon it, the Bohemian clergy were glad to
redeem their tythes by owning the doctrine
orthodox.——Thus the king played one party
againft the other; and left neither any caufe
to triumph. No man underftood better the
balance of parties, nor the advantages, which
might accrue from adjufting it properly.

About the time of this conteft with the
clergy, we find Hufs again in Prague, though
it does not appear, whether the king permitted, or connived at him.

Alexander V. the predeceffor of John
XXIII. had been chofen pope, we have feen,

to

to put an end to the fchifm, which raged in the Roman church; on which event it had been expected the other two popes would relinquifh their claims. So they had promifed at their election. But reftlefs ambition intervened. Neither of them would give up his power; and from that time the church was governed (if fuch anarchy can be called government) by three popes at once. Their names were now John, Gregory, and Benedict.

With a view to clofe this fatal fchifm; to remove fuch diforders in the church, as had fprung up during the continuance of it; and to bring about a thorough reformation of the clergy, the emperor Sigifmond, in the year 1414, convened a general council.

Sigifmond, the brother of Winceflaus, was the moft accomplifhed prince of the age in which he lived. To the virtues of a patriot he added a greatnefs of mind, and dignity of manner, which adorned a throne. It might perhaps be faid, that he excelled too in the princely art of diffimulation: that indeed was the great foible in his character. He was himfelf a man of letters; and gloried in being thought the patron of learning.

He

He had enobled, on the occasion of some solemnity, a learned doctor, who had spoken an eloquent oration.   In the procession, which followed, the doctor chose rather to walk among the nobility, than among his learned brethren.   " Sir, (said the emperor " observing it,) diminish not a body, which " it is not in my power to replenish: the " corps you have joined I can augment when " I please."   This prince was more successful in his negotiations than in his wars; and yet he was esteemed a better soldier, than a statesman.   In his cabinet he often blundered; but rarely in his camp.   His political errors were yet generally retrieved by a noble air of ingenuity, and an addrefs which nothing could withstand.   His manners were the most humane and gentle.   He would often say, " When I forgive an injury, I ac-" quire a friend."   But what is very surprising in a character of this liberal cast, he was a bigot.

Besides the reasons already mentioned for calling a general council at this time, Sigismond had other motives. The Ottoman arms having lately given a severe blow to the empire; and growing daily more formidable, he was very follicitous to oppofe them; and he could not fo effectually do it, while Europe continued in a divided ftate. This famous council was convened at Conftance, one of the moft fouthern towns in Germany, fituate on the confines of Switzerland, as nearly as might be, in the middle of Chriftendom. Hither from all parts of Europe princes and prelates, clergy and laity, regulars and feculars, flocked together. Mr. Fox hath given us an humourous catalogue of them. " There were, (fays he) archbifhops " and bifhops 346, abbots and doctors 564, " princes, dukes, earls, knights and fquires " 16000, common-women 450, barbers 600, " muficians, cooks and jefters 320."——Four prefidents were chofen from four nations, Germany, France, England and Italy,

Ceremonies and punctilios being fettled, the confultation opened. That a reformation of the clergy was neceffary, was agreed on all hands; but a debate arofe, in what part of the clerical fcale it fhould begin? While fome contended it fhould begin a minoritis, at the inferior clergy, the emperor replied brifkly, " Non a minoritis, fed a majoritis." They began therefore with pope John. This

unhappy

unhappy pontiff, being convicted of many crimes, was deprived, and imprisoned. Gregory was prudent enough to give in a refignation; and efcaped on eafier terms. But Benedict continued long obftinate. The king of Navarre efpoufed his caufe for fome time; but that prince forfaking him, he was deprived and excommunicated. In the room of thefe three Martin was chofen.— Thus at length was clofed the great fchifm of the Roman church; and here too ended the reformation of the clergy; a work begun indeed with fpirit; but unhappily left unfinifhed.—But this is anticipating the affairs of the council; for the depofition of the three popes was in fact conducted leifurely with the other bufinefs of it.

The next grand defign of the fathers in this council was to apply remedies to the diforders of the church. By the diforders of the church nothing more was meant than Wicliff's herefy; the extirpation of which took up a full moiety of the council's time. Wicliff was now dead : their rage therefore againft him wanted its full fcope. What was in their power however they did: they reviled his memory : they condemned his te-

                    nets :

nets: they burnt his books: nay they ordered his very bones to be dug out of the grave,
and confumed to afhes.

Their rage however, unavailing againft
him, fell with double weight upon his followers. Of thefe Hufs was the principal.
Some time before the council was opened,
application had been made to the emperor to
bring him to Conftance. The emperor engaged in the bufinefs, and fent two gentlemen into Bohemia to communicate the affair
to Hufs himfelf. Hufs directly anfwered,
" That he defired nothing more than to
purge himfelf publicly of the imputation of
herefy; and that he efteemed himfelf happy
in fo fair an opportunity of doing it, as the
approaching council afforded."

Before he began his journey, he thought
it proper to give notice, (which he did by
putting up papers in the moft public parts of
Prague) that he was going to Conftance; and
that whoever had objections againft him or
his doctrine, might make them there. He
provided himfelf likewife with proper tefti-
monials; and what is very remarkable, he
obtained one from the bifhop of Nazareth,
inquifitor general of herefy in Bohemia;

which

which is still extant. In this the bishop declares, that as far as he had any opportunity to know, (and he had had many opportunities) Huss had never shewn the least inclination to impugn any article of the Christian faith. He provided himself likewise with a passport from the emperor.

In october 1414, he set out for Constance, accompanied by two Bohemian noblemen, the barons of Clum, and Latzenbock; who were among the most eminent of his disciples, and followed their master merely thro' respect and love. Some writers say, they were required by the emperor to attend him.

Through whatever towns of any consequence he passed, he had the following paper posted up : " John Huss, B. D. is now upon " his journey to Constance, there to defend " his faith; which by God's help he will " defend unto death. Willing therefore to " satisfy every man, who hath ought to ob- " ject against him, he published in Bohemia, " and now doth publish in this noble and " imperial city his said intention. Whoever " therefore hath any error or heresy to lay " to the charge of the said John Huss, be it " known unto him, that the said John is

M 4   " ready

" ready to anfwer the fame at the approach-
" ing council."

The civilities, and even reverence, which
he met with every where, exceeded his imagination. The ftreets, and fometimes the
very roads were lined with people, whom
refpect, rather than curiofity drew together.
He was ufhered into towns with acclamations; and indeed paffed through Germany
in a kind of triumph. He could not help
expreffing his furprize at the reception he
met with. " I thought, (faid he,) I had
" been an outcaft; I now fee my worft ene-
" mies are in Bohemia." At Nuremburgh
he was received with particular diftinction;
the magiftrates and clergy waited upon him
in form; and being convinced of his innocence and integrity, affured him they had no
doubt but the council would difmifs him
with honour.—Thefe inftances of the refpect
he met with are worth mentioning, not only
as they fhew the veneration in which Hufs
was generally held; but as they fhew likewife how well-difpofed the Germans were,
even at that early day, to a reformation.
This fcene was acted about an hundred years
before the time of Luther.—In three weeks
Hufs

Hufs arrived at Conftance; where, no one molefting him, he took private lodgings. One of his hiftorians tells us, with an air of triumph, that his hoftefs's name was *Faith*.

Soon after Hufs left Prague, Stephen Paletz left it likewife; a perfon employed by the clergy there to manage the intended profecution againft him at Conftance. Paletz was a man of good parts, plaufible morals, and more learning than was commonly found among the churchmen of thofe days. He had contracted an early intimacy with Hufs: their ftudies had been nearly the fame: their opinions feldom oppofite. When John XXIII. fent his legate to Prague, to levy forces againft the king of Naples, his bulls were confidered as a party-teft in Bohemia;— a kind of fhiboleth, which diftinguifhed the papift from the gofpeller. Paletz having received favours from the pope, and expecting more, deliberated what he fhould do. In a queftion of *right* and *wrong*, he fhould have taken the *firft fuggeftion*, which is generally that of *confcience*: in a cool deliberation intereft is apt to interfere. He was guilty therefore of a common piece of felf-deceit; and miftook a point of confcience

for

for a matter of prudence. His deliberations therefore ended as such deliberations generally do: he made a matter of prudence of it. Having thus passed the barrier, every thing else was easy. The same prudence suggested to him, that what he had already done was insufficient;— that his offence in having at all communicated with the enemies of religion was great;— and that his atonement must be great likewise. He made his atonement, and with abundant zeal; and continued from that time the most forward of Hufs's persecutors.

On the same errand came to Constance, on the part of the court of Rome, Michael de Cassis; a person of a less solemn appearance, but of more dextrous talents. He had been bred a churchman, and was beneficed in Bohemia, which was his native country. But his abilities had been grosly mistaken. Formed by nature for business, he had an utter aversion to study, and the confined employment of a parochial cure. He was a subtle enterprising man, versed in the world, of courtly manners, and a most insinuating address. Finding his profession a curb upon his genius, he recommended

himself

himfelf to his fovereign under the title of a
projector. The king of Bohemia had a gold
mine in his poffeffion; which had been long
neglected, as having coft more than its produce. This mine de Caffis pretended to
work at an eafier expence; and dreffed his
tale in fo many plaufible circumftances, that
Winceflaus was thoroughly impofed upon;
and intrufted him with what money he defired, to the amount of a large fum, for the
execution of his project. Whether the artift
at firft meant honeftly, may be doubted; his
project however mifcarried: on which finding himfelf in a perplexity, he embezzled
what was left of the money, and efcaped
out of Bohemia. Rome was the afylum he
chofe. Here by an artful difplay of fome
new talents, of which he had a great variety,
he obtained not only the pope's protection,
but his favour; and became a very ufeful
perfon in the capacity of one, who was ready
for any employment, which nobody elfe
would undertake. When it was refolved in
the conclave to have Hufs brought before
the council of Conftance, this man was
tamper'd with. He made large promifes:
" He had formerly been acquainted with
Hufs

Hufs at Prague, and knew fuch things of him, as perhaps nobody elfe did." In fhort, being thought an excellent inftrument for the purpofe, and being well penfioned, and inftructed, he fet out among the pope's retinue.

When Hufs arrived at Conftance, he found the council almoft full: the more confiderable members of it were either already arrived, or arriving every day: the pope had been there fome days; and held his refidence in a caftle near the city.

Immediately after Hufs's arrival, his friend the baron de Clum notified it to the pope; whom he informed at the fame time, that Hufs had obtained the emperor's fafe conduct, to which he begged his holinefs would add his own. " If he had killed my bro- " ther, (anfwered John vehemently,) he " fhould have it."

Hufs depending upon his innocence, and ftill more upon the emperor's honour, ufed the fame freedom of fpeech at Conftance, which he had ever ufed at Prague. He fuppofed he fhould have been called upon to preach before the council; and had provided two fermons for that purpofe; in one of
which

which he made a confeffion of his faith;
and in the other fhewed the neceffity of a
reformation of the clergy. But the council
did not put him upon preaching; which
fhews, as Leufant feems to infinuate, that
they were predetermined to deftroy him.
They were unwilling to give him an opportunity of fpeaking, without interruption, to
the people; knowing that his noble fimplicity, his doctrine far from heretical, and the
engaging fweetnefs of his manner, would
have greatly conciliated the minds of men
in his favour.

In the mean time his adverfaries, particularly the two already mentioned, were inde-
fatigable. They were continually with the
leading members of the council, plotting,
contriving, and concerting in what way their
fchemes might run the leaft rifk of a mif-
carriage. Paletz took upon himfelf the tafk
of drawing up articles, which he did with
fuch acrimony, as left no room for the
amendment of others.—The effect of thefe
fecret negotiations foon appeared.

About the beginning of december, the
bifhops of Aufburgh and Trent came to
Hufs's lodgings, informing him they were

fent

fent by the pope and the college of cardinals; who were now difpofed to hear what he had to urge in his defence. Hufs excufed his attendance. " I came voluntarily hither, faid he, to be examined before the whole council; and to them only I will render myfelf accountable." The bifhops affuming a friendly air, began to prefs him : and after many affurances, on their part, of the purity of their intentions, and fome farther oppofition on his, he at length complied.

His examination before the pope and cardinals was a mere farce. They wanted him in their power; and even ftill feemed irrefolute how to act. Paletz preffed to have him imprifoned; and affured the cardinals, he was daily increafing his party by that unbridled liberty of fpeech, in which he was indulged.

While this point was debating, Hufs was engaged in the following fcene. As he waited in a gallery, a Francifcan came up to him; and, after many croffings, and gefticulations common among that fort of men, accofted him thus. " Reverend father, of whom the world fpeaketh fo loudly, excufe a poor friar's impertinence. All my

life

life long have I been enquiring after truth. Many difficulties have arifen in the courfe of my enquiries: fome I have conquered; others have been above my abilities.   Among the reft, none hath occafioned me fo much perplexity, as the doctrine of the facrament. How kindly fhould I take it, would you rectify my errors. I am informed, you hold, that the bread ftill remains material, after the words of the confecration ?"   Hufs told him, he had been mifinformed.   Upon which the Francifcan feeming furprized, repeated his queftion, and received the fame anfwer.   Afking the fame queftion a third time, the baron de Clum, who attended Hufs, turned to the friar, and faid with fome afperity, " Why, doft thou believe this reverend father would lie to thee? How many anfwers doft thou expect?"   " Gentle fir, (faid the Francifcan,) be not wroth with your poor fervant.—I afked but in mere fimplicity, and through a defire of knowledge.— May I then, (faid he, addreffing himfelf to Hufs) prefume to afk, what kind of union of the godhead and manhood fubfifted in the perfon of Chrift?"   Hufs furprized at this queftion, faid to the baron in the Sclavonian
tongue,

tongue, " This is one of the moſt difficult queſtions in divinity :" And then turning to the Franciſcan, told him, he did not believe him to be that uninformed perſon whom he pretended to be. The Franciſcan finding himſelf ſuſpected, went off with the ſame ſanctified grimaces, with which he had approached ; and the baron aſking a ſoldier of the pope's guard, who ſtood near him, if he knew the Franciſcan, the ſoldier told him, that his name was Didace ; and that he was eſteemed the moſt ſubtil divine in Lombardy. It afterwards appeared, that the whole was a formed ſcheme of the cardinals, who had ſent this perſon to endeavour to draw ſome new matter of accuſation againſt Huſs from his own mouth. The ſtory may give an idea of the unmanly artifices which were practiſed againſt him.

The friar was ſcarce gone, when an officer appeared with a party of guards ; and ſeizing Huſs, ſhewed his warrant to apprehend him. Aſtoniſhed at ſuch perfidy, the baron ran inſtantly to the pope, and demanded an audience, or rather indeed puſhed rudely into his preſence ; where with great heat of language, (for he was naturally a

warm

warm man) he remonftrated againft fo notorious a breach of faith. "Can your holinefs, (faid he) deny, that with your own mouth, you made me a formal promife, that Hufs fhould remain unmolefted at Conftance?" The pope was confounded: he fat fpeechlefs for fome time: at laft, he brought out by fyllables, — that it was the act of the cardinals; — that he had no hand in the matter; — that he could not help it.

In truth, the pope was an object of pity as well as blame. Forefeeing the ftorm, which was already gathering againft him, he was looking round for fhelter; and was become at this time fo difpirited, fo timid, fo fearful of giving offence, among the cardinals particularly, from whom he had fo much both to hope and fear, that he neither did; nor faid any thing but what he knew would be agreeable. The baron perceiving the pope would not interfere, left him with indignation, refolving to try his influence with the other members of the council.

In the mean time Hufs was conveyed privately to Conftance, where he was confined in the chapter-houfe of the cathedral, till a more proper place could be found.

N

Upon

Upon the banks of the Rhine, where that river leaves the lake of Conſtance, ſtood a lonely monaſtery, belonging to the Franciſcans, the whole intereſt of which order was bent againſt Huſs. Thither he was conveyed, and lodged in a noiſome dungeon.

Yet even here his active ſpirit could not reſt unemployed. By the help of a ſingle ray of light, which ſhone through an aperture in his cavern, he compoſed many little tracts; which afterwards found their way into Bohemia, and were in great eſteem among his followers. Of theſe one was a comment upon the commandments; a ſecond upon the Lord's prayer: a third was an eſſay upon the knowledge and love of God; and a fourth upon the three great enemies of mankind. Beſides theſe, were ſome others.

Whilſt Huſs was thus employed, the baron, and many of his other friends, were labouring for his liberty. They applied ſeparately to the leading members of the council; and addreſſed themſelves particularly to the four preſidents. All was in vain: effectual pains had been taken to fruſtrate their endeavours; every ear was

ſtopped.

ftopped, and every avenue barred. Baffled, and difconcerted, the baron was obliged to defift, full of reflections upon the horrors of ecclefiaftical tyranny.

In the midft of thefe endeavours for the recovery of his liberty, Hufs was feized with a violent diforder, probably brought on by unwholfome air, and want of exercife. His difeafe increafing, his life was in queftion. The pope alarmed, fent his own phyficians to attend him. A grand council was called. " What fhould be done? Should the heretic dye, himfelf and his doctrine yet uncondemned, what difcredit would arife to the church of Chrift?" They refolved therefore to draw up articles againft him, and condemn him in prifon. Articles accordingly were drawn up, and a formal citation fent.

The meffengers found him extended upon what ferved him for a bed. He raifed himfelf upon his arm. His eyes funk and languid, his vifage pale, and emaciated. " You fee, (faid he) friends, my condition. Do I feem like a man fit to defend a caufe in a public affembly? — Go — tell your mafters what you have feen.—But ftay; tell

 them

them likewife, that if they will only allow me an advocate, I will not fail, even in this condition, to join iffue with them."

This requeft occafioned a new debate. All were againft clofing with it; but they wanted a pretext. Fortunately an old canon was produced, which forbad any one to defend the caufe of an heretic. Though this was begging the queftion; yet it was the faireft pretence which could be found. Hufs was accordingly informed, that his requeft fhould have been complied with, but the orders of holy church forbad. — While this affair was in agitation, the following event checked its progrefs.

John XXIII. from many fymptoms at this time, forefeeing his fate, refolved, if poffible, to avoid it. He left Conftance therefore in difguife, and made towards Italy; flattering himfelf, that if he fhould be able to reach Rome, he might ftill contrive to baffle the council. But his hopes were too fanguine. The emperor, having early notice of his flight, with a fpeedy arm arrefted him near the alps. He was brought back to Conftance; and from that time every appearance of power fell from him.—This event put a ftop to the

profecution

profecution againſt Huſs; and his health afterwards growing better, it was for ſome time wholly laid aſide.

The Bohemian nobility having in vain made an application to the council, applied next to the emperor. That prince, when firſt informed of the impriſonment of Huſs, was greatly diſguſted at it. So notorious a breach of faith ſhocked the honeſty of his nature; and he ſent immediate orders to Conſtance, where he himſelf was not yet arrived, to have him inſtantly releaſed. But the fathers of the council ſoon removed his ſcruples; and he was, at the time of the pope's flight, ſo entirely devoted to their ſentiments, that he delivered Huſs into their hands. By them that unfortunate man was ſent to the caſtle of Gotleben, beyond the Rhine, where he was laden with fetters, and at night even chained to the floor:—to ſuch a determined height was the malice of his enemies at this time raiſed!

Nor was Huſs the ſingle object of their reſentment. Whoever in Conſtance was known to be of his party became immediately obnoxious. The populace were even mad with the prejudices of their leaders;

 had

had thoroughly imbibed their spirit, and turned it into fury: so that it became dangerous not only for Hufs's followers, but even for his favourers to appear in public. Seeing their presence therefore served only to exasperate, the greater part of them withdrew from Constance, leaving their unfortunate leader to abide his fate.

In the mean time, his friends in Bohemia were sufficiently active. The whole kingdom was in motion. Messengers were continually posting from one province to another. It appeared as if some great revolution was approaching. At length a petition was sent through the kingdom, and subscribed by almost the whole body of the Bohemian nobility, and gentry. It was dated in May 1415, and was addressed to the council of Constance. In this petition, having put the council in mind of the safe conduct, which had been granted to Hufs; and of their having, in an unprecedented manner, imprisoned him, before they had heard his defence; they begged a speedy end might be put to his sufferings, by allowing him an audience as soon as possible. The barons, who presented this petition, were

answered

anfwered in brief, that no injury had been done to their countryman; and that he fhould very fpeedily be examined.

Finding however that delays were ftill made, they prefented a fecond, and more explicit petition to the prefidents of the four nations: and not receiving an immediate anfwer, they prefented a third, in which they begged the releafe of Hufs in very preffing terms, and offered any fecurity for his appearance.

The Bohemian nobility were too much in earneft, and too inftant to be wholly neglected. As carelefs an ear as poffible had been thus far lent to their petitions. But their ardour was now too great to be eafily checked. The patriarch of Antioch therefore, in anfwer to this laft petition, made them a handfome fpeech; and in civil language informed them, that no fecurity could be taken; but that Hufs fhould certainly be brought to a hearing in lefs than a week.

When they prefented this laft petition to the council, they prefented another to the emperor; in which they preffed upon him, with great earneftnefs, his honour folemnly engaged for the fecurity of Hufs; and im-

plored

plored his protection, and his interest with the council.

As the affair of the safe conduct, in which the aggravation of the injuries done to Hufs so greatly depends, is placed in different lights by proteftant and popifh writers, it may not be improper to enquire into the merits of it ; and to lay before the reader the principal topics of the argument on both fides of the queftion.

In anfwer to the proteftants exclamations againft fo notorious a breach of faith, the papift thus apologizes.

" We allow, (fays Mainburgh,) that Hufs
" obtained a fafe conduct from the emperor:
" but for what end did he obtain it ?   Why,
" to defend his doctrine.   If his doctrine
" was indefenfible, his pafs was invalid.   It
" was always, (fays Rofweide, a jefuit,) *fup-*
" *pofed*, in the fafe conduct, that juftice
" fhould have its courfe. — Befides, (cry a
" number of apologizers) the emperor
" plainly exceeded his powers.   By the
" canon-law he could not grant a pafs to an
" heretic; and by the decretals the council
" might annul any imperial act. — Nay far-
" ther, (fays Morery,) if we examine the
" pafs,

" pafs, we fhall find it, at beft, a promife
" of fecurity only till his arrival at Conftance;
" or indeed rather a mere recommendation
" of him to the cities, through which he
" paffed: fo that, in fact, it was righteoufly
" fulfilled."

To all this the proteftant thus replies.
" Be it granted, (which is, in truth, grant-
" ing too much,) that the fafe conduct im-
" plied a liberty only of defending his doc-
" trine; yet it was violated, we find, before
" that liberty was given, — before that doc-
" trine was condemned, or even examined.--
" And though the emperor might exceed
" his power in granting a pafs to an heretic,
" yet Hufs was, at this time, only *fufpected*
" of herefy. Nor was the imperial act an-
" nulled by the council, till after the pafs
" was violated. Hufs was condemned in
" the fifteenth feffion, and the fafe-conduct
" decreed invalid in the nineteenth.—With
" regard to the deficiency of the fafe-con-
" duct, which is Morery's apology, it doth
" not appear, that it was ever an apology of
" ancient date. Hufs, it is certain, confi-
" dered the fafe-conduct as a fufficient fecu-
" rity for his return home: and indeed fo
" much

" much is implied in the very nature of a
" safe-conduct.   What title would that ge-
" neral deserve, who should invite his ene-
" my into his quarters by a pass, and then
" seize him ?   Reasoning however apart,
" let us call in fact.   *Omni prorsus impedi-*
" *mento remoto, transire, stare, morari, &*
" REDIRE, *liberè permittatis sibique et suis,*
" are the very words of the safe-conduct."

In conclusion therefore we cannot but judge the emperor to have been guilty of a most notorious breach of faith.   The blame however is generally laid, and with some reason, upon the council, who directed his conscience.   What true son of the church would dare to oppose his private opinion against the unanimous voice of a general council ?

On the first of June, the council had promised the Bohemian deputies, that Huss should be examined within the week.   They said *examined*; but they meant *condemned*. In the mean time, as if they had been suspicious of their cause, all probable means were used to shake his resolution, and make him retract : but his unaltered firmness gave them no hope of effecting their purpose.

On

On the 5th of June it was refolved, that the articles objected to him, fhould be produced, and in his abfence examined: when, after what they called a *fair hearing*, he fhould be fent for, and condemned.

There was attending the council, at that time, a public notary, whofe name was Madonwitz. This man, whether ftruck with the iniquity of their proceedings, or in his heart a favourer of Hufs, went immediately to the Bohemian deputies; and gave them a full information of the defigns of the council. The deputies had no time to lofe. They demanded an inftant audience of the emperor; and laid their complaints before him.

Sigifmond was at leaft a decent adverfary. The manners of a court had polifhed away thofe rough edges of bigotry in him, which appeared fo harfh in the cloyftered churchman. He was greatly offended at the grofs proceedings of the council; and fent them a very arbitrary meffage to defift. He would have nothing done, he told them, but with the defendant face to face. This meffage had its effect; and Hufs was fummoned to appear before them the next day.

The

The affembly was held in a large cloyfter belonging to the Francifcans. Here a new fcene, and of a very extraordinary kind, was prefented. The firft article of the charge was fcarce read, and a few witneffes in a curfory manner examined, when, Hufs preparing to make his defence, the tumult began. Loud voices were heard from every quarter; a multitude of queftions at the fame inftant afked, every one fpeaking, and no one heard, or heard but in one univerfal din of confufion. From many parts even re-proaches, and the moft opprobrious language broke out — Such, on this occafion, was the behaviour of the famous council of Conftance. No forum could produce more licentious inftances of popular tumult. If an interval of lefs diforder fucceeded, and Hufs was about to offer any thing in his de-fence, he was immediately interrupted: " What avails this? What is that to the " purpofe?" No appearance of argument was brought againft him.

Such aftonifhing licence moved, in fome degree, the moft difpaffionate of men. " In this place, (faid Hufs,) looking round him, I hoped to have found a different treatment."

His

His rebuke increased the clamour; so that finding it vain to attempt any farther defence, he held his peace. This was matter of new triumph: " He was now confounded, silenced, by confession guilty." Luther hath given us a strong picture of this unruly assembly. " *Ibi omnes,* (saith he) *aprorum more, fremere, setas à tergo erigere, frontem corrugare, dentesque acuere cæperunt.*"

There were some in that council, men of cooler temper, who foreseeing the ill effects of such violence, used what credit they had to check it. To divert the furious spirit, which had spread among those zealots, and to throw in so much moderation among them, as to bring them to debate calmly, was at this time impossible. All that could be done, was, to get the business postponed till another opportunity: which was at length, and with the utmost difficulty, effected.

The next morning they met again. They were hardly seated, when the emperor entered the council-chamber, and took his seat at the upper end of it. The disorder of the assembly, the day before, had greatly disgusted Sigismond; and he came now prepared

pared to awe them into a more decent be-
haviour. His end was in part obtained; Mere decency was at least observed.—It would be tedious to enter into a full detail of what passed upon this occasion: what follows is a summary of it.

The examination was opened by Du Cassis; the first article of which exhibited a charge against Hufs for denying the real presence. This was proved by a Dominican, from a sermon which Hufs had preached at Bethelem. He had only to answer, that he had always held the true catholic doctrine; which was a known truth among his friends; for he had ever believed transubstantiation.

He was next charged in general with maintaining the pernicious errors of Wicliff. To this he answered, that he never had held any error, which he knew to be such; and that he desired nothing more than to be convinced of what errors he might inadvertently have fallen into.—Wicliff's doctrine of tythes was objected to him; which, he owned, he knew not how to refute.—It was farther proved, that he had expressed himself against burning the books of Wicliff. To this he answered, that he had spoken against burn-

ing

ing them in the manner practifed by the late archbifhop of Prague, who condemned them to the flames without examining them.—— He was farther charged with faying, that he wifhed his foul in the fame place, where Wicliff's was. This expreffion, he owned, he had made ufe of; which afforded matter of great mirth to his hearers.

The next article charged him with fedition, in exciting the people to take arms againft their fovereign. But of this charge he entirely exculpated himfelf. Nothing indeed could be proved againft him, but that in a fermon, by no means temporizing, he had exhorted his hearers, in the apoftle's language, *to put on the whole armour of God*. This very frivolous charge gives us the moft adequate idea of the malice of his enemies.

The next article accufed him of forming diffentions between the church and the ftate; and of ruining the univerfity of Prague. The former part of the accufation alluded to a difpute between the pope and the king of Bohemia, which Hufs was faid, though unjuftly, to have fomented: the latter part to the affair of the Germans, which hath already been placed in its proper light.—— An

examination

examination of Hufs on thefe few articles employed the firft day.

The council rifing, he was carried back to prifon. As he paffed by the cardinal of Cambray, who fat near the emperor, the cardinal ftopping him, faid, " I have been informed, you have heretofore boafted, that unlefs you had chofen it yourfelf, neither the king of Bohemia, nor the emperor could have forced you to Conftance." " My lord cardinal, (anfwered Hufs,) if I faid any thing of this kind, I faid it not in the ftrong terms, in which it hath been reprefented to you. I might poffibly fpeak gratefully of the kind-nefs of my friends in Bohemia." Upon this the baron de Clum, who never left him, with a noble firmnefs, told the cardinal, that if what he had heard had been faid, it was only the truth. " I am far from being, (faid he,) a perfon of the greateft confequence in my own country: others have ftronger caftles, and more power than I have; yet even I would have ventured to have defend-ed this reverend father a whole year againft the utmoft efforts of both the princes you have mentioned."

The

The emperor then turning to Huſs, told him, that he had given him his ſafe-conduct, which he found was more than was well in his power, that he might have an opportunity to vindicate his character: " But depend upon it, (ſaid he) if you continue obſtinate, I will make a fire with my own hands, to burn you, rather than you ſhall eſcape."

To this zealous ſpeech Huſs anſwered, in few words, that he could not charge himſelf with holding any opinions obſtinately;—that he came thither with joy rather than reluctance; that if any better doctrine than his own could be laid before him in that learned aſſembly, he might ſee his error, and embrace the truth.—Having ſaid this, he was carried back to priſon.

His examination did not end here. He was called before the council again; and many articles, not fewer than 40, were brought againſt him. The chief of them were extracted from his books; and ſome of them by very unfair deduction.

The following opinions, among many others, which gave offence, were eſteemed moſt criminal.—" That there was no abſolute neceſſity for a viſible head of the church—

that

that the church was better governed in apos-
tolic times without one — that the title of
holiness was improperly given to man—that
a wicked pope could not possibly be the vicar
of Christ, and he denied the very authority
on which he pretended to act — that liberty
of conscience was every ones natural right—
that ecclesiastical censures, especially such as
touched the life of man, had no foundation
in scripture — that ecclesiastical obedience
should have its limits—that no excommunication should deter the priest from his duty—
that preaching was as much required from
the minister of religion, as alms-giving from
the man of ability; and that neither of them
could hide his talent in the earth without in-
curring the divine displeasure."—Paletz and
the cardinal of Cambray were the chief managers of this examination.

To these opinions, most of which were
proved and acknowledged, he added many
things in the course of his examination, which
were eagerly laid hold on; particularly against
the scandalous lives of the clergy of every
denomination; the open symony practised
among them, their luxury, lewdness, and
ignorance.

Huss

Hufs having now been examined on all thofe articles, which the niceft fcrutiny into his books, and the moft exact remembrance of his words, could furnifh, the cardinal of Cambray thus accofted him. "Your guilt "hath now been laid before this auguft "affembly with its full force of evidence. I "am obliged therefore to take upon me the "difagreeable tafk of informing you, that "only this alternative is offered to you: "either to abjure thefe damnable errors, and "fubmit yourfelf to the council; in which "cafe thefe reverend fathers will deal as "gently with you as poffible: or to abide "the fevere confequence of an obftinate "adherence to them." To which Hufs anfwered, that he had nothing to fay, but what he had often faid before; that he came there not to defend any opinion obftinately; but with an earneft defire to fee his errors, and amend them;—that many opinions had been laid to his charge, fome of which he had never maintained,. and others, which he had maintained, were not yet confuted;— that as in the firft cafe, he thought it abfurd to abjure opinions which were never his; fo

in

in the fecond, he was determined to fubfcribe nothing againſt his confcience."

The emperor told him, he faw no difficulty in his renouncing errors, which he had never held. " For myſelf, faid he, I am, at this moment, ready to renounce every hereſy, that hath exiſted in the Chriſtian church : does it therefore follow that I have been an heretic ?"

Huſs refpectfully made a diſtinction between abjuring errors in general ; and abjuring errors which had been falſely imputed : the latter he could not abjure ; but he prayed the council to hear him upon theſe points, which to them appeared erroneous ; were it only to convince them that he had ſomething to ſay for the opinions he maintained. To this requeſt however the council paid no attention.

Here Paletz and De Caſlis took an opportunity to exculpate themſelves of any appearance of malice in this difagreeable profecution. They both had entered upon the taſk with great unwillingneſs ; and had done nothing but what their duty required. To which the cardinal of Cambray added, that he could fufficiently exculpate them on that

head,

head. They had behaved; he faid, through the whole of this tedious bufinefs, with great humanity; and to his knowledge might have acted a much feverer part.

The emperor obferving, that every thing, which the caufe would bear, had now been offered, arofe from his feat, and thus addreffed himfelf to the council.

" You have now heard, reverend fathers,
" an ample detail of herefies, not only proved,
" but confeffed; each of which unqueftion-
" ably, in my judgment, deferveth death.
" If therefore the heretic continueth obftinate
" in the maintenance of his opinions, he
" muft certainly die. And if he fhould even
" abjure them, I fhould by no means think
" it proper to fend him again into Bohemia;
" where new opportunities would give him
" new fpirits, and raife a fecond commotion
" worfe than the firft.——As to the fate how-
" ever of this unhappy man, be that as it
" may hereafter be determined; at prefent,
" let me only add, that an authentic copy of
" the condemned articles fhould be fent into
" Bohemia, as a ground-work for the clergy
" there to proceed on; that herefy may at
" length

" length be rooted up, and peace reſtored
" to that diſtracted country."

The emperor having finiſhed his ſpeech, it was agreed in the council to allow Huſs a month longer to give in his final anſwer. With the utmoſt difficulty he had ſupported himſelf through this ſevere trial. Beſides the malice of his enemies, he had upon him the paroxiſm of a very violent diſorder. On this laſt day he was ſcarce able to walk, when he was led from the council. His conſolation in theſe circumſtances was a cold and hungry dungeon, into which he was inhumanly thruſt.

His friend, the baron, attended him even hither, and with every inſtance of endearing tenderneſs, endeavoured to ſupport him. The ſuffering martyr wrung his hand; and looking round the horrid ſcene, earneſtly cried out, " Good God! this is friendſhip " indeed!" His keepers ſoon after put him in irons; and none, but ſuch as were licenced by the council, were allowed to ſee him.

The generous nature of Sigiſmond, tho' he was not unverſed in the artifices of the cabinet, abhorred a practiſed fraud. The affair of Huſs, amidſt all the caſuiſtry of the council,

council,

council, gave him keen diftrefs; and he wifhed for nothing more ardently, than to rid his hands of it with honour.—On the other fide, his vanity and his intereft engaged him to appear the defender of the catholic caufe in Germany. If he fuffered Hufs to be put to death, one part of the world would queftion his honour; if he interfered with a high hand in preferving him, the other part would queftion his religion. The perplexity was great; from which he thought nothing could relieve him, but the recantation of Hufs.

To obtain this, he tried every mean in his power, he had already endeavoured to intimidate him with high language, which he had ufed, both in the council, and in other places. But this was ineffectual. He had now recourfe to foothing arts. The form of a recantation was offered; in which Hufs was required only to renounce thofe herefies, which had been fairly proved. But that undaunted man ftill continued inflexible. Several deputations were afterwards fent to him in prifon; and bifhops, cardinals, and princes in vain tried their eloquence to perfuade him.

                  Sigifmond

Sigifmond feeing the conclufion to which this fatal affair was approaching, might probably have interefted himfelf thus far, as thinking he had been too condefcending to the council. The flame too, which he faw kindling in Bohemia, where he had high expectations, and was willing to preferve an intereft, might alarm him greatly. He had gone too far however to recede; and knew not how to take Hufs out of the hands of the council; into which he had given him with fo much zeal and devotion.

In the mean time Hufs remained mafter of his fate; and fhewed a conftancy which fcarce any age hath excelled. He amufed himfelf, while it was permitted, with writing letters to his friends, which were privately conveyed by the Bohemian lords, who vifited him in prifon. Many of thefe letters are ftill extant. The following may be a teft of that compofed piety and rational frame of mind, which fupported him in all his fufferings.

" My dear friends, let me take this laft opportunity of exhorting you to truft in nothing here, but to give yourfelves up entirely to the fervice of God. Well am I

authorized

authorized to warn you not to truft in princes, nor in any child of man, for there is no help in them. God only remaineth ftedfaft. What *he* promifeth, he will undoubtedly perform. For myfelf, on his gracious promife I reft. Having endeavoured to be his faithful fervant, I fear not being deferted by him. Where I am, fays the gracious promifer, there fhall my fervant be. May the God of heaven preferve you!—This is probably the laft letter I fhall be enabled to write. I have reafon to believe I fhall be called upon to morrow to anfwer with my life.—Sigifmond hath in all things acted deceitfully.—I pray God forgive him! You have heard in what fevere language he hath fpoken of me."

The month, which had been allowed by the council, being now expired, a deputation of four bifhops came to receive his laft anfwer, which was given in the fame language as before.

The fixth of July was appointed for his condemnation; the fcene of which was opened with extraordinary pomp. In the morning of that day, the bifhops and temporal lords of the council, each in his robes,

affembled

aſſembled in the great church at Conſtance.
The emperor preſided in a chair of ſtate.
When all were ſeated, Huſs was brought in
by a guard. In the middle of the church,
a ſcaffold had been erected; near which a
table was placed, covered with the veſtments
of a Romiſh prieſt.

After a ſermon, in which the preacher
earneſtly exhorted his hearers to *cut off the
man of ſin*, the proceedings began. The
articles alledged againſt him were read aloud;
as well thoſe, which he had, as thoſe which
he had not allowed. This treatment Huſs
oppoſed greatly; and would gladly, for his
character's ſake, have made a diſtinction:
but finding all endeavours of this kind ineffectual, and being indeed plainly told by
the cardinal of Cambray, that no farther opportunity of anſwering for himſelf ſhould
be allowed, he deſiſted; and falling on his
knees, in a pathetic ejaculation, commend-
ed his cauſe to Chriſt.

The articles againſt him, as form required,
having been recited, the ſentence of his condemnation was read. The inſtrument is
tedious: in ſubſtance it runs, " That John
Huſs, being a diſciple of Wicliff of damnable

ble memory, whofe life he had defended, and whofe doctrines he had maintained, is adjudged by the council of Conftance (his tenets having been firft condemned) to be an obftinate heretic ; and as fuch, to be degraded from the office of a prieft; and cut off from the holy church."

His fentence having been thus pronounced, he was ordered to put on the prieft's veftments, and afcend the fcaffold, according to form, where he might fpeak to the people ; and, it was hoped, might ftill have the grace to retract his errors. But Hufs contented himfelf with faying once more, that he knew of no errors, which he had to retract; that none had been proved upon him; and that he would not injure the doctrine he had taught, nor the confciences of thofe who had heard him, by afcribing to himfelf errors, of which he had never been convinced.

When he came down from the fcaffold, he was received by feven bifhops, who were commiffioned to degrade him. The ceremonies of this bufinefs exhibited a very unchriftian fcene. The bifhops forming a circle round him, each adding a curfe took off

a part

a part of his attire. When they had thus ſtripped him of his ſacerdotal veſtments, they proceeded to eraſe his tonſure, which they did by clipping it into the form of a croſs. Some writers ſay, that in doing this, they even tore and mangled his head; but ſuch ſtories are unqueſtionably the exaggeration of zeal. The laſt act of their zeal was to adorn him with a large paper cap; on which, various, and horrid forms of devils were painted. This cap one of the biſhops put upon his head; with this unchriſtian ſpeech, " Hereby we commit thy ſoul to " the devil." Huſs ſmiling, obſerved, " It " was leſs painful than a crown of thorns."

The ceremony of his degradation being thus over, the biſhops preſented him to the emperor. They had now done, they told him, all the church allowed. What remained was of civil authority. Sigiſmond ordered the duke of Bavaria to receive him, who immediately gave him into the hands of an officer. This perſon had orders to ſee him burned, with every thing he had about him.

At the gate of the church a guard of 800 men waited to conduct him to the place of execution.

execution. He was carried firft to the gate of the epifcopal palace; where a pile of wood being kindled, his books were burned before his face. Hufs fmiled at the indignity.

When he came to the ftake, he was allowed fome time for devotion; which he performed in fo animated a manner, that many of the fpectators, who came there fufficiently prejudiced againft him, cried out, " What this man hath faid within doors we " know not, but furely he prayeth like a " Chriftian."

As he was preparing for the ftake, he was afked whether he chofe a confeffor? He anfwered in the affirmative; and a prieft was called. The defign was to draw from him a retractation, without which, the prieft faid, he durft not confefs him. " If that be your refolution, faid Hufs, I muft die without confeffion: I truft in God, I have no mortal fin to anfwer for."

He was then tied to the ftake with wet cords, and faftened by a chain round his body. As the executioners were begining to pile the faggots around him, a voice from the crowd was heard, " Turn him from the " eaft; turn him from the eaft." It feemed

like

like a voice from heaven. They who conducted the execution, ſtruck at once with
the impropriety, or rather prophanenefs of
what they had done, gave immediate orders
to have him turned due weſt.

Before fire was brought, the duke of
Bavaria rode up, and exhorted him once
more to retract his errors. But he ftill continued firm. " I have no errors, ſaid he,
to retract: I endeavoured to preach Chriſt
with apoſtolic plainnefs; and I am now prepared to ſeal my doctrine with my blood."

The faggots being lighted, he recommended himſelf into the hands of God,
and began a hymn, which he continued
ſinging, till the wind drove the flame and
ſmoke into his face. For ſome time he was
inviſible. When the rage of the fire abated,
his body half conſumed appeared hanging
over the chain; which, together with the
poſt, were thrown down, and a new pile
heaped over them. The malice of his enemies purſued his very remains. His aſhes
were gathered up, and ſcattered in the
Rhine; that the very earth might not feel
the load of ſuch enormous guilt.

From

From this view of the life and sufferings of Hufs, it is hard to fay what were the real grounds of the animofity he had raifed. His creed unqueftionably was far from being exactly orthodox; yet it is plain how very ill able his adverfaries were to gather from it offenfive matter enough for an accufation. He believed tranfubftantiation; he allowed the adoration of faints; he practifed confeffion; he fpoke cautioufly of tradition, and reverently of the feven facraments; and whatever latitude he might give himfelf on any of thefe articles, it was not more than had been often taken, inoffenfively taken, by Gerfon, Zabarelle, and other fpirited divines of the Roman church.

Befides, the great pains the council took to avoid a public queftion, and the great confidence with which Hufs defired one, are prefumptions very ftrong in his favour.

It is the opinion of Lenfant, that the great caufe of his condemnation was his introducing Wicliff's doctrine into Bohemia; and chiefly perhaps that offenfive part of it, which ftruck at the temporalities of the clergy. And indeed this is extremely probable from the whole conduct of the council;

cil; for though it is apparent, that he never adopted the entire fyftem of that reformer; yet his principles, it is certain, would have led him much farther, than they had hitherto done: and the fathers of the council being aware of this, feem to have determined, though at the expence of juftice, to crufh an evil in its origin, which appeared teeming with fo much mifchief.

Befides this, there feems to have been another caufe for that unabated prejudice, which ran fo high againft him. The warmth, with which he treated the corruptions of the clergy, and the ufurpations of the church of Rome, was a crime never to be forgiven by the ecclefiaftics of thofe times; and added the keeneft edge to their refentment.—But as this was an unpopular caufe to appear in, it is plain they wanted to have it believed their refentment arofe upon another account. This feems to have been the foundation of a fpeech, attributed by Varillas to cardinal Perron; " My learned friends, (he would fay,) you cannot employ your time worfe, than in giving the world any account of the affairs of Hufs."

His

His L I F E however was the severest satyr upon the clergy. It was a mirror, which reflected their distorted features. In him they saw the true ecclesiastic, and the real christian,—characters so different from their own. Gentle and condescending to the sentiments of others, this amiable pattern of virtue was strict only in his own principles. The opinions indeed of men were less his concern than their practice. His great contest was with vice; and he treated the ministers of religion with freedom, only as he thought their example encouraged, rather than checked, that licence, which prevailed. The great lines in his character were piety, and fortitude. His piety was calm, rational, and manly: his fortitude nothing human could daunt. The former was free from the least tincture of enthusiasm; the latter from the least degree of weakness. He was in every respect an apostolical man. "From his infancy, (says the university of Prague, in a voluntary testimonial,) he was of such excellent morals, that during his stay here, we may venture to challenge any one to produce a single fault against him."

P

As

As to his parts and acquirements, he seems to have been above mediocrity; and yet not in the higheſt form, in reſpect of either. A vein of good ſenſe runs through all his writings; but their diſtinguiſhing characteriſtics are ſimplicity and piety. In one of Luther's pieces we have the following teſtimony in their favour. " In a monaſtic library, (ſays that reformer,) a volume of Huſs's writings fell in my way; which I ſeized with great eagerneſs, ſurprized that ſuch a book had eſcaped the flames, and deſirous to know ſomething of the opinions of that hereſiarch. But who can expreſs my aſtoniſhment, when I found him by many degrees the moſt rational expounder of ſcripture I had ever met with. I could not help crying out, What could occaſion the ſeverity with which this man was treated! yet as the name of Huſs was ſo deteſtable; and as a favourable opinion of him was ſo utterly inconſiſtent with a Chriſtian's faith, I ſhut the book, and could find comfort only in this thought, that perhaps he wrote theſe things before his fall; for I was yet ignorant of what had paſſed at the council of Conſtance."

To .

To preserve the memory of this excellent man, the 6th of July was, for many years, held sacred among the Bohemians. A service, adapted to the day, was appointed to be read in all churches; and instead of a sermon, an oration was spoken in commendation of their martyr, in which the noble stand he made against ecclesiastical tyranny was commemorated; and his example proposed as a pattern to all Christians.

In some places large fires were lighted in the evening, upon the mountains, to preserve the memory of his sufferings; round which the country-people would assemble, and sing hymns in his praise.

A very remarkable medal was struck in honour of him, on which was represented his effigies, with this inscription, CENTUM REVOLUTIS ANNIS DEO RESPONDEBITIS ET MIHI. These words are said to have been spoken by him to his adversaries, a little before his execution; and were afterwards applied, by the zealots of his sect, as prophetic of Luther; who lived about an hundred years after him. The story carries with it an air of irrational zeal; and seems calculated only for the credulous.

The end.   *The*

The life of

JEROME *of* PRAGUE.

WE find very little relating to the early part of the life of this reformer. As he was a zealous follower of Hufs, and united with him in all his fchemes; the actions, in which they were jointly engaged, are afcribed by hiftorians to Hufs, as the more eminent leader. In general however, we find his youth fpent in an eager purfuit of knowledge; which he fought after in all the more confiderable univerfities of Europe; particularly in thofe of Prague, Paris, Heidelburgh, Cologn, and Oxford.

At Oxford, which feems to have been the laft feat of learning, which he vifited, he became acquainted with the works of Wicliff; and being a perfon of uncommon application, he tranflated many of them into his native language; having with great pains made himfelf mafter of the Englifh.

It

It is probable he had conceived an efteem for Wicliff, before he went to Oxford. At his return to Prague, he profeffed himfelf an open favourer of him; and finding his doctrines had made a confiderable progrefs in Bohemia, and that Hufs was at the head of that party, which had efpoufed them, he attached himfelf to that leader.

Hufs was glad of fo able an affiftant in his great work of reforming the clergy: for Jerome was inferior to none of his time, in point either of abilities, or learning;—fuperior certainly to his mafter in both. Hufs was however better qualified as the leader of a party; his gentlenefs, and very perfuafive manner conciliating the minds of men in his favour: whereas Jerome, with all his great and good qualities, wanted temper.

Of this we have fome inftances; one indeed very flagrant. He was difputing with two monks about reliques, whom he accidentally met on the banks of the Muldaw; and finding himfelf more warmly oppofed than he expected, he feized one of them by the middle, and threw him into the river. The monk recovered the fhore; but was in no condition to purfue his argument. So
Jerome

Jerome triumphed by the strength of his arm. Whether this story be a fact, as indeed Lenfant speaks very dubiously of the truth of it, we have however no reason to doubt, that Jerome was principally concerned in those passionate doings, which have been mentioned in the life of Hufs.

We find little more recorded of Jerome, till the time of the council of Conftance. When Hufs went thither, Jerome, we are told, very pathetically exhorted him to bear up firmly in this great trial; and in particular to insift strenuously upon the corrupt state of the clergy; and the neceffity of a reformation. He added, that if he should hear in Bohemia, that Hufs was overpowered by his adverfaries, he would immediately repair to Conftance; and lend him what affiftance he was able.

He promifed only what he fully intended. He no fooner heard of the difficulties, in which his mafter was engaged, than he set out for Conftance; notwithftanding Hufs wrote very preffing letters, infifting upon his putting off the defign, as dangerous, and unprofitable.

P 4

He

He arrived at Conſtance, on the 4th of April, 1415; about three months before the death of Huſs. He entered the town privately; and conſulting with ſome of the leaders of his party; whom he found there, he was eaſily convinced, that he could be of no ſervice to his friend: he found the council would not ſo much as give him an hearing; and that open violence was the only argument they uſed. He heard likewiſe, that his arrival at Conſtance had taken air; and that the council intended to ſeize him.

As this was the ſituation of things, he thought it prudent to retire. Accordingly the next day he went to Iberling, an imperial town about a mile from Conſtance; whither he fled, ſays Reichenthal, with ſuch precipitation, that he left his ſword behind him. Reichenthal was an officer, employed by the council, to give an account of all ſtrangers, who came to Conſtance.

From Iberling Jerome wrote to the emperor, and profeſſed his readineſs to appear before the council, if that prince would give him a ſafe-conduct. But Sigiſmond had the honeſty to refuſe. Jerome then
tried

tried the council; but could not obtain a favourable anſwer.

In this perplexity he put up papers in all the public places of Conſtance, particularly upon the doors of the cardinals houſes, in which he profeſſed his readineſs to appear at Conſtance, in the defence of his character, and doctrine, both which he heard had been exceedingly defamed; and declared, that if any error ſhould be proved againſt him, he would with great readineſs retract it; begging only that the faith of the council might be given for his ſecurity.

Theſe papers obtaining no anſwer, he ſet out upon his return to Bohemia. He had the precaution to carry with him a certificate ſigned by ſeveral of the Bohemian nobility then at Conſtance, teſtifying, that he had uſed all prudent means in his power to obtain a hearing.

But he did not thus eſcape. At Hirſaw he was ſeized by an officer of the duke of Sultzbach; who, though he acted unauthorized, made little doubt of the council's thanks for ſo acceptable a ſervice.

Reichanthal hath given us a more particular account of this matter. " At a village
upon

upon the borders of the black foreſt, (ſaith that ſtrenuous defender of the council,) Jerome fell accidentally in company with ſome prieſts. The converſation turning upon the council of Conſtance, Jerome grew warm; and among other ſevere things, called that aſſembly the *ſchool of the devil*, and *a ſynagogue of iniquity*. The prieſts, ſcandalized at this language, gave immediate information of it to the chief magiſtrates of the place, who arreſted Jerome, and put him into the hands of the duke of Sultzbach.—This ſtory hath by no means an improbable air; as it is rather characteriſtic; though Lenfant treats it as a fable.

The duke of Sultzbach, having gotten Jerome in his power, wrote to the council for directions. The council, expreſſing their obligations to the duke, deſired him to ſend his priſoner immediately to Conſtance. The elector-palatine met him, and conducted him in triumph into the town; himſelf riding on horſe-back, with a numerous retinue, who led Jerome, in fetters, by a long chain, after him.

He was brought immediately before the council. Here a citation was read to him;
which,

which, it was said, had been posted up in Constance, in answer to the papers, which he had sent from Iberling; and he was questioned about his precipitate flight from that town. To this he answered, that he had waited a reasonable time for an answer to his paper; but had never heard of any such answer till that moment. He added, that if he had heard of it, he would have returned to Constance, though he had been upon the confines of Bohemia.

Great was the clamour which ensued on this declaration. So eager was every mouth to open upon him, that the impartial spectator saw rather the reprefentation of the baiting of a wild beast, than a wife assembly enquiring after truth. Nothing indeed more disgraceth the popish cause, than the grofs indecency, which, in a manner, was authorized on these solemn occasions. A good cause hath never recourse to tumult.

Among those, who clamoured loudest against Jerome, we find a person, whom we are unwilling to see mixing in such a scene of disorder;— John Gerson, chancellor of the university of Paris, one of the most learned, as well as the most knowing men

of

of his time, but without that candour which usually attends knowledge. With great acrimony he reproached Jerome for the novel opinions he had introduced in Paris, while he studied there. Jerome answered with equal spirit, that it was hard to object opinions of so long a date;—that it was well known the disputations of young students were meant rather as the exercise of genius, than as strict disquisitions of truth;—that no exceptions, at this time, had been made to the opinions, which he had maintained;—so far from it, that he had been honoured with a degree;—but that however, if the chancellor would make his objections, he would be ready either to defend, or retract what he had said.

As the chancellor was about to reply, an inundation of furious language broke in upon their discourse. The rectors particularly of the universities of Cologn, and Heidelburgh, following the track of Gerson, made lamentable complaints of the pestilent heresies which Jerome had maintained in those places; one of them in particular dwelt much upon an impious idea he had given of the Trinity, comparing it to water, snow,

and

and ice. Jerome had no opportunity of anfwering.   A thoufand voices burft out from every quarter, " Away with him : " burn him : burn him."

This confufion continued nearly the fpace of half an hour. Jerome ftood amazed at the grofs indecency of the fcene. As foon as he had collected himfelf, and could in any degree be heard, he looked round the affembly with a noble air, and cried out aloud, " Since nothing can fatisfy you but my " blood, God's will be done !"

Thus ended his firft hearing. He was carried from the affembly into a dungeon, under the cuftody of a guard, till it could be determined how to difpofe of him.

As he was fitting here, ruminating upon his approaching fate, a voice ftruck him, calling out in thefe words, " Fear not, " Jerome, to die in the caufe of that truth, " which, during thy life, thou haft defend- " ed." Jerome looking up to a dark window, from whence the voice feemed to come, cried out, " Whoever thou art, who " deigneft to comfort an abject man, I give " thee thanks for thy kind office. I have " indeed lived defending what I thought the " truth:

" truth : the harder tafk yet remains, to die
" for its fake : but God, I hope, will fup-
" port me againft flefh and blood."

This converfation alarmed the guard, who rufhing in difcovered the offender. He appeared to be that Maddonwitz, whofe fervices to Hufs have already been mentioned.

The affair was ufed as a pretence for more feverity againft Jerome, who was immediately conveyed to a ftrong tower, where his hands being tied behind his neck, he was left to languifh in that painful pofture, during the fpace of two days, without any aliment, but bread and water.

Thefe feverities, and others, which were inflicted upon him, were intended to force a recantation from him; a point which the council exceedingly laboured. Nothing, in the way either of promifing or threatening, was omitted, which, it was thought, might be effectual to that end.

His confinement brought upon him a dangerous illnefs; in the courfe of which he fent preffing inftances to the council for a confeffor. This afforded a proper occafion to work upon him; and he was given to
underftand,

underſtand, upon what terms he might be gratified.   But he remained immoveable.

The next attempt upon him, was immediately after the death of Huſs.   The circumſtances of that affair were laid before him, and the fatal example preſſed home in the moſt affecting manner.   Jerome liſtened without emotion; and anſwered in ſuch reſolute language, as afforded little hopes of his ſudden converſion.

His conſtancy, however, at length gave way.   Fleſh and blood could not ſupport him longer.   The ſimple fear of death he withſtood; but to endure impriſonment, chains, hunger, ſickneſs, and even torture, through a ſucceſſion of many months, was too great a trial for human nature.   But though he fell in this conflict, yet he fell not, till he had made a noble ſtand.   He was three times brought before the council; and having as often withſtood the fury of intemperate zeal, retired, maſter of himſelf, to the horrors of his dungeon.

On the 11th of September his judges firſt had hopes of his recantation.   He began to waver; and talked obſcurely of his having miſunderſtood the tendency of ſome of the

tenets

tenets of Hufs.   Promifes and threatenings were now redoubled upon him; and the 20th was appointed for a more ample confeffion of his herefies.   He was founded the night before; but not being yet brought to a proper flexibility, another day was appointed.   That fatal day was the 23d of September; when he read aloud an ample recantation, of all the opinions he had maintained, couched in words directed by the council.   In this paper he acknowledged the errors of Wicliff, and of Hufs, entirely affented to the condemnation of the latter, and declared himfelf, in every article, a firm believer with the church of Rome.

Having thus acted againft his confcience, with a heavy heart he retired from the council.   His chains indeed were taken from him; but the load was only transferred from his body to his mind. Vain were the careffes of thofe about him : they only mocked his forrow. His prifon was now indeed a gloomy folitude.   The anguifh of his own thoughts had made it fuch.

Paletz,   and Du Caffis, who were the chief managers againft him, as they had been againft Hufs, foon obferved this change.
His

His recantation, they said publicly, came only from his lips; and they determined, to bring him to a second hearing. It is probable indeed they acted in this business only an under-part. The pretence for a new trial was a new accusation. Some Carmelite friars, just arrived from Bohemia, laid before the council many strong articles against Jerome, which had not yet appeared. Paletz taking up the affair, seconded the Carmelites with great zeal: others again, as the scheme had been laid, harangued on different articles.

The managers however of this business soon found, they were likely to meet with a warmer opposition than they had imagined. The cardinals particularly of Cambray and Florence, and others, who had been appointed judges by the council in the cause of Jerome, loudly exclaimed against a second trial. " He hath submitted, (said they,) to " the council;—he hath acknowledged his " errors in particular, as well as in general, " what can we expect more? Hitherto we " have acted with credit: let us stop here, " and not suffer an intemperate zeal for truth " to carry us beyond the bounds of justice."

Whether

Whether the love of juftice was the only motive with thefe cardinals may be queftioned.   It is probable they were influenced by motives of policy alfo.   The death of Hufs had occafioned a greater commotion in Bohemia than had been forefeen.   Nothing was heard in the ftreets of Prague, but clamour againft the council, which was every where reprefented as an affembly of perfecutors.   The council, it feems, had written a letter, in very fmooth language, to palliate what had been done in the cafe of Hufs : but it had little effect.   On the contrary, the principal Huffites, (for by that name the party became now diftinguifhed,) affembled in the church of Bethelem, where they decreed the honour of martyrdom to their mafter.   They went farther : they fent a letter to Conftance ; in which, having given ample teftimony to the merits of Hufs, they reproached the council with his death ; expreffing at the fame time their devotion to the fee of Rome, when the confufion, with which it was diftracted, fhould be at an end. This letter was figned by 54 of the firft nobility in Bohemia, and Moravia : fome Polifh lords too fubfcribed it.   Nor was it

thought

thought that Winceflaus himfelf, though no way attached to the caufe of Hufs, had interfered in checking the difturbance occafioned by his death.   It is certain, he had taken great offence at the council for the affront, which he thought they had put upon him ; and wanted only an opportunity of fhewing them how much he was offended.

From the determined fpirit of this letter, it was eafy to obferve the feeds of fire fcattered in Bohemia, which a fingle breath might excite into flame ; and how general this flame might afterwards become, it was impoffible to forefee. All well-wifhers therefore to the peace of Chriftendom, thought it prudent to refrain from counfels of an inflammatory kind.

Among thefe, it is probable, were the cardinals juft mentioned ; who laboured, with what addrefs they were able, to prevent a fecond trial.   But their endeavours were ineffectual.   A torrent of zeal and bigotry bore down all oppofition. Even the learned Gerfon joined in this unmanly clamour ; and with great indecency employed his pen, as well as his tongue, upon the occafion.   A treatife of his was made public, in which he

Q 2   fhewed

fhewed how little ftrefs could be laid upon the recantation of heretics. To fuch an height ran diffention on this occafion, that the cardinal of Cambray was even reproached in public, on a fuppofition of having taken money from the king of Bohemia.

He, and his colleagues, finding themfelves unable to ftem fo furious a tide, at length gave way to it. They entered their proteft however againft thefe violent proceedings, and laid down the commiffion, with which the council had intrufted them. It was immediately taken up, with the general approbation of all the zealot-party, by the patriarch of Conftantinople; who having fufficiently fhewn his fpirit in the affair of Hufs, was confidered as a man prepared to go any lengths.

While thefe things were in agitation, a full half-year elapfed; during which time Jerome's enemies had influence enough to continue his confinement, till fome end fhould be put to the affair.

It was not till the May of the year 1416, that Jerome was called again before the council. He had long been apprized of the defign of bringing him to a fecond trial

upon

upon fome new evidence which had appeared. This, amidft all his diftreffes, was his
great confolation; and he rejoiced at an opportunity of acknowledging publickly that
fhameful defection, which hung fo heavy
upon him.

A little before the day of trial, he was informed, that proctors were appointed, by
whom he might urge his defence. But he
infifted pofitively upon making no defence
in any form, unlefs the council would give
him an audience; and let him anfwer for
himfelf. This, after much difficulty, and
long debatings, was at length allowed.

When he was brought to an audience, he
was charged with various articles; the chief
of which were,—His adherence to the errors
of Wicliff,—his having had a picture of that
heretic in his chamber, arrayed in the common ornaments of a faint,—his counterfeit-
ing the feal of the univerfity of Oxford in
favour of Wicliff,—His defpifing the authority of the church after excommunication,—
and his denial of tranfubftantiation.

On all thefe articles of accufation, and
what others of lefs moment were objected
to him, he anfwered with great fpirit.

Q 3

"That

" That he thought well of Wicliff, and of
his doctrine, he said, he scrupled. not to
own; but that he thought him infallible, as
seemed to be insinuated, was false; — that
many of his books he had never seen; and
that he could not subscribe in all points. to
those he had: but that in general he believed
many errors had been laid to his charge, of
which he was innocent; for he was too wise
a man, he said, to be the author of grofs
absurdities, many of which his enemies had
inserted in his creed. — With regard to his
having had a picture of Wicliff in his poffef-
sion, he said, it was very true; and that he
had the pictures likewise of many other
learned men; but he remembred not, he
said, that Wicliff's portrait was dreffed in
any faint-like ornaments; — that as to the
charge of his having counterfeited the feal
of the univerfity of Oxford, he had feen, he
said, a teftimonial under that feal, in favour
of Wicliff, which he had been made to believe was authentic: he owned too, that he
had read it publickly; but that as to his
having counterfeited either the feal, or the
inftrument, he was totally innocent of the
charge; and it refted upon his opponents to
prove

prove the allegation. This affair of a falfe teftimonial made much noife, it feems, at that time. But from the general temper of the univerfity it is probable, the inftrument was authentic; and the evidence of hiftory confirms its authenticity.—Finally, Jerome declared folemnly, that he had never defpifed the authority of the church: he could prove, he faid, that he had ufed every probable method in his power to be reconciled to it;— and that laftly, he had never, either in con- verfation, or writing, oppofed the doctrine of tranfubftantiation.

Having thus protefted his innocence, he gave the council a circumftantial detail of his coming to Conftance; and of all that had fince befallen him. Then raifing his voice, and expreffing himfelf firft with fome afperity againft his accufers, he told them, he was now going to lay himfelf more open to them, than he had yet done. He then, with great emotion, declared before the whole affembly, that the fear of death only had induced him to retract opinions, which from his heart he maintained;—that he had done injuftice to the memory of thofe two excellent men, John Wicliff, and John

Hu

Hufs; whofe examples he revered; and in whofe doctrine he was determined to die. He concluded with a fevere invective againft the clergy; the depravity of whofe manners, he faid, was now every where notorious.

It may truly be lamented, that the whole of his fpeech, upon this occafion, hath not been preferved. It is faid to have been a model of true eloquence. The minds of his hearers were fo captivated with it, that, in fpite of themfelves, they were attentive. Once or twice he was interrupted; but the interrupters paid feverely for their impertinence: they were foon lafhed into confufion by the acrimony of his language, and the fpirit, with which he fpoke. So collected was he, fo entirely mafter of himfelf; and of every topic, on which he difcourfed, that it feemed as if heaven had indulged him, on this folemn occafion, in the exertion of more than natural powers. It is faid, that many in the council, while he was fpeaking, became fo prejudiced in his favour, that they fat with a dread upon them, left he fhould utter fomething, which might throw him beyond a poffibility of obtaining mercy.

His

His speech however was not calculated to move pity. On the same day, or a few days after, sentence passed upon him, by which he was condemned for having held the errors of Wicliff; and for apostatizing. He was immediately, in the usual stile of popish affectation, delivered over to the civil power. As he was a layman, he had no ceremony of degradation to undergo. The same sort of cap was put upon his head, with which Hufs had been adorned; and so attired he was led to execution.

When he came to the place, he could not but smile to see the malice of his enemies appearing in a shape too grotesque for so serious an occasion. The post, to which he was chained, was hewn, it seems, into a monstrous, and uncouth figure of Hufs, and ornamented into a ridiculous likeness of him.

A little before the fire was kindled, he told the people, that he believed the established creed, and that he knew not for what he suffered death, unless because he had not subscribed to the condemnation of Wicliff, and of Hufs; which he could not do with
a safe

a safe confcience; becaufe he firmly believed them both to be pious men.

The wood beginning to blaze, he fang an hymn, which he continued with great fervency, till the fury of the fire fcorching him, he was heard to cry out, " O Lord God! " have mercy upon me! have mercy upon " me!" And a little afterwards, " Thou " knoweft how I have loved thy truth." The wind parting the flames, his body, full of large blifters, exhibited a dreadful fpectacle to the beholders; his lips continued ftill moving, as if actuated by intenfe devotion. During a full quarter of an hour, he difcovered the figns not only of life, but of intellect.——Even his enemies thought the rage of his judges purfued him too far, when they faw his wretched coverlet, and the other miferable garniture of his prifon, by their order, confumed in the fire after him; and his afhes, as thofe of Hufs had been, thrown into the Rhine.

From this account of the trial, and death of Jerome, it feems as if the leading members of the council were determined, at any rate, to put him to death. We cannot otherwife fee the reafon of their bringing him to

a fecond

a fecond hearing. They had already obtained a triumph over him. A fecond trial made that again doubtful, which his recantation had decided in their favour. But it hath been the notorious practice of the church of Rome, in her dealings with capital offenders, to put them firft to fhame, and afterwards to death.

Among thofe, who have treated of the death of Jerome, none hath done him more honour than Poggè the Florentine. The anecdotes of him preferved by this writer have not yet been laid before the reader. As Poggè was not only a man of fome eminence, but an adverfary likewife to the caufe of Jerome, his teftimony is of too much confequence to be kneaded with the mafs of other authorities; and will appear to moft advantage by itfelf.

This eminent perfon had been bred in the court of Rome; and having been fecretary under two popes, was well inftructed in its defigns. Here too he had every opportunity of gratifying his inclination for ftudy; and was verfed alike in bufinefs, and in letters. He had a tafte for poetry likewife; and gained great credit by fome fatyrical compofitions,

which

which he publifhed in the early part of his life. To his other praifes he added that of an hiftorian. His hiftory of Florence is efteemed an elegant at leaft, though a partial compofition. But the world is moft indebted to him as an antiquarian. To his induftry we owe many noble remains of antiquity, which he redeemed from that obfcurity, in which barbarifm had involved them; particularly the works of Quinctilian; which he had the happinefs to find compleat in a ruined monaftery.

In what capacity he attended the council, we have no account. As he relates matter of fact only, it is of little confequence. The examination, and death of Jerome, of which he was an eye-witnefs, affected him in fo ftrong a manner, that he gave a full account of both to his friend Aretin at Rome, as the moft extraordinary events he had met with, during his refidence at Conftance. The reader will confider his letter on this occafion, as a portrait warm from the life; and, if not a finifhed picture, at leaft a very fpirited fketch. It was written originally in Latin. The following is not meant as a literal tranflation. Thofe circumftances, with which

the

the reader hath been already made acquainted, in the courfe of the narrative, are
omitted.

A letter from Poggè of Florence to Leonard Aretin.

" In the midft of a fhort excurfion into
" the country, I wrote to our common
" friend; from whom, I doubt not, you
" have had an account of me.

" Since my return to Conftance, my at-
" tention hath been wholly engaged by Je-
" rome, the Bohemian heretic, as he is
" called. The eloquence, and learning,
" which this perfon hath employed in his
" own defence are fo extraordinary, that I
" cannot forbear giving you a fhort account
" of him.

" To confefs the truth, I never knew the
" art of fpeaking carried fo near the model
" of ancient eloquence. It was indeed
" amazing to hear with what force of ex-
" preffion, with what fluency of language,
" and with what excellent reafoning he an-
" fwered his adverfaries; nor was I lefs ftruck
" with the gracefulnefs of his manner; the
                                    " dignity

" dignity of his action; and the firmnefs,
" and conftancy of his whole behaviour. It
" grieved me to think fo great a man was la-
" bouring under fo atrocious an accufation.
" Whether this accufation be a juft one,
" God knows: for myfelf, I enquire not
" into the merits of it; refting fatisfied with
" the decifion of my fuperiors.——But I will
" juft give you a fummary of his trial.

" After many articles had been proved
" againft him, leave was at length given
" him to anfwer each in its order. But Je-
" rome long refufed, ftrenuoufly contending,
" that he had many things to fay previoufly
" in his defence; and that he ought firft to
" be heard in general, before he defcended
" to particulars. When this was over-ruled,
" Here, faid he, ftanding in the midft of
" the affembly, here is juftice; here is equity.
" Befet by my enemies, I am already pro-
" nounced a heretic : I am condemned, be-
" fore I am examined.——Were you God's
" omnifcient, inftead of an affembly of fal-
" lible men, you could not act with more
" fufficiency.——Error is the lot of mortals;
" and you, exalted as you are, are fubject
" to it. But confider, that the higher you

" are

" are exalted, of the more dangerous con-
" fequence are your errors. — As for me, I
" know I am a wretch below your notice:
" but at leaft confider, that an unjuft action,
" in fuch an affembly, will be of dangerous
" example."

" This, and much more, he fpoke with
" great elegance of language, in the midft
" of a very unruly and indecent affembly :
" and thus far at leaft he prevailed; the
" council ordered, that he fhould firft anfwer
" objections ; and promifed that he fhould
" then have liberty to fpeak.   Accordingly,
" all the articles alledged againft him were
" publicly read ; and then proved ; after
" which he was afked, whether he had ought
" to object ? It is incredible with what acute-
" nefs he anfwered ; and with what amazing
" dexterity he warded off every ftroke of his
" adverfaries.   Nothing efcaped him : his
" whole behaviour was truly great and pious.
" If he were indeed the man his defence
" fpoke him, he was fo far from meriting
" death, that, in my judgment, he was not
" in any degree culpable. — In a word, he
" endeavoured to prove, that the greater
" part of the charge was purely the inven-
" tion

" tion of his adverfaries. — Among other
" things, being accufed of hating and de-
" faming the holy fee, the pope, the cardi-
" nals, the prelates, and the whole eftate of
" the clergy, he ftretched out his hands,
" and faid, in a moft moving accent, " On
" which fide, reverend fathers, fhall I turn
" me for redrefs? whom fhall I implore?
" whofe affiftance can I expect? which of
" you hath not this malicious charge entirely
" alienated from me? which of you hath it
" not changed from a judge into an invete-
" rate enemy?—It was artfully alledged in-
" deed! Though other parts of their charge
" were of lefs moment, my accufers might
" well imagine, that if this were faftened on
" me, it could not fail of drawing upon me
" the united indignation of my judges."

" On the third day of this memorable
" trial, what had paft was recapitulated :
" when Jerome, having obtained leave, tho'
" with fome difficulty, to fpeak, began his
" oration with a prayer to God ; whofe di-
" vine affiftance he pathetically implored.
" He then obferved, that many excellent
" men, in the annals of hiftory, had been
" oppreffed by falfe witneffes, and con-
" demned

" demned by unjuſt judges. Beginning
" with profane hiſtory, he inſtanced the
" death of Socrates, the captivity of Plato,
" the baniſhment of Anaxagoras, and the
" unjuſt ſufferings of many others: he then
" inſtanced the many worthies, of the old
" Teſtament, in the ſame circumſtances,
" Moſes, Joſhua, Daniel, and almoſt all
" the prophets; and laſtly thoſe of the new,
" John the baptiſt, St. Stephen, and others,
" who were condemned as ſeditious, pro-
" phane, or immoral men. An unjuſt judg-
" ment, he ſaid, proceeding from a layic
" was bad; from a prieſt, worſe; ſtill worſe
" from a college of prieſts; and from a ge-
" neral council, ſuperlatively bad.—Theſe
" things he ſpoke with ſuch force and em-
" phaſis, as kept every one's attention awake.

" On one point he dwelt largely. As the
" merits of the cauſe reſted entirely upon
" the credit of witneſſes, he took great pains
" to ſhew, that very little was due to thoſe
" produced againſt him. He had many
" objections to them, particularly their
" avowed hatred to him; the ſources of
" which he ſo palpably laid open, that he
" made a ſtrong impreſſion upon the minds

R

" of

" of his hearers ; and not a little ſhook the
" credit of the witneſſes. The whole coun-
" cil was moved ; and greatly inclined to
" pity, if not to favour him. He added,
" that he came uncompelled to the council ;
" and that neither his life nor doctrine had
" been ſuch, as gave him the leaſt reaſon to
" dread an appearance before them. Dif-
" ference of opinion, he ſaid, in matters of
" faith had ever ariſen among learned men ;
" and was always eſteemed productive of
" truth, rather than of error, where bigotry
" was laid aſide. Such, he ſaid, was the
" difference between Auſtin and Jerome :
" and though their opinions were not only
" different, but contradictory, yet the im-
" putation of hereſy was never fixed on
" either.

" Every one expected, that he would
" now either retract his errors, or at leaſt
" apologize for them : but nothing of the
" kind was heard from him : he declared
" plainly, that he had nothing to retract.
" He launched out into an high encomium
" of Huſs ; calling him a holy man ; and
" lamenting his cruel, and unjuſt death.
" He had armed himſelf, he ſaid, with a
                                    " full

" full refolution to follow the steps of that
" bleffed martyr; and to fuffer with con-
" ftancy whatever the malice of his enemies
" could inflict.   " The perjured witneffes,
" (faid he,) who have appeared againft me,
" have won their caufe : but let them re-
" member, they have their evidence once
" more to give before a tribunal, where
" falfhood can be no difguife."

    " It was impoffible to hear this pathetic
" fpeaker without emotion.   Every ear was
" captivated; and every heart touched. —
" But wifhes in his favour were vain : he
" threw himfelf beyond a poffibility of
" mercy.   Braving death, he even provoked
" the vengeance, which was hanging over
" him.   " If that holy martyr, (faid he,
" fpeaking of Hufs,) ufed the clergy with
" difrefpect, his cenfures were not levelled
" at them as priefts, but as wicked men.
" He faw with indignation thofe revenues,
" which had been defigned for charitable
" ends, expended upon pageantry, and
" riot."

    " Through this whole oration he fhewed
" a moft amazing ftrength of memory.   He
" had been confined almoft a year in a dun-

" geon

" geon : the feverity of which ufage he
" complained of, but in the language of a
" great and good man.   In this horrid place
" he was deprived of books and paper. Yet
" notwithftanding this, and the conftant
" anxiety, which muft have hung over him,
" he was at no more lofs for proper authori-
" ties, and quotations, than if he had fpent
" the intermediate time at leifure in his
" ftudy.

" His voice was fweet, diftinct, and full :
" his action every way the moft proper either
" to exprefs indignation, or to raife pity ;
" though he made no affected application to
" the paffions of his audience. Firm, and
" intrepid he ftood before the council ; col-
" lected in himfelf ; and not only contemn-
" ing, but feeming even defirous of death.
" The greateft character in ancient ftory
" could not poffibly go beyond him. If
" there is any juftice in hiftory, this man
" will be admired by all pofterity.—I fpeak
" not of his errors : let thefe reft with him.
" What I admired was his learning, his elo-
" quence, and amazing acutenefs.   God
" knows whether thefe things were not the
" ground-work of his ruin.

" Two

" Two days were allowed him for re-
" flection; 'during which time many perfons
" of confequence, and particularly my lord
" cardinal of Florence, endeavoured to bring
" him to a better mind. But perfifting ob-
" ftinately in his errors, he was condemned
" as an heretic.

" With a chearful countenance, and more
" than Stoical conftancy, he met his fate;
" fearing neither death itfelf, nor the horri-
" ble form, in which it appeared. When he
" came to the place, he pulled of his upper
" garment, and made a fhort prayer * at
" the ftake; to which he was foon after
" bound with wet cords, and an iron chain;
" and inclofed as high as his breaft with
" faggots.

" Obferving the executioner about to fet
" fire to the wood behind his back, he cried
" out, " Bring thy torch hither. Perform
" thy office before my face. Had I feared
" death, I might have avoided it."

" As

---

* *Flexis genibus veneratus eft palum* (faith the original.)
This certainly muft have been a falfe interpretation of his
praying *with his face turned towards the ftake.* But other
hiftorians, on Poggè's authority, have taken up the notion,
that he *prayed to the ftake.*

" As the wood began to blaze, he fang
" an hymn, which the violence of the flame
" fcarce interrupted.

" Thus died this prodigious man. The
" epithet is not extravagant. I was myfelf
" an eye-witnefs of his whole behaviour.
" Whatever his life may have been, his
" death, without doubt, is a noble leffon of
" philofophy.

" But it is time to finifh this long epiftle.
" You will fay I have had fome leifure upon
" my hands: and, to fay the truth, I have
" not much to do here. This will, I hope,
" convince you, that greatnefs is not wholly
" confined to antiquity. You will think me
" perhaps tedious ; but I could have been
" more prolix on a fubject fo copious.—
" Farewell my dear Leonard."

Conftance May 20.

Such was the teftimony born to an adverfary by this ingenuous papift. His friend
Aretin was lefs candid. " You attribute
" more, fays he, to this man, than I could
" wifh. You ought at leaft to *write* more
" cautioufly of thefe things." And indeed,

it

it is probable, Poggè would have written more cautioufly, had he written a few days afterwards. But his letter is dated on the very day, on which Jerome fuffered, and came warm from the writer's heart. It is fufficiently plain, what Poggè himfelf thought of the council, and its proceedings. His encomium on Jerome, is certainly a tacit cenfure of them.

The end.   The

ZISCA

The Life of

Z I S C A.

IN the lives of John Hufs, and Jerome of Prague, we have feen great inftances of the violence and injuftice of the council of Conftance. That bigotted affembly ap-peared ready to embrace any meafures, and to run any lengths, to eftablifh the tyranny of the church of Rome. The life of Zifca exhibits thofe fcenes of diforder and ruin, which might be expected as the natural confequences of fuch furious zeal.

The real name of this eminent perfon was John de Troeznow. The epithet Zifca was given him from his having loft an eye; that word, in the Bohemian language, fignifying one-eyed. He was a native of Bohemia; born of a good family, remarkable rather for its credit, than its wealth.

In the early part of his life Zifca was in-troduced to Winceflaus, whom he ferved in

the

the capacity of a page: but being tired of a subjection to the capricious and trifling humours of that prince, he gave up all expectations from royal favour, and left his country, with a resolution to seek his fortune abroad. His intention was to enter into some military service; having from his earliest youth discovered a strong inclination to the profession of arms.

He lived some time in Denmark, and afterwards in lower Saxony; but we find him not in any employment, till the breaking out of the wars in Poland, against the knights of the Teutonic order.

The Poles embracing Christianity earlier than their neighbours, suffered from some of them a sort of national persecution. The irruptions of the Prussians were particularly formidable; with which hardy people they waged a long and unsuccessful war. At length finding themselves reduced, they called to their assistance the knights of the Teutonic order; by whose alliance being strengthened, they soon brought their enemies to terms.

To recompence these foreigners, or more probably to fulfil a previous engagement,

they

they allowed them to settle in Poland, and distributed lands among them. But the Poles had soon reason to repent of their civility. These insolent inmates made early incroachments upon their benefactors; and matters proceeding to extremity, a bloody war broke out. Neither side had much reason to boast, till the year 1410; when the knights suffered a total defeat: their grand-master was killed, and their whole army very severely handled.

Zisca, who had entered, at the begining of the war, into the service of the king of Poland, distinguished himself greatly in this battle. He led a battalion in that wing, which first turned the fortune of the day. The king presented him with a purse of ducats for his services; and accompanied his liberality with a badge of honour.

The Polish generals however not pursuing their victory as they ought, the knights so far collected themselves, as to enter with a good face into negotiation. A treaty was soon afterwards concluded; and Zisca finding his sword of no farther use in Poland, returned into Bohemia; where we meet him again, notwithstanding his former prejudices, in the court of Winceſlaus; and in office about his perſon.

Upon the tragical fate of Huſs, which threw all Bohemia into confuſion, no one felt more acutely than Ziſca. He did not however vent his indignation, like others, in clamour and threatening language; it ſat in a melancholy gloom upon his brows, and ſunk into his heart. The king, we are told, ſeeing him, from a window of the palace, walking in a thoughtful poſture, aſked him, upon what ſerious ſubject he was meditating? " Upon the bloody affront, anſwered Ziſca, which your majeſty's ſubjects have ſuffered at Conſtance." " It is true, replied Win-ceſlaus; but, I fear, it is neither in your power, nor in mine, to revenge it." This circumſtance, we are told, firſt inſpired Ziſca with a reſolution to aſſert the religious liber-ties of his country.

Beſides the affair of Conſtance, he wanted not other motives to incite him to this enter-prize. Though a man of no great know-ledge in matters of divinity, he had ſagacity enough to ſee the neceſſity of a thorough reformation in the diſcipline of the church. He had conceived likewiſe a ſteady diſlike to the clergy; founded more upon the corruption of their lives, than of their doctrine. We are told too, he had personal cause of resentment; a favourite sister having been debauched by a monk.

But with whatever zeal Zisca and his friends were animated in private, in public they observed a commendable temper. While the council still sat, they had hope that some healing expedient might be found. Were the fathers there assembled in earnest, it was impossible, they imagined, but something would be done to remove abuses, and allay distempers, become now so flagrant, and alarming. They resolved however to wait the event.

With these vain hopes they were deluded, till the dissolution of the council, in the beginning of the year 1418. Their eyes were now fully opened. That great assembly of Christian bishops, from the result of whose counsels, a full reformation of all abuses was expected, were so far from answering those sanguine hopes, that they left things very little better than they found them; many things worse, as sanctifyed by a new authority. " Thus ended, (says the
" impartial

" impartial Lenfant, in the conclufion of his
" hiftory,) the famous council of Conftance;
" in which it cannot be denyed, but that
" fome things were done truly commend-
" able, though that affembly by no means
" anfwered the general expectation of the
" world. It condemned men, who at worft
" were only fomewhat too forward in their
" zeal againft abufes, which all ferious men
" acknowledged, and which even the coun-
" cil itfelf difapproved. It fpared errors
" likewife, which certainly tended to the
" deftruction of all true religion. But what
" placed it in the worft light, were the feeble
" efforts it made towards a reformation of
" the clergy; though it is evident, from the
" teftimony of all writers, that the refor-
" mation of the clergy was the avowed, and
" principal end it had in view."

The council being diffolved, the heads of
the reforming party in Bohemia knew what
they had now to expect. They knew they
had nothing to depend upon for the pre-
fervation of their religious liberties, but their
own ftrength, and fpirit.

If any hope of favour from the court of
Rome ftill remained, it was wholly diffipated
by

by a letter, which the new pope, Martin V. sent into Bohemia, soon after his election. This letter was directed to the Huffites, whom he charges with many and great herefies. In particular, he tells them, they had trampled upon the ftatues of the faints, and the ceremonies of the church; — that they had celebrated the feafts of John Hufs, and Jerome of Prague;—that the facrament under both fpecies had been adminiftred among them;—and, in one word, that the church was never worfe treated under Nero, than it had been by them. He ftill however gives them hopes of favour, if they would return again within their ancient pale; but threatens, if they continued obftinate, to cut them off entirely from the church, and give them as a prey to their enemies.

Martin not refting his caufe entirely upon this letter, fent the cardinal Dominictis, as his legate, into Bohemia. This minifter foon informed himfelf of the temper of the country; and, after a fhort and fruitlefs negotiation, wrote letters to the pope, and to the emperor Sigifmond, (who claimed the crown after Winceflaus, and was of courfe greatly interefted in the affair,) acquainting them,

them, it was in vain to expect any submission from that country, through means less effectual than open force.

During this negotiation, the heads of the reforming party, foreseeing the evil at a distance, concerted measures for their safety. In the summer of the year 1418 they had a general meeting at the castle of Wisgrade; the design of which was, to deliberate on the best means of preserving the liberties of the church of Bohemia. They had no reverence for the pope; and very little for the emperor: with their own sovereign they were desirous of keeping terms. Their first resolution therefore was to sound the inclinations of Winceslaus; that capricious prince having yet given them no certain evidence either of his favour, or aversion. With this view, they sent deputies to the king; who, in the name of the assembly, acquainting him with the increasing numbers of their sect, requested the use of more churches.

Winceslaus was surprized rather at the spirit in which the request was made, than at the request itself. He was dissatisfied, as much as they were, with the affair of Constance; but he chose to have the resentment

due

due upon that occasion to appear as coming
from himself; and he had no inclination, at
this time, to shew it. On the other hand,
here was a violent party, which would take
no denial; whose strength he knew as well
as his own comparative weakness; and tho'
it was hard for a monarch to receive law from
his subjects, (for he could not but consider
their request as a demand,) yet the remembrance of past misfortunes had taught him
to put many restraints upon himself.

Agreeable to this perplexity, and to the
darkness of his own character, he answered
the deputies evasively. He was greatly inclined, he said, to favour them; but disap-
proved passion and tumult. He required
them therefore to rely upon his honour;
and, as a pledge of their good intentions,
to deposit their arms with him.

With this answer the deputies returned.
It was by no means satisfactory; and the
more violent were for breaking all measures
forthwith. The debates of these fierce spirits
becoming tumultuous, Zisca suddenly start-
ing up, cried out, Gentlemen, "I have long
" known the king, and am thoroughly ac-
" quainted with his temper: arm yourselves,
S" and

" and follow me." Thus attended he ftood
before Winceflaus : " Behold, (faid he,) a
" body of your majefty's faithful fubjects :
" we have brought our arms, as you com-
" manded : fhew us your enemies ; and you
" fhall have reafon to acknowledge, that our
" weapons can be in no hands more faithful
" to you, than in thofe, which hold them."
In a capricious, unprincipled mind, a fudden
evafion hath often the weight of argument.
It had on this occafion. Struck with the
heroic language, and appearance of thefe
brave men, the king cried out, " Take your
" arms, gentlemen, and ufe them proper-
" ly."—This action firft recommended Zifca
to the confidence of his party ; and gave an
earneft of thofe ftrokes of policy, which his
mind, fruitful of expedients, was afterwards
found fo capable of difplaying.

The reftraint however, which Winceflaus
put upon the reformers was foon removed.
Tired with the paft, and dreading the future,
which he faw approaching in a ftorm, that
unhappy prince at length gave way to the
anguifh of his fpirit, and funk under a
weight of grief. His death was accelerated
by a violent fit of paffion, in the agony of
                                    which

which he expired; leaving it a conteft among hiftorians, whether the man, or the prince was more contemptible in his character.

Upon the death of Winceflaus, the crown of Bohemia was claimed, as hath been faid, by his brother, the emperor Sigifmond. This claim made an entire change in the fyftem of the reformers. They now faw their civil, as well as religious liberties in danger; and came to an unanimous refolution to oppofe the emperor at the hazard of their lives. They were perfuaded they had a conftitutional right to elect their own prince; and againft Sigifmond they had many objections. The fhare he had in the bufinefs of Conftance had rendered him odious to the whole reforming party. But his avowed principles in favour of the court of Rome, were the grand obftacle.

On the other hand, the friends of the emperor, at the head of whom was the queen dowager, who had been appointed regent, took meafures to fupport his title. They proclaimed him at Prague; adminiftred oaths to thofe in office about the court; and re-moved fuch as were thought ill-affected to his government.

The

The reformers, unwilling to give the queen any advantage by their delay, took arms without farther hesitation; and chosing Zisca their general, declared war against all the adherents of the emperor, and upholders of the tyranny of the church of Rome.

The regular clergy felt the first effects of this commotion. These, wherever found, Zisca treated with sufficient severity. "Let "us, said he, encouraging his men, drive "these fatted hogs from their sties."

The queen regent alarmed at these proceedings, wrote an account of them to the emperor; intreating speedy aid, and assuring him, that the insurrection was by no means trivial.

Sigismond was, at that time, engaged in an expedition against the Turks; and could not immediately, without some discredit, turn his arms towards Bohemia. The queen, thus left to herself, exerted a spirit proportioned to the emergence; and drawing together what troops she was able, strengthened the works of Prague, and shut herself up in it with a good garrison. She was well assured however the city was not wholly hers, the new town being chiefly inhabited by reformers.

formers.   With great ſkill therefore ſhe fortified all the avenues, which led from one
town to the other; and in particular the
bridge over the Muldaw.

The ſtandard of the reformers having
been erected only a few weeks, Ziſca found
himſelf at the head of 40,000 men; a body
of troops leſs formidable for their numbers,
than for their martial ardour.   Well knowing that action is the life of a tumultuary
army, he took the field without delay; and
finding himſelf in want of garriſons, for almoſt every fortreſs in the kingdom was in
the hands of the Imperialiſts, he reſolved to
open the campaign by the ſiege of Pilſen.
This town lay conveniently for him, as it
was in the midſt of a country greatly devoted
to his intereſt.   Here his troops firſt ſignal-
ized their courage.   Though few of them
had ſeen action before, they mounted the
wall like veterans; and after a ſhort diſpute
became maſters of the fortreſs.   Ziſca having added to its works, put a garriſon into
it, and made it a place of arms.

From hence he ſent out parties, and took
in the caſtles, and ſtrong holds in the neighbourhood: ſo that in a little time he found

all the south-west part of Bohemia in his hands; and his army greatly increased by these conquests.

While Zisca was thus employed, his friends in Prague were endeavouring their utmost to make themselves masters of that city. Notwithstanding the watchful eye, which was continually upon them, they had their private meetings; and having formed a scheme, they made a desperate attempt to pass the Muldaw, where that river divides, at the isle of St. Benedict. The encounter was sharp, and bloody: the imperialists however maintained their post.

The reformers, not discouraged, made their next attempt upon the bridge. Here they fought with incredible firmness, and with more success. Five days, and five nights, with little intermission, the dispute lasted: during which time, both parties, as may be imagined, suffered greatly; and some of the fairest buildings of the town, particularly the great council-chamber, were destroyed. The reformers at length carried their point; and the imperialists took shelter in the castle.

The

The emperor was now alarmed in earneſt, He withdrew his troops ſuddenly from the confines of Turkey, and making haſty marches towards Bohemia with part of his cavalry, appointed his army to follow his rout.

At Brin in Moravia he halted; and being greatly deſirous of bringing matters to a fair accommodation, he ſent deputies to Prague to treat of peace.

At the head of theſe deputies was Gaſpar Selic, one of the moſt accompliſhed ſtateſmen of his time. His father was a German, and his mother an Italian. From theſe he inherited the good qualities of each people; the ſolidity of the one; the inſinuating manners of the other; and the characteriſtic foibles of neither.

This artful miniſter ſoon put the emperor's affairs into a hopeful train. He managed all parties with ſuch dexterity, convincing them how much it was their intereſt to coaleſce; that he ſoon brought on a treaty. As a preliminary, Ziſca gave up Pilſen, and all the other fortreſſes he had taken. He ſeems indeed to have been influenced by the citizens of Prague; who, having ſeen their town miserably harrassed in the late commotions, were already weary of the dispute.

In this hopeful way were the affairs of the emperor, when an unhappy letter, which he wrote to the magistrates of Prague, ruined all. In this letter, after congratulating them on the prospect of a speedy peace, which he mentions as an event equally advantageous to all parties, he tells them, he hopes, they shall never have occasion to repent the confidence they had placed in him; and promises to govern, after the model of his father, the emperor Charles. Whether by governing after the model of his father, Sigismond meant only in civil matters, which is most probable; or whether he insinuated his intention with regard to religion, it is certain he expressed himself either negligently or imprudently. It was presently caught up, and propagated among the reformers, that the emperor had at last dealt honestly with them; — that he had now shewn his full intention; — that he could not even keep on the disguise, till he had them fairly in his power; — but, they thanked God, they had yet time to take other measures.

If

If any thing was wanting, after this imprudent letter, to ruin the interests of Sigismond in Bohemia, his impolite behaviour afterwards compleated the work. Having put the treaty of Prague, as he hoped, on a good footing, he went to Breslaw; where, it seems, the spirit of Zisca had diffused itself; and the citizens had shewn some zeal in his cause. They opened their gates however to the emperor; and received him with great appearance of devotion. Sigismond, instead of taking these half-formed subjects under his protection, and caressing them with tenderness, began with a strict enquiry into the authors of the late disturbances, many of whom he treated with severity enough. The impolitic monarch was yet unacquainted with the spirit of these men: he had not yet learned, that persecution in no shape could subdue them; and that nothing could work upon them, but gentle treatment, and great toleration.

The conduct of Sigismond at Breslaw was an alarm-bell from one end of Bohemia to the other. Not a man but was ready to take arms. "What! shall we see ourselves tame-
" ly slaughtered like sheep? Let us shew this
" haughty

" haughty tyrant, that we are not yet victims
" deftin'd to his knife."

The high fpirit, which was thus raifed among the reformers, foon fhewed itelf in action. Their firft attempt was on the caftle of Prague; of the town they were already in poffeffion. This ftrong fortrefs was maintained for the emperor by Zincho, a German officer, in whom the queen had great confidence. But he deceived her expectation. Zifca, who knew the governor's foible, bad fo high for his virtue, that he became mafter of the caftle without ftriking a blow.

Sigifmond by this time faw his errors; and had only left, if poffible, to retrieve them. The hopes of peace, he obferved, had greatly diffipated the tumultuary army of the reformers. He refolved therefore to attack them with what troops he had about him, which confifted only of a few regiments of horfe, the grofs of his army not being yet arrived; and, if poffible, to crufh them, before they could well affociate.

But Zifca, fufficiently upon his guard, retreated before his unfkilful enemies into a mountainous and rocky country, where he
knew

knew their horfe would only be an incumbrance to them. Having thus chofen his ground, he drew up his fmall army, which was compofed entirely of infantry, in a very advantageous manner; and, on the 19th of Auguft, 1420, prefented himfelf to the enemy.

The imperial generals faw their danger, but knew not how to avoid it. To fight on horfeback was impracticable: to retreat, barely poffible. Difmounting they formed on foot. But Zifca feconding his conduct with his bravery, fell on them with fuch irrefiftible fury, that the imperialifts were immediately thrown into confufion; and were all either cut to pieces on the fpot, or flaughtered in the defiles.

The fabulous writers of thofe times attribute this victory to a very improbable device of Zifca. He ordered the women, we are informed, who attended his camp, to ftrew their handkerchiefs and aprons in the front of the army, in which the fpurs of the imperialifts being intangled, the reformers had an eafy victory.

Zifca, whofe army daily increafed, purfuing his conqueft, appeared fuddenly before
Aufca.

Aufca. This town had little favour to expect, having always treated the reformers with more than usual severity; at the instigation chiefly of Ulric, the governor, a man of a savage disposition. The formality of a siege not suiting the circumstances of Zisca, he made a general assault; and after a sharp dispute carried the town. He gave orders, the same day, to set it on fire, and level it with the ground; leaving behind him a monument of his vengeance, ill-becoming the cause in which he fought. The unhappy Ulric, falling into his hands, was put to an ignominious death.

Zisca employed the short respite, which his enemies, at this time, allowed him, in fortifying a camp. Though the summer was wearing apace, yet he had reason to expect the emperor would lie quiet only till he had collected his troops. The push, he doubted not, would be vigorous; and if any sinister event should await him, he foresaw, that all would be ruined, if he had no retreat. Pilsen he had given up: Prague indeed was in his hands; but Prague was a divided town; too extensive for a garrison, and too populous.

Near

Near Bechin, the provincial town of its circle, about 40 miles south of Prague, an arm of the Muldaw, winding round a craggy hill, forms a peninsula, the neck of which is scarce 30 feet broad. The hill itself is accessible on one side only. This was the place which Zisca chose for his camp; a place, which nature had nobly fortified to his hand. The declivity he assigned to his companions, on which they pitched their tents; at the summit he erected his own; inclosing the whole with a good rampart; and fortifying the neck of the peninsula with a broad ditch, and two strong towers. In time their tents became houses, his own pavilion a castle, and the ramparts and ditches, impregnable walls. To this fortress he gave the name of Tabor, alluding to the hill on which it stood. It makes, at this day, an appearance in the maps of Bohemia.

While Zisca was employed in this business, he had intelligence, that a body of imperial horse lay in the neighbourhood, observing his motions. He took his opportunity, and surprizing them at midnight, surrounded the village in which they were

quartered;

quartered ; and made the whole party, confisting of a thoufand men, prifoners of war.

The action was trifling, but had confequences, which Zifca did not forefee. He had long wanted a body of horfe, which, in the necessity of his affairs, he had never been able to raife ; and thought the fuits of armour and horfes, which, on this occasion, fell into his hands, were a very valuable prize, as they might become a good foundation for a body of Cavalry; without which he never afterwards took the field. He was himfelf an excellent horfeman, fond of horfes, and of the management of them; and if in any one part of the general's duty he laid himfelf more particularly out, it feems to have been in that of forming his cavalry.

The attention of Zifca was, at this time, for a few days, engaged in a very extraordinary manner. An enthufiaftic Picard ; or, as others call him, a Fleming of the name of Picard, leaving his own country, and paffing the Rhine, wandered into Bohemia. On his journey, he had drawn many followers of both fexes after him ;
whom

whom he deceived by a ſtrange volubility of rhapſody; and pretences to a power little leſs than almighty; of which he ſeemed to give many very ſurprizing inſtances. Whatever his impoſtures were, they were ſufficiently adapted to the credulity of his followers; with whom, and ſuch proſelytes as he gained in the country, he ſeized an iſland upon the Muldaw, not far from Tabor, where he ſettled in the form of a ſociety.

Here he began to unfold his doctrines; which differed little from thoſe of the old Adamites, and were in a high degree impious and deteſtable. He declared himſelf the ſon of God, called himſelf Adam; and profeſſing he was ſent to revive the law of nature, made his religion to conſiſt chiefly in the entire diſuſe of cloaths, and in the free indulgence of promiſcuous luſt. The children, thus born, were accounted free; all mankind beſides were conſidered as ſlaves.

Theſe vile ſectaries ſoon became a general peſt. Among their other horrid extravagancies, they made an excurſion into the country, and put to the ſword not fewer than 200 of the peaſants: "They were

"ſlaves,

" flaves, and did not deferve the breath of
" God."

Zifca being now at leifure, was eafily wrought on by the defires of the country, to extirpate thefe execrable wretches. The peafants furnifhing boats, he invaded the ifland; and the Adamites, except a few, who died in arms, were all taken. They were equally involved in guilt, and, after a very fummary form of juftice, were all put to death.

While Zifca was thus engaged, the emperor was making preparations for a more formidable attempt than he had yet made. Roufed by the late fucceffes of his antagonift, he began now to think the affair grew ferious; and having drawn together his whole force, and preffed into his fervice a body of Silefians, he entered Bohemia, on the fide of Glatz; which town, with many other places, fubmitted. In a few days, he arrived before Prague, and encamped within half a league of the city. As he had many friends in the place, he chofe to make his firft effort in the way of negotiation.

Upon the earlieft news of the emperor's march, Zifca, with an equal army, was in motion.

motion. He was secretly glad to hear, that Sigifmond had made an attempt on Prague; not doubting but he would be obliged to wafte the remaining part of the fummer in a fruitlefs fiege. It was matter therefore of equal concern and aftonifhment to him, to fee from the heights, as he approached the town, the emperor's ftandard erected on the caftle. He was foon informed, that Sigifmond had followed the example, which himfelf had fet; and, upon a good underftanding with the governor, had found the means of introducing 4000 men into that fortrefs, the evening before. He was informed too, that the Imperialifts had made an attempt upon the town that morning, and were in hopes of maftering it, before relief fhould arrive.

Zifca had now an opportunity of difplaying his great talents. Upon reflection he began to hope, that if the town only could hold out, he might yet, by an after-game, recover all. Being acquainted with every defile, and fpot of ground in the neighbourhood, he harraffed the Imperialifts with continual alarms, beat them from their works, feized every poft as they deferted it,

T

and allowing them only a very difadvantage-
ous field of battle, which it had been ruin
to accept, obliged the whole body of them
at length to retire into the caftle. He had
now compleated half his work: what remained was as expeditioufly performed.
With great art and induftry he fo entirely
blockaded the place, that the emperor in
the fame inftant faw the neceffity, and the
impracticability of a retreat.

Sigifmond was now in great perplexity.
Pent up in ftraitened quarters, with a numerous garrifon, no magazines provided, and
no profpect of relief, he had nothing before
him, but famine and peftilence; or, what
he dreaded as much as either, the vengeance
of Zifca, who would certainly make him
pay the utmoft price of the advantage he
had gained. Full of thefe racking thoughts,
he put on however an air of compofed dignity, which no man could better affume:
and to divert the melancholy of thofe about
him, and intoxicate the imaginations of the
foldiery, he ordered himfelf to be crowned
king of Bohemia. This vain piece of
pageantry was performed by the archbifhop
of Prague, who had thrown himfelf under

his

his protection. The marquifs of Brandenburgh, the elector of Saxony, and the arch-
duke of Auftria, who ferved under Sigifmond, affifted at the ceremony.

- Zifca's joy, upon this happy crifis of his
affairs, paffed the bounds of his ufual moderation. " Now, my friends, he would
fay to his officers, it is ours to give law.
From this glorious day, let Bohemia boaft
the eftablifhment of her liberties." In the
mean time he remitted nothing of his accuftomed vigour. His works were carried
on with unabated ardour; he vifited every
poft himfelf; and hourly expected, as the
reward of his labours, that his prey would
fall into his hands.

But Zifca's conduct, able as it was, was
ineffectual. Sigifmond fummoned all his
fortitude; and knowing he had nothing to
depend on but the edge of his fword, in
circumftances, which would have added
ftrength to the feeble, he determined to hazard all upon one defperate pufh. He had
the beft intelligence, from his friends in the
city, of all that paffed in Zifca's quarters;
which he fuddenly attacked at midnight,
with all his forces, where he was well in-

 formed

formed the poſt was weakeſt. The Taborites, by which name Ziſca's adherents began
now to be diſtinguiſhed, were not ſurprized.
Each ſide fought, like men, who had their
religion, and liberty at ſtake. The imperialiſts in the end prevailed by mere ſuperiority
of numbers; and opened the paſs, before
any reinforcement could arrive.

The riſing ſun diſcovered the ſlaughter,
and horrible confuſion of the night; and
did full credit to the bravery of the Taborites, who with a handful of men had reſiſt-
ed an army: and Ziſca, though unfortunate, made ſuch an impreſſion upon his enemies, by the firmneſs of his troops, as was
never afterwards forgotten.

Some authors relate, that Sigiſmond
eſcaped by means of a very extraordinary
ſtratagem. He got together a quantity of
combuſtibles, in which he mixed a drug of
ſuch a nature, that when fired, it emitted
a moſt peſtilential ſtench. The ſmoke of
this, ſay theſe writers, being driven in the
faces of the enemy, occaſioned them immediately to abandon their poſt. This improbable tale ſeems to have ariſen, from the
emperor's making his attack under the cover

of

of ſmoke; or invented from a belief, that
Ziſca could not be conquered by any ordinary means.

The poſt, which the imperialiſts had thus
forced, was not far from the camp of the
Taborites, which was the head quarters of
Ziſca. Prompted by his ſucceſs, the emperor came to a ſpeedy reſolution, at day-
break, to endeavour to force this likewiſe.
Not ſatisfied with an eſcape, he now ſtrove
for maſtery; and encouraging his men ſtill
covered with duſt, and blood, he led them
to the aſcent, on which Ziſca lay encamped.
" Yonder, cryed he, lye your proviſions."
The hungry veteran preſſed on; the camp,
thinned by numerous out-poſts, was inſtantly entered; and the Taborites could only die
in its defence. As we are not informed that
Ziſca was in the action, it is probable he was
in ſome other quarter at the time of the
attack.

This was a cruel ſtroke upon him. His
hopes were now entirely blaſted. A favourable opportunity had been wreſted from him;
his camp had been deſtroyed, and his baggage plundered. But theſe were trivial loſſes.
Another opportunity might offer; his tents

and baggage might eafily be replaced. But the lofs of his credit in arms he dreaded as an irreparable lofs. His being thought invincible, he well knew, could only fupport his caufe; and he had fufficient reafon to fear, that if his troops efteemed him lefs the favourite of heaven, than they had hitherto done, they would inftantly defert.—— Thefe were the mortifying reflections, which accompanied his retreat.

In the mean time Sigifmond made the utmoft of his advantage. The principal of Zifca's pofts he feized; and returning to his old enterprize, he blocked up the city. Here divifion reigned. The emperor's party was ftrong; but Zifca's prevailed to keep the gates fhut: and fuch was the extreme diforder of the place, and the rancour, which appeared on both fides, that fober men had juft grounds to fear the worft from the fuccefs of either.

While Sigifmond was thus engaged in the fiege of Prague, Zifca was employed in recruiting his army; in which he had better fuccefs than he expected. The fpirit of his adherents was of too high a temper to be cooled by one finifter event. The quarrel
was

was important.   Their interests were deeply embarked; and there was no reason yet to give up all for lost.   They fully confided in their general; and seemed to make it a point to shew that confidence by their activity in raising troops.   So that in fact before Zisca could feel his loss, it was repaired.

Sigismond had now lain six weeks before Prague, harrassed daily by the army of Zisca, which seemed to have recovered fresh spirits from its defeat.   The posts of the imperialists were attacked; their foraging straitened; and their provisions cut off.   Once Sigismond had the mortification to see a considerable part of his troops defeated, and very roughly handled.   His supplies too from Germany came in more leisurely than he expected. These things abated greatly that eagerness, with which he began his design.   But an event soon afterwards totally discouraged him.

Near Prague stood a craggy hill, which Zisca, thinking it a post of advantage, had seized, and fortifyed.   From this eminence he greatly annoyed the emperor; so that Sigismond at length found, he must either give up all hopes of taking the city, or make

T 4

himself

himself master of this post. His efforts were ineffectual: the post was stronger than he supposed, when he attempted force; better guarded, when he attempted surprize. One effort more he was determined to make. With this view he sent the marquis of Misnia with a large body of men, sufficient, as he thought, to force it. The marquis met with little to oppose him in his march. The Taborites, except a few cautious skirmishers, lay close in their Trenches. The Imperialists, misjudging this the effect of fear, ascended with the more presumption. They now approached the craggy part of the top, overcome with toil; when on a sudden the Taborites leaping out, with loud shouts, from every part of the intrenchments, fell on them with all the fury of impatient ardour. Amazement checked the Imperialists, and the first shock obliged them to give ground. They would have retreated, but their able adversary had made sure work,— their retreat was intercepted. They had only to chuse the manner of their death. On one hand were the swords of an enraged foe; on the other a precipice. The whole affair was instantly decided; and before mercy

could

could take place, scarce an object of mercy remained. The marquis himself, with a few of his followers, escaped.

This terrible disaster, by which the emperor lost near one third of his army, reduced him to the necessity of raising the siege. He gave all necessary orders by sunset; and, at the close of the evening, drew off his troops in silence, without drum or trumpet, accompanied with all those signs of mute dejection, and terrors of alarm, which commonly attend disgraced armies. Zisca pursued his rear; but with little advantage, the emperor conducting his retreat in a very masterly manner.

Thus ended this momentous affair; in which great military skill, and great courage had been shewn on both sides. So equal indeed the contention had been, that it is hard to say, whether Sigismond deserved more praise by obliging Zisca to raise the siege of the castle; or Zisca by obliging him to raise the siege of the town. Undistinguishing fame however blew her trumpet over the banners of the successful hero; and gave Zisca that full glory, which his noble adversary should have divided with him.

Such

Such was the firſt ſummer of the war; in which Ziſca ſufficiently tried his ſtrength, and found the courage of his men proportioned to any ſervice. He had the ſatisfaction likewiſe of finding himſelf, notwithſtanding his many loſſes, at the head of a greater army when he cloſed, than when he opened the campaign.

Early in the ſpring, of the next year, 1421, Ziſca took the field; and began this campaign, as he had begun the laſt, by deſtroying all the monaſteries, which he met with in his march. His deſign was upon the caſtle of Wiſgrade, a ſtrong fortreſs near Prague, where Sigiſmond had placed a numerous garriſon. He endeavoured firſt to take it by ſtorm; but loſing many men in the attempt, and ſeeing little likelihood of ſucceeding in that way, he turned the ſiege into a blockade. The magazines of the beſieged growing ſcanty, and their very horſes being now conſumed, they began to think of a capitulation; and propoſed to deliver up the caſtle within ſuch a time, if the emperor did not relieve it. The condition was accepted, and the time being nearly elapſed, Ziſca had intelligence, that Sigiſmond was

approaching

approaching with his army. He put himself immediately in a posture to receive him; and sent advice of his march to Prague. The Taborite party there instantly taking arms, posted themselves according to Zisca's direction, in some defiles, through which the Imperialists were obliged to pass. Sigismond, not expecting hostilities from that quarter, and having his eye fixed on Zisca, fell into the snare. It was a massacre, rather than a battle; and the emperor escaped with a remainder of his army, only because his enemier were too much fatigued to urge the slaughter farther. The severity of this action fell chiefly upon the Hungarian, and Moravian troops; whose officers, the prime nobility of their respective countries, distinguishing themselves with great spirit, if any distinction could be made in such confusion, were almost entirely cut off. Some writers give the credit of this action to Zisca in person. He retreated, we are told, at the emperor's approach; and in the security of the night returning, attacked his camp with such fury, as soon ended the contest.

The emperor, thus maimed, was in no condition to keep his appointment with the

castle

caftle of Wifgrade; which immediately furrendered upon the news of his defeat. This was the moft valuable acquifition which Zifca had made, no garrifon in thofe parts holding a larger territory in devotion.

Zifca was now at leifure to attend a little to the work of reformation; a work which he had exceedingly at heart. For himfelf, tho' he was more a foldier than a divine; yet he had in general an utter deteftation of the fupremacy of the court of Rome, and a high efteem for the memory of Hufs. What he aimed at therefore was to give a form, and fettlement, to the opinions of that reformer. With this view he confulted thofe efpecially, for whom he knew Hufs had ever had the higheft regard; and fhewed he could, on this occafion, exert as much prudent caution, as on other occafions he had exerted vigour, and activity.

While Zifca was thus employed in eftablifhing a church, like the Jews in Ezra's time, he kept his fword continually drawn. Sigifmond, tho' he durft not fairly meet him, would harrafs him with conftant alarms. Nor was Zifca, in his heart, difpleafed at thefe frequent vifits. " It is friendly, faid
" he,

" he, in the emperor, to keep our fwords
" from rufting in their fcabbards."

Indeed Zifca had lefs to fear from the enemy than from inaction. Danger was the great central force, which drew men to him; and his authority rofe in proportion to the fears of the multitude. Of courfe, he dreaded no artifice like a falfe peace. He well knew how eafily the minds of the people were deluded; and he wanted thofe neceffary means of keeping a body of men together, which his adverfary poffeffed; a military law, and a military cheft. Mere native authority ftood in lieu of both.

He had an evil too of another kind to contend with. The Bohemian clergy were in general, beyond conception, ignorant: and too many of thofe, who came over to the reformed opinions, brought nothing with them, in fupport of the new caufe they had adopted, but an inflamed zeal againft the pope, and the emperor. Not a few of thefe bigots followed the camp of Zifca; and having great influence upon the people, which they were forward, on all occafions, to fhew, they frequently interfered with his fchemes, and oppofed his meafures.   A

feftival,

feftival, or a faft-day, was improper for action ; the eaft-fide of a town was never to be attacked ; an encampment was to be formed, and an army drawn up, as nearly as could be, in the form of a crofs. Thefe were, in general, points not only of moment, but of indifpenfible neceffity.

Indeed Zifca had never more occafion for his addrefs, nor, upon any occafion, more fhewed it, than in the management of thefe mifguided zealots. In trifles he conformed, with great deference, to their humours, that he might with a better grace remonftrate in matters of importance. The influence however which he had from the firft over the foldiery, fettled by degrees into a confirmed authority ; and in proportion as more weight was thrown into his fcale, the other afcended. The clergy had befides made themfelves fo contemptible in many inftances, that even the common foldiers began to detect their folly. Hiftory takes notice of a ridiculous accident, which contributed not a little to deftroy their credit. They had expreffed their diflike to a piece of ground, where Zifca lay encamped ; and with great haughtinefs had ordered the intrenchments to be
                                        razed.

razed. Zifca, unwilling to relinquifh a fituation, which was very advantageous, with equal firmnefs perfevered. But he was given to underftand, that all remonftrance was to no purpofe;—that fire would certainly the next day defcend from heaven upon that accurfed fpot;—and that he muft inftantly decamp, unlefs he chofe to fee his men burnt alive before his face. This dreadful prediction of divine wrath fpread an alarm through the camp, which Zifca had not influence to withftand: the foldiers fcarce waited for orders: the tents were inftantly torn up, and the ground entirely deferted. In the morning, when every one expected to fee the devoted fpot overwhelmed with a tempeft of fire, fuch a deluge of rain fell, as if fent on purpofe to turn the prophecy into ridicule. The troops were afhamed of their folly in liftening to fuch teachers; and it became a common jeft in the army, that the prophecies of their clergy, and the completion, were as oppofite to each other, as fire and water.—In the infancy however of his affairs, thefe people had given great difturbance to Zifca; whofe ufual method was, when he obferved any fymptoms of uneafi-

nefs

nefs in his camp, to fpread alarms, and draw his men into action. He thought it imprudent to fuffer the quarrel to languifh, till the full eftablifhment of peace; and when the enemy did not find him employment, he found it for himfelf; making expeditions into the country, and deftroying the caftles, and ftrong holds, wherever he became mafter.

One of thefe expeditions almoft proved fatal to him. He was incamped before the town of Rubi, which he had almoft reduced to extremities. As he was viewing a part of the works, where he intended an affault, an arrow, fhot from the wall, ftruck him in the eye. The wound being thought dangerous, the furgeons of the army propofed his being carried to Prague, where he might have the beft advice. In reality they were afraid of being cut to pieces by the troops, if he fhould die under their hands. When his removal to the capital was refolved on, it was difficult to check the conteft among the foldiers, who ftrove for the honour of carrying their wounded general. At Prague the arrow was extracted; which being barbed, tore out the eye with it; and it was feared,

the

the fever which fucceeded, might prove fatal
to him. His life however, though with
difficulty, was faved.

He was now totally blind: his friends
therefore were furprized to hear him talk of
fetting out for the army; and did what was
in their power to diffuade him from it. But
he continued refolute: " I have yet, faid
" he, my blood to fhed; let me be gone."
He fuffered himfelf however to undergo the
affected formality of being intreated by a
deputation from the army; and enjoyed the
pleafure of hearing the foldiers, in tumults
around his quarters, cry aloud, " They
would throw down their arms, unlefs their
general were reftored."

In the mean time Sigifmond had lain
quiet: at leaft his army, fince its defeat
before Wifgrade, had appeared in no fhape
in Bohemia, but in that of fcouting parties.
This calm in the emperor's quarters was only
that lowring ftillnefs, which is the prelude
of a ftorm. Sigifmond had been making
preparations during the fummer. At Nuremburgh he convened the ftates of the empire. Here, in full convention, (for, it
feems, no prince except the elector of Treves

was abfent,) he opened to them his embar-
raffed circumftances; and intreated them
for the fake of their fovereign, for the honour of the empire, and in the caufe of their
religion, to put themfelves in arms. His
harangue had its effect. Proper meafures
were concerted; and the affembly broke up,
with a unanimous refolution to make this
audacious rebel feel the full weight of the
empire: and that the blow might fall the
more unexpected, it was refolved to defer it
till the end of the year; when, it was hoped,
that Zifca might the more eafily be furprized,
as great part of his troops left him in the
winter, and returned again in the fpring.

The campaign, as that chief imagined,
was now over, when he was fuddenly alarmed
with the report of thefe vaft preparations;
and foon after with the march of two
powerful armies againft him; one of which
was compofed of confederate Germans,
under the marquifs of Brandenburgh, the
archbifhop of Mentz, the count-palatine of
the Rhine, and other princes of the empire;
the other of Hungarians and Silefians, under
the emperor himfelf. The former were to
invade Bohemia on the weft; the latter on

the

the east. They were to meet in the middle; and, as they affected to give out, would crush this handful of vexatious sectaries between them. At the head of such a force, the emperor could not avoid being sanguine.

They, who are acquainted with the nature of armies intended to march in concert, know the difficulty of making such unweildy bodies observe those exact laws of motion, which prudent generals trace out in councils of war. Some unforeseen event generally creates some unavoidable difficulty.

It happened thus on the present occasion. Sigismond, disappointed in a contract for forage, was obliged to defer his march. He was retarded too by the Austrian and Hungarian nobility, who entring as volunteers into his service, and being suddenly called upon, had not gotten their equipages and dependants, without which their dignity could not take the field, in such readiness as it was thought they might have had them.

The confederate princes, in the mean time, began their march; and were already advanced a considerable way into Bohemia, before they heard of the emperor's disappointment. Sigismond gave them hopes,

that

that he would prefently join them; and advifed them to form the fiege of Soifin. They intrenched themfelves accordingly, and began an attack, for which they were not in the beft manner provided, againft what was then efteemed one of the ftrongeft fortreffes in Bohemia. The befieged laughed at their vain efforts, and kept their ufual guard; while wet trenches, a hungry camp, the fevereties of an inclement winter, and above all, the emperor's delay, introduced mutiny into the tents of the befiegers, and diffention into their councils.

In this fituation were they, ready to catch any alarm, when Zifca approached with his army. The very fight of his banners floating at a diftance, was fufficient. They ftruck their tents, and retreated with precipitation; burning the country as they fled; and curfing the emperor's breach of faith.

About the end of December, a full month after his appointed time, the emperor began his march. As he entered Bohemia, he received the firft account of the retreat of the confederates; yet he determined to proceed. He was at the head of a gallant army, the flower of which were 15,000 Hungarian horfe, horse, esteemed, at that time, the best cavalry in Europe, led by a Florentine officer of great experience. The infantry, which consisted of 25,000 men, were provided, as well as the cavalry, with every thing proper for a winter's campaign.

This army spread terror through all the east of Bohemia; Zisca being still in the west pursuing the Germans. Wherever Sigismond marched, the magistrates laid their keys at his feet; and were treated with severity, or favour, according to their merits in his cause.

His career however was presently checked. Zisca with speedy marches approached; and threw a damp upon him in the midst of his success. He chose his ground however as well as he was able; and resolved to try his fortune, once more, with that invincible chief.

No general paid less regard to the circumstances of time and place than Zisca. He seldom desired more than to come up with his adversary: the enthusiastic fury of his soldiers supplied the rest. There was not a man in his army, who did not meet his enemy with that same invincible spirit, with

which

which the martyr meets death; who did not in a manner prefs to be the foremoft in that glorious band of heroes, whom the Almighty fhould deftine to the noble act of dying for their religion.——Such were the troops, which the ill-fate of Sigifmond brought him now to encounter.

On the 13th of January, 1422, the two armies met, on a fpacious plain, near Kamnitz. Zifca appeared in the centre of his front line; guarded, or rather conducted by a horfeman on each fide, armed with a poll-ax. His troops having fung an hymn, with a determined coolnefs drew their fwords, and waited for the fignal.

Zifca ftood not long in view of the enemy. When his officers had informed him, that the ranks were all well clofed, he waved his fabre round his head, which was the fign of battle.

Hiftorians fpeak of the onfet of Zifca's troops, as a fhock beyond credibility; and it appears to have been fuch on this occafion. The imperial infantry hardly made a ftand. In the fpace of a few minutes they were difordered beyond a poffibility of being rallied. The cavalry made a feeble effort; but

feeing

feeing themfelves unfupported, they wheeled round, and fled upon the fpur.—Thus fuddenly was the extent of the plain, as far as the eye could reach, fpread with diforder; the purfuers and the purfued mixed together, the whole one indiftinct mafs of moving confufion. Here and there might be feen, interfperfed, a few parties endeavouring to unite; but they were broken as foon as formed.

The routed army fled towards the confines of Moravia; the Taborites, without intermiffion, galling their rear. The river Igla, which was then frozen, oppofed their flight. Here new difafters befel them. The bridge being immediately choked, and the enemy prefling furioufly on, many of the infantry, and in a manner the whole body of the cavalry, attempted the river. The ice gave way; and not fewer than 2000 were fwallowed up in the water.

Here Zifca fheathed his fword, which had been fufficiently glutted with blood; and returned in triumph to Tabor, laden with all the fpoils, and all the trophies, which the moft compleat victory could give.

 The

The battle of Kamnitz having put Zifca in peaceable poffeffion of the whole kingdom of Bohemia, he had now leifure to pay a little more attention to his defigned eftablifhment of a church.

He began now to abolifh, in all places, the ceremonies of the popifh worfhip. Prayers for the dead, images, holy-water, auricular confeffion, holy-oil, facerdotal veftments, fafts, and feftivals, all thefe things he totally forbad. The pope's name he rafed out of all public inftruments; and denied his fupremacy. Merit alone, he faid, fhould give diftinction among the priefts of Bohemia; and they fhould gain the reverence of the people by the fanctity of their lives, not by their luxurious manner of living. Churchyards were forbidden alfo; as they had been brought into ufe, he thought, only to enrich the clergy. Purgatory too was expunged from the articles of belief.

From thefe things we may judge how much farther Hufs would, in all probability, have carried reformation; if he had had it in his power: for we may confider Zifca, as acting by his authority, and doing nothing,

but

but what was confonant to his exprefs doctrine; or might by fair inference be deduced
from it.

We have no grounds to fuppofe this military reformer had any bigotry in his temper:
he feems not to have fhewn any inclination
to force the confciences of any differing fect;
but to have left men at liberty to like or diflike, to unite with him, or leave him, as
they thought beft.   Nor was he by any
means arbitrary in his impofitions; but confulted his friends, and fixed on nothing, but
what found at leaft a general concurrence.——
He had the misfortune, notwithftanding this
moderation, to give great offence to many
of the Bohemian reformers.

A variety of fects is the natural confequence of religious liberty; and mutual animofity is too often the confequence of a
variety of fects.   The mifchief is not, that
men think differently, which is unavoidable;
it is, their refufing others, that liberty,
which they take themfelves.   To reftrain
therefore the bad effects of bigotry, the prudent legiflator protects an eftablifhment; and
whatever toleration he may allow to fectaries, (and the wifeft hath generally allowed
the

the moſt,) he will however keep ſuch a reſtraint upon them, as may preſerve the tran-
quility of the whole.

Among the ſeveral ſects, for there were
ſeveral, which the reformation produced in
Bohemia, one only was able to diſpute the
point of ſuperiority with the Taborites. It
was that of the Calixtins, ſo called from the
word *calix*, a cup. They adminiſtred the
Lord's ſupper in both kinds; but in other
points receded leſs from the church of Rome,
than any other Bohemian reformers.

The ſeeds of animoſity had long been
ſown between this ſect, and the Taborites;
but each was reſtrained by its fears of ex-
ternal danger. When an appearance of
greater tranquillity ſucceeded; and Ziſca,
taking the opportunity, began to innovate,
and form the ſcheme of an eſtabliſhment,
he ſoon found how warm an oppoſition he
was likely to meet with from the Calixtins,
whoſe party was by no means contemptible.
Theſe ſectaries, who were chiefly confined
to Prague, and its diſtrict, (and being the
more embodied, could act with the greater
force,) were highly offended at being leſs
taken notice of, than ſo conſiderable a party,

in

in their own eyes, fhould have been. Their clamour foon began, and in language fufficiently warm : " Here, faid they, is a re-
" formation indeed ! inftead of weeding and
" pruning the Lord's vineyard, as ought to
" have been done, the fence is totally taken
" away, and the wild boar of the wood is
" fuffered to root it up. The church of
" Rome, however culpable in many ref-
" pects, is at leaft decent in its worfhip :
" but the prefent fyftem of reformation hath
" not even decency to boaft of."—From violent language, they proceeded, in the ufual progreffion, to violent actions.

John the Premonftratenfian, (fo called from an order of monkery, in which he had fpent a novitiate,) was the principal abettor of the Taborite party in Prague. He was a man of family, fortune, and character ; all which confpired to give him influence. This perfon, confidering Zifca, during the prefent unfettled ftate of Bohemia, as the leader, from whom he was properly to look for inftructions, employed his whole intereft in favour of that chief ; and endeavoured to introduce the fame regulations at Prague,
which

which Zifca had eftablifhed in other parts of the kingdom.

The principal magiftrates of Prague were Calixtins ; and unhappily men of little temper.   It doth not appear, that John had dif- covered any unbecoming zeal ; yet he foon found, that he had given great offence ; and had fufficient reafon to fear, that if he brought himfelf within the fhadow of a law, that law would be made to crufh him.

Late one evening, he and nine others, all chiefs of the Taborite party, were fent for, by the magiftrates, to the council-chamber, upon a pretence of fettling fomething with regard to public peace.   They came without fcruple ; but found, on their entrance, an affembly, which they little expected ; — a court fitting in form ; before which they were immediately arraigned.   The chief magiftrate, without further ceremony, ac- quainted them, that in all ftates it had been the practice, upon emergent occafions, to difpenfe with the formalities of law ; — that their behaviour had been fuch, as very great- ly endangered the tranquillity of the city ; — that fufficient matter for the moft public trial

could

could be brought againſt them;—but that it was rather choſen, for the ſake of peace, to proceed againſt them in this more private way.

Vain were all remonſtrances againſt theſe lawleſs proceedings: witneſſes were immediately called; and, the facts alledged being proved, ſentence of death was haſtily paſſed upon them; and they were as haſtily hurried into an inner court of the building; where, without any of the uſual circumſtances of decency, they were put to death.

It was impoſſible, that ſo horrid a maſſacre, however privately tranſacted, ſhould eſcape the public knowledge. By noon the next day it was known in all parts of the city. Some authors mention its being diſcovered in a very extraordinary manner. The blood, which ran in ſtreams from the headleſs trunks of theſe unfortunate men, having been forgotten in the confuſion of the action, made its way through the drains into the ſtreet, and plainly diſcovered the horrid deed. The populace, by whatever means acquainted with the affair, were immediately in an uproar: all parties were ſcandalized: even the Calixtins were too

much

much confounded to make refiftance; while the Taborites took an ample revenge. They were not now actuated by thofe mild virtues, which Hufs had difcovered on a like occafion. The fpirit of the times was changed. They affembled with loud clamours before the houfes of the magiftrates; forced open the doors; dragged them from their concealments; and haled them into the ftreets; where, having expofed them as fpectacles, and reproached them with their crimes, they put them to a cruel death.

When the tumult of this affair was over, and men began to think coolly upon the matter, the Calixtins plainly faw how much injury their caufe had fuffered. It was true, that outrages had been committed on both fides. But the fcale was by no means equal. The world would certainly be moft forward to condemn the aggreffor; and a manifeft diftinction would be made between an act of magiftracy, and an act of mere popular fury. They concluded therefore, that the breach between them and the Taborites was irreparable; and that it was impoffible for them to live happily under any government, in which Zifca prefided.

Thefe

Thefe were the fentiments of the fenate of Prague; in which affembly, after long deliberation, it was refolved to fend deputies to the grand duke of Lithuania, and to offer him, in the name of the capital of Bohemia, the crown of that kingdom. The duke accepted their offer; and immediately fent troops to fupport his title.

This fatal diffention was looked upon as the expiring pang of the liberties of Bohemia. It was not doubted but the emperor would feize this favourable opportunity; and, having fuffered the two parties thoroughly to weaken themfelves, would fuddenly crufh them both. It happened otherwife. Animated as thefe fectaries were againft each other, they were ftill more fo againft the common enemy. Zifca indeed fatisfied himfelf with protefting againft the refolutions of the fenate of Prague; and, bearing, with his accuftomed firmnefs, the ingratitude of his country, lay quiet in his camp at Tabor: while the Calixtins, in concert with the Lithuanians, feeing themfelves unmolefted by him, began immediately to act againft the emperor.

This

This party affected now to take the lead in all public affairs. But their fuccefs was not anfwerable to their prefumption. The firft enterprize they attempted was the fiege of Charles-ftone, a fortifyed poft, where the emperor had found an opportunity to introduce a garrifon of 400 men. Before this place, which was by no means confiderable, they confumed full fix months; and at length gave up the affair. The garrifon, during the whole fiege, held them in the utmoft contempt. Having taken fome prifoners, in a fally, they hung one of them over the wall, where the affault was fierceft, with a fly-flapper in his hand, intimating, that this was fufficient to baffle the utmoft efforts of the befiegers. Zifca, in the mean time, fat by, a calm fpectator of what paffed. There were fome diftempers, which, he thought, beft cured themfelves; and he confidered this diforder as one of them. He knew the Calixtins had among them no leader of any capacity, in military affairs efpecially; and he doubted not but they would foon feel the bad effects of ill-concerted meafures.

Indeed

Indeed the Calixtins were not a little chagrined at the difgrace they had fuffered before Charles-ftone. The fuccefs of the invincible Zifca, from whofe aufpices they had now withdrawn themfelves, was, on this occafion, an unpleafing retrofpect: but they had foon feverer caufe for reflection.

On the frontiers of Hungary Sigifmond had a conference with the king of Poland; the fubject of which was the ill-ufage he had received from the duke of Lithuania. Sigifmond pufhed the affair with fo much force of argument, and infinuating addrefs, that upon a proper application from his fovereign, the duke gave up his title to the crown of Bohemia, and withdrew his forces. It is probable he had now leifure to fee things in a different light; and could difcern more thorns than flowers fcattered in the path-way to a throne; which he had not before obferved, while dazzled with the glare of royalty. The Calixtins thus deprived of foreign aid, immediately funk into their former infignificance. They became the objects alfo of that contempt, of which the world is commonly fo liberal upon the baffled fchemes of imprudence, and folly.

X

Zifca

already at its gates; and he determined to rifk all, rather than leave it a prey.

Zifca, who carried on his works with his ufual vigour, had brought the fiege to its laft ftage, when the marquifs appeared at the head of a great army, and offered him battle. Zifca, whofe maxim it was, never to decline fighting, accepted the challenge, though he had many difficulties to encounter. The marquifs had a fuperior army, and Zifca was obliged ftill more to thin his troops by leaving a large detachment to obferve the town. The Saxons befides were advantageoufly pofted, having taken poffeffion of a rifing ground, which fecured their flanks. A ftrong wind alfo blew in the faces of the Taborites; which greatly weakened the flight of their arrows, while it added new force to thofe of the enemy.

But Zifca had little confidence in miffive weapons. His whole line, with their poll-axes and fabres, in their accuftomed manner, made an impetuous attack upon the enemy. The Saxons, receiving them in good order, ftood firm, and gave them a very fevere check. This was a reception wholly unkown to the Taborites; who had ever been ufed

to

to bear down all before them; and in these
new circumſtances were at a loſs how to act.
They retreated ſome paces, as if aſtoniſhed
at the novelty of the thing.—This critical
moment the Saxons ſhould have ſeized, while
the blaſt, yet fluttering in the ſails, ſeemed
to heſitate, on which ſide to give the ſwell.
Had they moved forward at this inſtant, it is
probable the Taborites had never recovered
from their ſurprize. But inſtead of a general charge, they ſtood motionleſs; looking
upon the enemy, as if they had done enough
by not ſuffering themſelves to be beaten.—
Ziſca, little leſs than inſpired, had a compleat idea of the whole affair; and being
conducted to the front line, which ſtood yet
unbroken, he cried out, as he rode along,
" I thank you, my fellow-ſoldiers, for all
" your paſt ſervices,—if you have now done
" your utmoſt, let us retire." This noble
rebuke ſtung them to the ſoul. Every veteran gnaſhed his teeth with indignation,
graſped his ſword, and preſſed forward;
cloſing, hand to hand, with the enemy, in
the true temper of determined courage.

The combat, thus renewed, became ſoon
unequal. For ſome time the Saxons ſtill

 maintained

On the other fide, Zifca was not back-ward in his preparations. He had fome time before fent Procop, an excellent young offi-cer, to command in Moravia; in whom he had entire confidence, and to whofe ma-nagement he wholly intrufted the military affairs of that country; recommending to him particularly a cautious behaviour, and meafures merely defenfive.

Procop was a citizen of Prague, of ordi-nary parentage; but his fprightlinefs and beauty recommending him in his childhood to an affluent family, he had been adopted into it. His new father fpared no expence in his education; and having given him the beft, which his own country afforded, fent him to travel into Spain, Italy, and other parts of Europe. After a confiderable ftay abroad, he returned home, a very accom-plifhed perfon. The religious war foon after breaking out, he attached himfelf, as his inclination led him, to the fortunes of Zifca, under whom, he not only expected to learn the rudiments of war, his favourite ftudy; but refolved to practife them likewife, in the fervice of his country. From the moment he entered a camp, he gave himfelf up en-

irely

tirely to his profeffion ; in the knowledge of which he made a rapid progrefs. Zifca foon difcovered the uncommon talents of his young pupil; employed him frequently in matters, which required courage and punctuality; and, at an age when men feldom arrive at the command of a regiment, fet him over a province. His abilities indeed were fuch, that Zifca was in little pain about Moravia; at leaft he hoped, that Procop would be able to keep the emperor employed, till he himfelf fhould return from the frontiers of Saxony; whither he marched, with all his force, upon the firft notice of the enemy's preparations.

The marquifs had not yet taken the field. Zifca, to ftrike a terror into his troops, ravaged his borders; and boldly, in the face of his army, fat down before Aufig.

Aufig is a ftrong town fituate upon the Elbe, nearly where that river leaves Bohemia. It had always fhewn a particular attachment to the emperor ; and was recommended by him in ftrong terms, together with the bridge in its neighbourhood, to the protection of the marquifs. It was a fenfible mortification therefore to that general to fee an enemy

Zifca, in the mean time, was in full credit with his party, and was earneftly requefted to affume the crown of Bohemia himfelf, as a reparation for the infult he had received. No one in the kingdom, they affured him, had the power, if he had the inclination, to make the leaft oppofition; and as for the emperor, they hoped he would foon be induced to drop his claim. But Zifca, whom even his enemies neither tax with avarice, nor ambition, fteadily refufed. "While "you find me of fervice to your defigns, "faid the difinterefted chief, you may freely "command both my counfels, and my "fword; but I will never accept any eftab-"liſhed authority. On the contrary, my "moft earneft advice to you is, when the "perverfenefs of our enemies fhall allow us "peace, to truft yourfelves no longer in the "hands of kings; but to form yourfelves "into a republic; which fpecies of govern-"ment only can fecure your liberties."

It was near Chriftmas 1422, when the Lithuanian army evacuated Bohemia. Sigifmond was folicitous to have this impediment removed before the fpring, when he propofed to open a very active campaign. He

had

had made, as usual, great preparations; and intended once more to enter Bohemia with two separate armies. With this view, he set the marquifs of Mifnia at the head of a confiderable body of Saxons, which were to penetrate by the way of Upper Saxony; while himfelf, at the head of another army, fhould enter Moravia, on the fide of Hungary. His defign was, when he had over-run that country, which, upon the matter, was wholly in the intereft of Zifca, to join the marquifs in the centre of Bohemia. This was Sigifmond's laft effort; upon which he had exhaufted his whole ftrength. It is furprizing indeed, how he had thus far found refources in this ruinous and deftructive war; confidering him already in fome degree impoverifhed by an expenfive expedition againft the Turks. But the amiable Sigifmond could do what the authority of the emperor could not have done. So infinuating were his manners, fo gentle and affable his behaviour, that he won the hearts of men, and drew them as he pleafed. Had not religion oppofed, nothing could have withftood the claim of this accomplifhed prince to the crown of Bohemia.

 On

maintained a feeble fight. Four of their principal officers, endeavouring to reſtore the battle, were cut to pieces at the head of their diſmayed battalions. The whole army ſoon after, in every part, gave ground : a retreat, a rout, a maſſacre ſucceeded. The carnage of the field was terrible. Not fewer than 9000 Saxons were left dead upon the ſpot. Ziſca is taxed, however juſtly, with great cruelty, after all reſiſtance was over. It is certain he never bought a victory ſo dear,

From this ſcene of blood he recalled his troops to new fields of glory. "We muſt " ſleep to night, cryed he, within the walls " of Auſig." Thither the triumphant army carried the news of their victory. Ziſca would grant no conditions : the governor was allowed half an hour to deliberate, whether he would ſurrender at diſcretion, or take the conſequence. He choſe the ſafer meaſure ; and the Taborites were quietly in their quarters in Auſig before the cloſe of the evening. — Theſe two great events conſecrated the 22d of April, for many years, in Bohemia.

The

The next day Zifca ordered the town to be difmantled ; that it might no longer be a receptacle to his enemies : he broke down likewife the ftately bridge over the Elbe ; to cut off, as much as poffibe, all communication with Saxony.

Having thus fettled every thing in the eaft of Bohemia, where he had been kept longer than he expected, and having freed that country even from the apprehenfion of danger, he returned with his victorious army to the affiftance of Procop.

That general had fufficient bufinefs upon his hands. The emperor appeared early upon the frontiers of Moravia ; and after fome irregular motions, fat down before Pernitz.

Procop with his little army attended all his movements ; and practifed with admirable fkill thofe leffons, which he had juft received. He was confined however to the minutiæ of war : he could not hurt, he could only teize, his unweildy adverfary. If the emperor offered him battle, his Parthian brigades, unincumbered with baggage, retreated fuddenly to the mountains. If the emperor returned to his former enterprize, Procop was inftantly in his rear ; and, being

acquainted

prefently beaten off; and the Taborites gal-
lantly fought their way through all oppofition.

In the middle of the ftreet their impetu-
ofity received a check. There a barricado
had been begun, the hafty work of that tumultuous morning. The materials indeed
had been rather brought together, than put
into form. It ferved however to retard the
violence of *Zifca*. Many of his foldiers
were obliged to difmount, to clear the paffage; and could not afterwards recover their
horfes: all order was broken; and, the
enemy clofing on every fide, a fcene of great
confufion enfued.

At length the fortune of *Zifca* prevailed,
with the lofs of fome men, though of fewer
than might have been expected, he forced
the barricado, and made his way to the
gate.

Here the enemy endeavoured to form a
fecond time; and a new fcene of tumult
followed. But the gate was at length burft
open; and *Zifca*, at the head of his little
troop, fallied out in triumph. He was purfued by all the force, that could be brought
out againft him; which confifted of fome
thoufands;

thoufands ; againſt whom he maintained a flying fight with ſuch intrepidity, as made none of them very forward to cloſe in upon him. His diſmounted troopers, who had been of ſo much ſervice in opening a paſſage, were now of equal diſadvantage in retarding his march : notwithſtanding which, the order of it continued unbroken.

In the midſt of this victorious retreat, an unforeſeen accident almoſt proved fatal to him. The enemy were making one of their boldeſt efforts, when Ziſca being ſeparated from his company in the confuſion of the attack, his horſe, undirected, plunged into a moraſs. His perſon being conſpicuous, he was preſently ſurrounded ; and a furious conteſt enſued ; in which the Taborites were victorious ; and had the good fortune to recover their fainting general.

The route, which the Taborites took, led acroſs a fair plain, or rather valley, environ- ed with riſing grounds, which, approaching each other, at the farther end, formed a narrow paſs. Here Ziſca, who had been miſerably harraſſed along the plain, and had more open country beyond the defile, de- termined to make a ſtand ; thinking his deſ-
perate

ple; which he had the magnanimity to dif-regard, still expecting it would wear off. On the contrary, it increased daily, discovering itself in the most gross affronts, and at length in the most violent outrages.

At a very unseasonable hour, somewhat after midnight, he was alarmed by an officer of his guard; who entering his chamber, with a disturbed countenance, acquainted him, that he had no time to lose,——that the perfidious townsmen were preparing to seize him. Zisca asking a few questions, and receiving such answers as left him little room to doubt, immediately got on horse-back; ordering, at the same time, a hasty trumpet to sound *to horse*, through the quarters. The troops, which consisted of about 400 men, repaired directly, with such circumstances of disorder, as may be imagined, to the great square. Not a man knew the cause of this sudden alarm. While they stood inquiring one of another, and each forming such con-jectures, as his imagination suggested, their ears were suddenly struck with the sound of bells, which burst instantaneously from every tower of the city, in one general peal. Im-mediately on this signal, they were attacked

by

by multitudes of people, crouding through every avenue and ftreet; but in that tumultuary manner, which plainly difcovered a difconcerted fcheme. The Taborites, placing their father, as they commonly called Zifca, in the centre, formed round him, as the exigence would allow; and defended themfelves with great firmnefs. Indeed the enemy made no extraordinary efforts; they feemed contented with blocking up the avenues of the fquare, and throwing a few weapons, which did little execution. If any approached nearer, and attempted a ruder affault, a few horfemen were ordered to ride in among them; who generally drove them back fome paces. But this was only the reflux of a tide, which prefently returned.

In the mean time day-light appeared; and fhewed the Taborites the defperate circumftances of their fituation. Zifca, who was exactly informed of every thing, having called his officers about him, refolved (as the only expedient in the prefent exigence,) to endeavour to force a way through the high ftreet, which led to the camp.

In confequence of this refolution a vigorous attack was made. The citizens were

prefently

acquainted with the country, befet every avenue to his camp with fo much judgment, that Sigifmond was obliged to fend large detachments, and often to run great hazard in procuring provifions. In a word, Procop fhewed himfelf, during the whole campaign, a compleat mafter of defenfive war; and gave the emperor fuch a check, as he little expected from fo inferior a force.

In the mean time the town behaved with equal fpirit. Sigifmond had now lain eight weeks before it, and had not yet made the leaft impreffion either upon the walls, or the garrifon; though he had endeavoured his utmoft, by his engines and his menaces, to fhake both. He was obliged therefore to fubmit to his ill-fortune; and, drawing lines round the place, contented himfelf with ftraitening its quarters, and fhutting it up by a blockade.

In this defign he was again unfortunate. He had reduced the town to great extremity, when, by one of thofe mafterly ftrokes, which may deceive the greateft captain, Procop drawing his attention to another quarter, forced his lines in an unfufpected part, and threw fuccours into the place.

This

This was a fevere blow to Sigifmond. His work was entirely to begin anew; the fummer was wearing apace; the Saxons were totally defeated; and Zifca was returning with a victorious army. — Agitated by thefe reflections; and having nothing in profpect but new difafters, he gave up his defign, and retreated.—Thus was Bohemia delivered once more from the fear of her enemies; and her champion, after a fhort but active campaign, was allowed to fheath his fword.

The news of Sigifmond's retreat met Zifca near Prague. As the troops, having made forced marches from Aufig, had been harraffed with intolerable fatigue, he thought it proper to give them a few days reft. He incamped therefore within three leagues of Prague; and attended by a fmall body of horfe, took up his own refidence in the city. He had not been at Prague, fince the late difturbances, and hoped, by his prefence, to diffipate what might ftill remain of ill-humour in the minds of the inhabitants. He was however miftaken. His prefence, inftead of reftoring harmony, appeared plainly to give new offence. He foon had flagrant inftances of the diftafte of the peo-

ple;

perate circumstances a sufficient apology for the appearance of rashness. Having drawn up his little troop therefore with all the advantage, which accrued from his situation, he presented himself to the enemy; who did not decline an engagement.

Historians relate this battle with very improbable circumstances. We are told, that Zisca not only gained the victory, but that he put to the sword above 3000 of the enemy. It is not unlikely, that if the slaughter from the beginning be taken into the account, the Calixtin party might lose that number.—It is certain however, that Zisca made good his retreat; and arrived in safety at his camp.

Great was the consternation in Prague, when the fugitives from this unfortunate attack returned without their prey. The Calixtin-party at first intended to have crushed Zisca without disturbance; not doubting but the dissipation of his sect would follow. When that was found impracticable, they determined, at any rate, to crush him. Their fraud and force being equally ineffectual, they saw themselves in desperate circumstances. They had provoked a very

powerful

powerful enemy, whom they could not withstand; and from whom they had every thing to fear.—The die however was thrown; and they muſt accommodate their game, as they were able.

In the mean time Zifca, calling his troops together, acquainted them in form with the whole tranſaction; and having raiſed in them ſuch ſentiments of indignation as he wiſhed to inſpire, he immediately ſtruck his tents, and like the injured Roman of old, marched directly to the city, and incamped under its walls.

Before he attempted force, he ſent in a trumpet, requiring, in very ſtern language, that the adviſers, and chief inſtruments of the late villainous aſſault ſhould be put into his hands. But the guilt of that action was ſo univerſal, that it was impoſſible to ſay, who was involved the deepeſt. Inſtead of complying therefore with the order of Zifca, the miſerable inhabitants choſe rather to try perſuaſive arts; endeavouring by every me-thod to ſoften the chief, and move the com-paſſion of the troops. Intreaties, promiſes, and prayers were addreſſed by the magiſtrates to Zifca; while the populace, from the

Y

walls,

walls, made the same earnest application to the soldiers. Some pleaded kindred, or alliances, or the rites of hospitality affectionately performed. Many with tears deplored their wretched fate; protesting before God and man, that they had no hand in the late commotion: while numbers, who had a right to the protection of Zisca, from their adherence to his cause, were describing their doors, and houses, or agreeing upon secret marks, and pledges, by which they might escape the impending vengeance; intreating, at the same time, one for a friend, another for a son, or near relation, whom his unhappy fate had involved in the general guilt.

But Zisca continued stern and immoveable. He was persuaded the Calixtin-party could, by no means, be depended on; and that they would never unite in any friendly league. He determined therefore to take this opportunity of leisure from his other enemies, to subdue them thoroughly; assuring himself, that till this should be effected, the accomplishment of his great designs would remain uncompleat.

The troops were more flexible. They considered not the affair with the foresight of their chief; and having only before their eyes the prefent fcene of diftrefs, began to murmur at the work, in which they were engaged; and at the feverity of him, who had engaged them in it. "They would "not be the inftruments of the deftruction "of a city, which was the glory of their "country.—Their general might feek other "minifters of his vengeance.—They would "offer their lives a willing facrifice againft "the unjuft attempts of their enemies; but "no one fhould oblige them to take up arms "againft their brethren."

Thefe whifpers foon reached the ears of Zifca,—the firft feditious whifpers he had ever heard. His orders he found hourly lefs punctually obeyed; he was accofted with infolent fpeeches, as he paffed along the lines; and mutinous tumults gathered about his tent. In a word, he faw the contagion fpreading apace; and the immediate need of a remedy. Calling his troops therefore together, he endeavoured to affuage the rifing mutiny, by fhewing them the neceffity of fevere meafures. The Calixtins had now twice, he told them, almoft ruined the com-mon caufe; and would be ready to ruin it

again on any future occafion. The emperor,
he faid, was always on the watch; and
would be glad to widen their mifunderftand-
ings, and take the advantage of them for
himfelf; he had no intention, he told them,
to lay the city in blood and defolation. All
he propofed was to make himfelf entire
mafter of it; and when he had it in his
power, he would liften to the fuggeftions
of pity, and would temper feverity with
mercy.

" This, my fellow-foldiers, faid he, con-
" cluding his fpeech, is my intention : but if
" it fhall feem more agreeable to you to act
" with greater lenity; if you fhall chufe to
" reach out to thefe bloody men even an
" unlimited mercy, I fhall confider myfelf
" only as your minifter : and whether you
" chufe war, or peace, I am ready with my
" utmoft power to fecond that choice. —
" One thing only let me requeft, for the
" fake of all our mutual labours, and mutual
" glories, let me requeft, that thefe unhappy
" divifions amongft us may ceafe ; and that
" whether we fheath our fwords, or keep
" them drawn, the world may know, that
" we are united in our councils, as well as
" our

" our arms; and that Zifca, and his com-
" panions, have only one common caufe."

In fuch foothing language did the prudent chief addrefs himfelf to the prejudices of his foldiers. His fpeech had the defired effect. They who did not hear it, caught the fire from thofe who did. The whole army was inftantly animated with a new fpirit; and the camp rang with profeffions of obedience, and acclamations of praife.

It was now near funfet; too late to take the full advantage of the ardour of the troops. Orders therefore were given for an affault early the next morning. Every thing was prepared. The regiments, in their feveral ftations, refted upon their arms; and Zifca retired to his tent, big with the thoughts of the fucceeding day.—Many were the reflections he made; and many the compunctions he felt, when he thus found himfelf upon the point of laying wafte the capital of his country.—But the liberties of Bohemia urged him upon this harfh fervice.

As he was ruminating on thefe things, it being now paft midnight, a perfon was introduced to him by the officer of his guard, who earneftly defired a private audience.

 Zifca

Zifca prefently knew him to be the celebrated Roquefan; an ecclefiaftic, who, from
the meaneft circumftances of birth and fortune, had raifed himfelf, by his great talents,
to have the moft perfonal confequence of any
man in Prague. Roquefan came a deputy
from his fellow-citizens, now reduced to the
loweft defpair. They had good intelligence
from Zifca's camp; and well knew the fatal
refolution of the preceding evening.

Of what paffed between thefe two chiefs,
on this occafion, we have no particulars.
Roquefan however infifted on fuch arguments, as over-powered the refolution of
Zifca; and a thorough reconciliation took
place. An anonymous French hiftorian,
who wrote the life of Zifca, mentions terms
of agreement; but as thefe are unlikely, and,
as far as appears, unauthorized, it is of little
moment to infert them. It is probable, that
Zifca would not fo eafily have been brought
to a reconciliation, had not the late mutiny
among his troops given a new turn to his
counfels.

While thefe things were acting at Prague,
the diftreffed Sigifmond was in great perplexity. The battle of Aufig had greatly
fhaken

shaken that constancy, which had thus far supported him. Six times, in three campaigns, he had been vanquished in the open field: his towns had been ravished from him, and his provinces laid waste. He acknowledged the superior talents of his adversary; and was quitted by that noble and unconquered spirit, which animated the cause of liberty. The late dissention had, in some degree, revived his hopes: but he was scarce informed of the circumstances of the quarrel, when he was informed of the reconciliation likewise. Every ray of hope therefore being now excluded, he submitted to his hard fate; and resolving on any terms, to give peace to his bleeding country, sent deputies to Zisca, requesting him to sheath his sword, and name his conditions; offering him, at the same time, for himself, what might have satisfyed the most grasping ambition.

Zisca was equally desirous of a reconciliation. He had taken up arms with a view only to obtain peace, and was heartily glad of an occasion to lay them down. He returned a message to the emperor, full of that respectful language, with which the great

can

can eafily cover enmity; tho' at the fame time breathing that fpirit, which became a chief in the caufe of liberty.

After a few couriers had paffed, a place of congrefs was appointed; and *Zifca* fet out to meet the emperor, attended by the principal officers of his army. It gave Europe a fubject for various converfation, when this great man, whom one unfortunate battle would have reduced to the condition of a rebel, was feen paffing through the midft of Bohemia, to treat with his fovereign, like a fovereign, upon equal terms.

But Zifca lived not to put a finifhing hand to this treaty. His affairs obliged him to take his route through a part of the country, in which the plague at that time raged. At the caftle of Prifcow, where he had engaged to hold an affembly of the ftates of that diftrict, the fatal contagion feized him, and put an end to his life, on the 6th of October 1424,——at a time, when, all his labours being ended, and his great purpofes almoft compleated, (fuch was the courfe of providence) he had only to enjoy thofe liberties, and that tranquillity, which his virtue had fo nobly purchafed.

Some

Some authors write, that, being afked by thofe around him, a little before his death, where he would have his remains depofited? he anfwered, Where they pleafed — that it was indifferent to him, whether they were thrown out to the vultures, or configned to the tomb.

We are informed too, that upon his death-bed he ordered his fkin to be made into a drum; " The very found of which, added " he, will difperfe your enemies." It is probable this fpeech is a mere fiction: fuch vaunting, agreeing ill with that referved cha-racter, which Zifca had ever maintained. Morery indeed tells us, that the drum was actually made; that it was ufed in battle by the Taborites; and that it had the full effect expected from it; though at the fame time, with a ridiculous gravity, he informs us, that he doth not fuppofe it was owing to any fu-pernatural power, with which that inftru-ment was endowed.—The whole feems an idle tale. It may even be queftioned, whe-ther the fkin of a body, in that morbid ftate, which the plague occafions, is capable of being cured; or if it were, we can hardly imagine, that any people could be fo infa-

tuated

tuated, as firſt to manufacture, and afterwards to carry about with them the remains of an infected carcaſe.

The beſt accounts inform us, that he was buried in the great church at Czaſlow in Bohemia; where a monument was erected to his memory, with an inſcription to this purpoſe;

HERE LIES JOHN ZISCA;
WHO HAVING DEFENDED HIS COUNTRY
AGAINST THE ENCROACHMENTS
OF PAPAL TYRANNY,
RESTS IN THIS HALLOWED PLACE
IN DESPITE
OF THE POPE.

The greateſt, indeed the only ſtain on the character of Ziſca, is his cruelty. Of this his enemies make loud complaints; and his friends, it muſt be confeſſed, are very ill able to clear him. Againſt the popiſh clergy, it is certain, he acted with great ſeverity. Many of them he put to death, and more he baniſhed; plundering and confiſcating their poſſeſſions, without any reſerve.

They

They who are the moſt inclined to exculpate this rigour, perſuade us, that he conſidered theſe eccleſiaſtics not as heretics, but as civil offenders;—as men, who were accountable for all the blood, which had been ſpilt in Bohemia; and on whoſe heads the juſtice of an injured nation ought deſervedly to fall.

But the beſt apology perhaps may be taken from the manners of the age, in which he lived. In thoſe barbarous times, and among thoſe barbarous nations, rough nature appeared in its rudeſt form. Friends and enemies were treated from the heart, without that gloſs of decency, which arts, and civility have introduced.

Some allowance alſo may be made for the peculiar violence, which naturally attends civil diſſentions; in which every injury is greatly heightened, and every paſſion immoderately moved.

Upon the whole, Ziſca was by no means animated with that true ſpirit of Chriſtianity, which his amiable maſter, Huſs, had diſcovered on all occaſions. His fierce temper ſeems to have been modelled rather upon the old Teſtament, than the new; and the

genius

genius of that religion in a great degree to have taken hold of him, which in its animosities called down fire from heaven.

His capacity was vaſt; his plans of action exťnſive; and the vigour of his mind in executing thoſe plans aſtoniſhing. Difficulties with him were motives. They rouſed up latent powers, proportioned to the emergence. Even blindneſs could not check the ardour of his ſoul; and what was ſaid of the Grecian Timoleon, under the ſame misfortune, (whoſe character indeed he reſembled in many inſtances) may with equal juſtice be applyed to him; *hanc calamitatem ita moderate tulit, ut neq; eum querentem quiſquam audierit, neq; eo minus privatis, publiciſq; rebus interfuerit.* His military abilities were equal to what any age hath produced; and as ſuch they are acknowledged by all hiſtorians. Nor do we admire him leſs as a politician. If the great man was ſeen in the conduct, and courage, which he diſcovered in the field; he was equally ſeen in governing, by his own native authority, a land of anarchy; and in drawing to one point the force of a divided nation.

Nor

Nor was the end, which he propofed, unworthy of his great actions. Utterly devoid both of ambition and avarice, he had no aim but to eftablifh, upon the ruins of ecclefiaftical tyranny, the civil and religious liberties of his country.

The End.

BOHEMIAN AFFAIRS.

HAVING thus brought the affairs of the Bohemian reformers to a glorious issue under Zisca, it may be proper to continue the narration, in few words, till this great struggle between the contending parties was decided.

After the death of Zisca, the flames of war kindled anew. It is probable, the emperor, on this great event, might suspend, and finally break off the treaty, expecting better conditions.

Procop, who had so greatly distinguished himself in Moravia, and was esteemed the ablest of Zisca's generals, naturally took the lead after his decease. This chief sustained the character he had acquired. Indeed the Taborite armies were now so formed, and disciplined by the care, and abilities of Zisca; so inured to all the difficulties of their pro-

fession

feffion, and fo formidable to their enemies, that the reputation of future generals was in a great meafure Zifca's due; who had laid a foundation, on which even inferior talents might fuccefsfully build.

But Procop had talents to form a fcheme, which fortune had given him only to compleat. Yet he had ftill great difficulties to encounter. To the old enemies of his caufe a new one was added. The pope, incited by the clamours of the religious, reared his holy banners; and a formidable army, under a cardinal-general, was fent into Bohemia. But his eminence fhared the fate of all his predeceffors in this war; and the Bohemian arms triumphed, wherever they were oppofed.

To the military inventions of Zifca, Procop added an improvement of his own. He introduced armed chariots into his lines, which ferved as a fort of moving rampart; through the interftices of which his troops charged, and retired at pleafure. On other occafions, his chariots would take a fudden wheel, and inclofe whole battalions of the enemy; which, thus environed, were deftined to certain flaughter. He found them

ftill

ftill more ufeful in his ravaging excurfions. They ferved, at the fame time, as a defence to his marauders, and as waggons to carry off the plunder.

Procop had now continued in arms fix years. His campaigns, though not diftinguifhed by thofe illuftrious actions, which had marked the campaigns of Zifca, were however generally fuccefsful. He had not indeed thofe opportunities of performing fplendid actions. The emperor, wafted by his vaft expences, had of late fuffered the war to languifh; hoping to procure thofe advantages from repofe, which he could not force by his arms. He was well acquainted with the mutual animofities of the Taborites, and the Calixtins, who agreed in nothing, but in oppofing him: and he thought a little leifure, as it had hitherto done, might ripen their diffentions. Procop, he knew, was an able general; but he had a mean opinion of him, as a politician—as a man either of temper, or addrefs to affuage or manage the rage of parties. Upon the whole, he had reafon to hope, that time might produce fome happy crifis in his favour. That crifis now approached.

In

In the year 1431, the council of Bafil affembled. Hither the Taborites were invited with a profufion of civil language. But they received the fummons with great indignation. It was the univerfal cry, " That " general councils were general pefts;— " that they were called only in fupport of " ecclefiaftical tyranny;—and that no credit " was due to fuch partial conventions."

Procop however, with a magnanimity which could not brook the imputation of refufing a challenge of any kind, determined to attend the council: and when his friends urged the danger; and advifed him at leaft to fecure himfelf by a fufficient pafsport; they only made him the more refolute in his purpofe: " Paffport! cried he, need we " other than our fwords?"

Thus refolved, and accompanied by Cofca, another leader of the Taborites, he fet out, at the head of a regiment of horfe. The whole city of Bafil came out to meet fo extraordinary a deputation. Every one was earneft to compare the faces of thefe gallant heroes with the actions they had performed; and faw, or thought they faw, fomething more than human in thofe countenances,

the

the very appearance of which had put armies to flight. The two deputies were received by the magiftrates at the gate of the city; and the fathers of the council (fo great a change, fince the times of Hufs, had the influence of power produced) paid them fuch honours, as were paid only to crowned heads. After many conferences, which ended in attaching them the more firmly to their own opinions, they returned into Bohemia.

The council however had an aftergame to play. Upon the departure of the Taborite chiefs, they fent deputies, chofen from the moft eminent of their body, into Bohemia; who had in charge (out of the great regard the council had for the Bohemians, and their earneft zeal to draw them to the true faith) to difcufs thofe points at full leifure in Prague, which the multiplicity of affairs would not allow at Bafil.—This was their pretence: their real defign was, to divide the Bohemians; and to kindle again the old animofity, which had fo nearly proved fatal to both parties.

This bufinefs was carryed on with that fingular addrefs, for which the court of

Rome

Rome hath ever been remarkable in negotiations of this kind; and was at length, by the affiduity of thefe good cardinals, brought to a happy iffue. A great party, under Mignard, a man of courage and abilities, appeared in arms againft Procop; and the fury of civil difcord began to rage in all its violence.

The Taborites had now ample occafion to regret the clemency, which had formerly been fhewn at Prague; and remembered, with compunction of heart, how often their great chief would infift, that no peaceful fettlement could be obtained, till the factious fpirit of that city fhould be fubdued.—But it was now too late for reflection.

Procop however, unconcerned, at the head of veterans, whofe valour he had known during ten campaigns, met his adverfary with affurance of fuccefs. " You have not now, " my fellow-foldiers, cryed he, difciplined " Imperialifts, and hardy Saxons to oppofe. " Thofe hoftile banners belong to troops " enervated by city-luxury; and infpired by " faction, inftead of courage. You have " only to begin the attack: their own guilty " confciences will do the reft."

The

The cautious Mignard felt, with secret joy, the prognostics of success: he saw the confidence of his impetuous enemy; and with the address of a more experienced leader improved it fully to his own advantage.

On the plains of Broda this fatal quarrel was decided. Here the Taborite army, drawn by their ardour into insuperable difficulties, after a well-fought day, was exterminated. Here fell the gallant Procop, vainly endeavouring to restore a broken battle; and with him fell the liberties of his country.

The battle of Broda opened an easy way to the succession of Sigismond. The Calixtin party having gratifyed their revenge, now paid the price. Reduced by their victory, they were no longer in a condition to oppose the emperor. Conquerors, and conquered submitted to his yoke; and he was crowned peaceably at Prague, amidst the acclamations of his enemies.

It would be unpardonable ingratitude in a protestant writer not to acknowledge the lenity, which attended this sudden revolution. Sigismond, with a magnanimity, which few princes could exert, (it would be invi-

                    dious

dious to afcribe his behaviour to meaner motives) entered Bohemia, not as a conquered
province, but as a patrimony, which had defcended to him quietly from his anceftors.
Such of the Taborites as had efcaped the
carnage of that fatal day, confifting chiefly
of a few thin garrifons, in all about 6000
men, he took under his protection; fuffered
them to live peaceably at Tabor; and fhewing them favour beyond any of the Bohemian reformers, (many of whom met with
rougher ufage) allowed them with unparal-
lelled generofity, the ufe of their own religion.

Some years after, Eneas Sylvius, refiding,
with a public character, in Bohemia, had
the curiofity to vifit Tabor. The account
he hath left us of the remains of this brave
people is not a little entertaining. The reader
will make allowance for the zeal of a popifh
writer.

Returning, fays he, to Prague, our route
brought us near Tabor, which we had all
an inclination to vifit: but not knowing
what fort of reception we might meet with,
we fent a meffenger to acquaint the magiftrates of the town with our names, and

our

our intentions. We had a very obliging anſwer; and the principal inhabitants came out to meet us. But ſo wretched a ſet of people I never ſaw. Their dreſs was rude, beyond what is commonly ſeen among the loweſt vulgar; ſome of them were clad even in ſkins. They rode on horſeback; but their horſes, and furniture were of a piece with their dreſs. Their perſons too were juſt as extraordinary: ſcarce one of them, but was disfigured by ſome frightful maim. One wanted an eye, another an arm, a third a leg. Their reception of us was equally void of every appearance either of form or politeneſs. In their rude manner, however, they offered us each a trifling preſent; and brought us, by way of refreſhment, wine and fiſh. We then entered the town. Over the gate ſtood a ſtatue of Ziſca; and near it an angel holding a cup; as an emblem of their maintaining the doctrine of the two ſpecies. Their houſes were very ordinary; built chiefly of clay, and wood; no regularity, no form of ſtreets; but every houſe ſtanding by itſelf. The inſides however were better furniſhed than the outſides ſeemed to promiſe: they were inriched with the

Z 4

ſpoils

ſpoils of conquered provinces; which, to
the everlaſting diſgrace of the emperor Sigiſmond, were never reſtored. In their great
ſquare ſtood various forms of military engines; with a view, as we ſuppoſe, to ſtrike
a terror into the neighbouring country: tho'
the people were become quite pacific, applying themſelves only to huſbandry, and me-
chanic arts.   In this ſquare too ſtood their
temple, as they call it; a wooden ſtructure,
ſcarce ſuperior to a country barn.   Here they
preached to the people: here they expounded
their doctrines; here ſtood their unconſecrated altar; and here even the holy ſacra-
ment was adminiſtred.   Their prieſts were
unornamented, except by beards of an im-
moderate length.   Tythes were entirely diſ-
allowed. The clergy had no property.   They
were ſupply'd with all neceſſaries, in kind,
by the people.   Images were wholly forbidden.   No prayers to ſaints were permitted;
no holidays; no ſet faſts; no canonical
hours.   Half the ſacraments were diſcarded.
Religious houſes were abominations.   Their
baptiſmal font was unconſecrated: their dead
buryed in unhallowed ground.   They were
punctual however in their attendance upon
divine

divine fervice; and had very fevere penalties to inforce a reverence to it.

The next day, upon our departure, the magiftrates of this wretched town came again to wait upon us, and returned us thanks for our vifit. Their fpeech, on this occafion, had more of politenefs in it, than their appearance feemed to promife.

The End.

A

POSTSCRIPT.

HAVING thus given the reader what appeared moſt worthy of his notice, with regard to theſe eminent reformers, whoſe lives I have attempted, it may be proper to acquaint him with thoſe helps, and authorities, which I have commonly uſed. I have indeed taken from other writers, beſides thoſe I ſhall mention; but I have generally in that caſe quoted them in the text, if the incident was of conſequence.

In the life of Wicliff, the labour of collecting was made very eaſy to me by the induſtry and accuracy of Dr. Lewis, who hath brought together, in his life of that reformer, great plenty of materials. Had he been as happy in the diſpoſition of them, I ſhould not have thought the new lights, which I have endeavoured to throw upon this great

character

character, a sufficient apology for my engaging in the same work.

Lord Cobham's life was collected from the rolls of parliament, Bale's chronicle, Fox's martyrology, and our earliest English historians. With relation both to Wicliff and Lord Cobham, I examined the manuscripts of the British museum, where I hoped to have found a great variety of materials. I found some; but fewer than I expected.

Lenfant's very accurate, and judicious history of the council of Constance, was of great use to me in the lives of John Hufs, and Jerome of Prague. I examined the earliest and best accounts I could meet with, of the progress of the reformation in Bohemia; but in all contested points I relyed chiefly on Lenfant's judgment, whom I may venture to call my principal guide.

With regard to Zifca, I was more at a lofs. It hath been the misfortune of this chief to have had no sober historians. Eneas Sylvius, the principal, and from whom the generality of writers have taken their leading facts, though a courtier, seems to have written in the spirit of a monk. Credulous, and

prejudiced,

prejudced, he appears scarce to deserve a higher rank in letters than our own legendary writers. Where Lenfant's judgment assisted me, I followed without fear; but where he forsook me, I was obliged to wander among a variety of strange, and inconsistent accounts; and with some difficulty picked out a probable road. I make no question but Zisca won as many battles, and took as many towns as are ascribed to him; and that the constituent parts of his history rest upon a good foundation of credit; but his actions are related so much in the air of romance, that I found it necessary, in the painter's language, to *keep down* the colouring as much as possible. Livy, speaking of some romantic writings of his own country, from which he was obliged to copy; cries out, *Hæc ad ostentationem scenæ gaudentis miraculis apticra, quam ad fidem.* I am afraid in some instances, this character is too nearly allied to the writings I have been describing.

I cannot close this postscript without a few strictures on the moral, as well as literary character of Eneas Sylvius. This zealot, in his usual exaggerated manner, hath taken great liberties with the reformers; indulging

himself

himself in a rancour of language against them, which must be offensive to every sober Christian.   I could produce a variety of examples; but shall content myself with one. The reader may recollect the account he gives of the Taborites, after the ruin of their affairs; from which any impartial person would be led to conclude, that they were a brave, liberal, inoffensive, hospitable, and religious people.   How greatly therefore are we surprized to find our author concluding to this effect.

"I have now given you, says he, some account of this habitation of the devil, this temple of Belial, this kingdom of Lucifer.—— I had imagined indeed, that this people differed from us only in one, or two points: but I find them confirmed heretics, mere infidels, little better than atheists, and without any form of religion.—— Every heresy, every impiety, every blasphemy, which hath infected Christendom, hath fled hither for refuge; and hath here met with a safe asylum. —— For my own part, I thought myself in a land beyond the frozen ocean, among Barbarians, even among Cannibals; for in all the earth there are surely no such mon-

strous

ftrous people as the Taborites.—Yet even to thefe facrilegious, and moft abominable men did the emperor Sigifmond grant a city; nay he allowed their liberty to wretches, whom not to exterminate was a fcandal to Chriften-dom."

With fuch freedom does the licentious pen of this writer treat the reformers. His cenfures are entirely founded on their opini-ons. Of their practice he fays nothing. That indeed was irreprehenfible. But among bigots, morals are always infinitely lower rated than opinions. Had the faith of the Taborites been unqueftioned, their practice however licentious, had been unqueftioned too.—But to fee the real value of the invec-tives of this author, let us examine him a little clofer; and inftead of condemning him in the grofs for his opinions, let us treat him more fairly, and try his opinions by his practice.

A volume of his familiar letters furvived him: fome of which appear to have *efcaped* into public among the croud. In thefe let-ters, among other paffages, the following will fufficiently fhew, what licence he in-dulged in point of morals; fome of which

paffages

paſſages fell from him even in his more advanced age.

Adviſing a friend about a wife, he thus ſpeaks, (epiſt. 45.) *Ego de me facio conjecturam: plures vidi, amavique feminas, quarum exinde potitus, tædium magnum ſuſcepi: nec ſi maritandus fierem, uxori me jungam, cujus conſuetudinem neſciam.*

In his 15th letter he tells a long ſtory of his debauching an Engliſh lady in the low countries; and triumphantly thus exults, *ſcis qualis tu gallus fueris; nec ego caſtratus ſum, nec ex frigidorum numero.*

Repining at the approach of age, *Mihi herculè,* (ſays he,) *parum meriti eſt in caſtitate; nam, ut verum fatear, magis me venus fugitat, quam ego illam horreo.* epiſt. 92.

Deſcribing the ſupple methods, by which he propoſed to obtain preferment, *Me regi,* (ſays he,) *inſinuabo, regi parebo, regem ſequar, quod is volet, et ego volam, nulla in re adverſus ero, nec attingam aliquid, quod ſtatum meum non reſpiciat. Ego peregrinus ſum: conſultum mihi eſt Gnathonis officium ſuſcipere; aiunt, aio; negant, nego.* Epiſt. 45.

Of the pleaſures of wine he ſpeaks in ſuch feeling language, as only a profeſſed voluptuary

tuary could ufe. *Vinum me alit, me juvat, me oblectat, me beat.* Epift. 92.

And that we may not be at a lofs for a key to all thefe illuftrious paffages, he takes care to give us one himfelf. *Non fieri poteft*, fays he,) *quin animum fuum prodat is, qui plurima fcribit.——Nudus fum, et aperte loquor. Veftem omnem rejicio, nec laboro, cum fcribo.* Epift. 402.

Such is the teftimony, which Eneas Sylvius hath given us of himfelf. It may ferve to invalidate what he hath faid of others; as it feems entirely to fhew that his cenfures are founded upon a mere difference of opinion, without any regard to practice; which is one of the characteriftics of bigotry.

They, who are not acquainted with the hiftory of this writer, will be furprized to hear, that the man of whom we have this authentic character, was not only a pope; but was acknowledged by the generality of the popifh writers, as one of the moft refpectable of all the Roman pontiffs.

The End.

AN EXPLANATION

OF THE

PLATES.

I.

THE works of Wicliff are reprefented as founded on fcripture. The fcourge is meant to characterize the acutenefs and fpirit of his contefts with the regular clergy of his time. The taper reprefents him as deftined to the work of enlightening mankind.

II.

A pillar, (the emblem of chriftian fortitude) adorned with a crown of martyrdom, fupports lord Cobham in his fufferings. The other appendages point out his knighthood, peerage, and profeffion of arms.

A a

III

III.

Hufs is reprefented as refting firm upon the anchor of faith. The poft, the manacles, chain, and crown of martyrdom fhew his fufferings, and their reward.

IV.

The dragon fpending his fruitlefs rage againft the medallion of Jerome reprefents the unavailing fury of Romifh perfecution. The flaming fire-brand characterizes the genius of popifh bigotry.

V.

The fword of Zifca is drawn in the defence of religion ; which is characterized by a bible, untied to diftinguifh it as a proteftant one. His medallion, refting upon arms, reprefents him as a military reformer.

ERRATA.

Read *great* for *egrat,* page 15———*cautious* for *cautions,* 16———*this reformer* for *the reformer,* 32———a period after *to the clergy,* 58———*a mean* for *a means,* 66———*through avarice* for *thought avarice,* 68———*futurorum* for *inturorum,* 86———a comma after *no cause why,* 95—*peire* for *peirc,* 95—*Lenfant* for *Leufant,* 189———comma after *on his arm,* 195———*and that he denyed* for *and he denyed,* 210———*To this* for *to which,* 211———period after *his power,* 215———*at the time,* for *at this time,* 236———*Trocznow* for *Troeznow,* 265———*Dominichi* for *Dominictis,* 271———*these tents* for *their tents,* 285———period after *Zisca prevailed,* 334———period after *advantage of them,* 340———*quelled* for *quitted,* 343.

www.ingramcontent.com/pod-product-compliance
Lightning Source LLC
Chambersburg PA
CBHW051526100726
47898CB00005B/1589